VALOR

The Custos Saga

Jessica Tastet

This is a work of fiction. All the characters and events
portrayed in this novel are fiction.

Publications

Valor
Copyright 2017 Jessica Tastet

Cover Design by Ashley Comeaux-Foret
Formatting by Polgarus Studio

ISBN 978-0-9986173-0-5
ISBN 978-0-9986173-1-2

One

The screams through the black metal door were high pitched and skin-raising. Alert in the darkness of the empty room, Kline tilted his stool slightly off-balance to distract himself. The trick was to imagine he was stuck in a horror movie. One of those bad ones that just left you bored.

A long stretch of silence commenced. There may have been soft muffled sobs drifting from the cracks, but he dismissed them as he had all the others who'd cried in that room.

A motion near the entrance drew him to his feet. Lucilius filled the doorway with his bulk, and Kline's gut throbbed once. Fear. His abs clenched tightly against it. He despised it. Everyone feared this man but it offered no consolation. Lucilius exuded power from the sleekness of his black clothing to the broadness of his chest. His long face was chiseled with hardness and intimidation. He was a force; one that Kline knew couldn't be tangled with without incurring a few scars.

"From the sounds of it, I believe she's nearly broken."

There was a matter of factness to his voice, as if he was announcing that the fridge was out of mayo. Death as casual as let's fix her a sandwich and kill her with the same knife.

Kline nodded and followed him to the metal door. The door

shuddered under Lucilius's grip and pulled free of its latch. A massive individual scurried into the corner leaving a grimy spotlight illuminating the surgical table and the blood stained instruments on a nearby cart.

Kline stepped inside the room and took his place in the corner. As a guard he was here to watch, to report back to the elders that all protocols had been followed. As a new guard with very little power, he was simply to stay out of Lucilius's way and keep quiet.

The young woman trembled as Lucilius stepped between her and the light. Her hands tugged at their leather restraints, and her sobs were silent.

"Now, now. Everything will be better now that I'm here." Lucilius's voice was a gentle melody, so different from the coldness that was usually there. It was chilling. Kline tensed.

She squirmed and the eye that wasn't swollen shut widened. Two hours ago she'd had a neat plaited braid and a clean white t-shirt. Now strands of ebony hair stuck out in all directions, her shirt was splattered with blood, and inflicted injuries were beginning to swell and make her unrecognizable.

Lucilius continued in that mesmerizing voice. "Don't you want things to be better? I'm sure this can't be what you want. To be taunted and tortured. The pain unbearable. No, I'm sure you want to rest."

He paused and a soft ticking of a clock was amplified. She'd been quite pretty before, for a human girl. Not that Kline was afforded the privilege of seeing many females in his position for comparison. He didn't imagine that the blood red tears, battered cheek, and shaky gasps would be considered attractive though.

"Good." Lucilius smiled. "Now in order to do that, I need you to answer a few questions."

Kline tensed and clenched his fists behind his back, focusing on his own self-control. His instincts throbbed to intervene.

Her good eye closed and a grimace appeared.

"You are an apprentice of sorts to Madame Lulu, correct?"

Her eye flew open, fear bright and clear. As a Custos, Kline could hear her internal dialogue. She didn't know who she feared more— Madame Lulu or Lucilius.

She nodded as she decided that this threat was more imminent.

"Good." Lucilius nodded his head. "Now, Madame Lulu has some information that I need about the whereabouts of a certain book. Do you know what I'm talking about?"

Kline's eardrum echoed with her heartbeat and the grip of his fists became painful. Chemicals flooded her body with fear, and he couldn't hear any of her thoughts above the rattle of panic that had seized her. Humans broadcasted so loudly with no filter. Custos avoided humans when possible.

"Answer carefully," Lucilius said, taking her hand in his. Kline noticed the slow squeeze and the whitening of her fingers. She couldn't feel the pain beyond her panic though. "I know you have my answer. You see, I chose you specifically and sent Gint to retrieve you for me."

Kline looked toward the far corner where Gint had retreated. His nearly seven-foot massive size didn't allow for him to disappear, even in the shadows of the room. He was a monstrosity with his milk complexion and oversized arms. Despite his lack of human appearance, it was his eyes that gave away that something wasn't right with him. Under any other leadership, Gint would have been eliminated for his homicidal tendencies, but Lucilius had found his special talent of inflicting pain and breaking down those who resisted, a great tool.

She sputtered and then coughed. "I don't know… she didn't tell me."

"Shhh." Lucilius leaned in. "I know she wouldn't tell you where it is. You aren't important enough for that, Child. I want to know who. Who does she protect? Who does she believe has it?"

She shook her head. "I don't know. She says she wants to stay out of it."

Lucilius's thumb covered her one good eye and he pushed down with what Kline could tell wasn't his full strength. She screamed and squirmed and gasped for air.

"Do not lie to me. Who does she help most often?"

"Her... her granddaughter." She sobbed.

"Who else?"

"John Landon."

"And?"

She shook her head. "I don't know who the girl is."

"The girl?

"I don't know. I just know there is a girl. Please, I don't know anything. I've only been in training a few months."

"Very well." Lucilius released her hand and stepped away from her. "It's unfortunate you couldn't be more helpful."

Lucilius motioned for Gint. "Finish her."

He then turned and walked toward the door whistling. Kline dutifully followed, his insides burning with the need to release the girl as the code of conduct required. But Lucilius ran things these days. The rules of the elders meant nothing to him, and no one lived after they challenged him, not that many of them tried. Kline rationalized that this was self-preservation, but his mind wasn't fooled. But he'd promised. The time wasn't right yet.

Kline stopped near his stool. He didn't trust himself to walk further. "Is her life not worth anything?"

Lucilius paused at the doorway, but didn't face him. "Human life means nothing compared to what we seek. Do not forget that you

4

aren't human. If you remember that your loyalty is to the Custos people, you will have no problems. Do not forget."

Kline remained quiet, understanding the message behind the words. Agree with Lucilius or die. It's how things were around here these days. Lucilius disappeared around the corner.

The scream was short and piercing. The silence echoed.

Two

The house hadn't changed. Angelica swatted at a persistent mosquito buzzing around her ear. The roof looked as though it had been re-shingled and the weathered clapboard siding had broken off at places along the ground, but the hand-stitched lace curtains still hung half-closed in the attic window. The garden hose was still in the rusty basket near the screen door that led to the back porch, where a woman sat hunched over in a rocking chair. The boards creaked beneath her weight.

Angelica hid among the gardenia and evergreen bushes. She doubted the old woman could see. Should she stay hidden though? She'd debated that question for twenty minutes, and she hated indecision. The woman stared straight ahead, her thinning gray hair pulled into a tight bun at the base of her neck.

Angelica had needed to see if this place was real. She'd needed to know it wasn't a figment of her seven-year-old imagination, and now she stood staring at the looming object straight from her dreams.

What now? What had been the grand plan for the confirmation? She hadn't planned that far ahead. The clouds darkened to a slate gray, and still, nothing came to mind.

A door slammed and Angelica eased back into the bushes. A short blond girl approached the woman. Their voices traveled to her in the eerie quiet.

"Mom, you should come inside."

The rocking chair creaked.

"I'm coming." A gravely voice answered. "Why don't you go run my bath?"

The daughter hovered over her a moment longer, a hand resting on the back of the rocker in a protective grip. After a moment, she returned inside, her slippers slapping against the wood.

Angelica moved closer to the edge of the bushes to see better. Everything was as she remembered it fourteen years ago. She'd dismissed the house, the woman, and the man that she'd known here years ago as just a sign of her overactive imagination. She'd told herself each time she'd shaken herself awake from another nightmare that none of it had been real. As the years had passed, it had become easier for her to believe her own reassurances. But there'd always been that thought, that inner voice that told her she was only lying to herself.

"You can come out now."

Angelica twitched and a branch rustled. She stopped breathing and glanced around the yard for a visitor.

"It's not nice to keep an old lady waiting."

Angelica's search turned up empty. No one else was here. The woman meant her. She took a deep breath and stepped out, hearing the bushes rustle behind her, closing her hiding spot. She'd known that Angelica was there.

She took an uneasy step toward the porch, and then quickly closed the gap before her instincts kicked in and she ran for it. Angelica focused on the clear, unmoving bright blue eyes on the porch. She looked harmless. Angelica couldn't really be in danger. Could she?

Angelica squinted at the glassiness of her eyes until it registered that the lady was blind.

Angelica's words stumbled out. "How did you know I was here?"

Her laugh trickled through the screen door, a sound like wind chimes. Angelica had remembered that laugh and dreamed of it often with this house. Angelica stayed behind the door, seeing the woman's distorted image through the screen.

"I'm the same as you, but I've lived more years. Means you can't fool me easily. Did you come for some reason?"

Now that she was close, the details of the woman from a hazy dream became sharply focused. There'd once been less wrinkles, and her blue eyes had given away every emotion, but for all of that, she was the same.

"I think I was here a long time ago," Angelica struggled out, the words catching in her throat. Why was this so difficult? "I was with a woman, Lily."

The rocking chair stilled and her breath rattled in her chest. Angelica felt a pain jolt through her as the shock of loss hit her. She quickly slammed the door shut on the part of her brain that felt other people's emotions; this woman's emotions at the mention of Lily. She'd been caught off guard, and the barrier must have gone down. She was usually diligent about keeping it in place. What was wrong with her today? She could feel the past pulling at her self-control as it had been doing the last three weeks.

The woman's voice scratched, but there was a hardness there that hadn't existed before. "Why have you come?"

Angelica's chest compressed. This time it was her own pain jolting through her. "I just needed to know if it was real."

The old woman gasped, her hand lifting to her thin lips. "How can you ask that? My husband is dead because of *you*. I can no longer see because of *you*. How can you not know that it was real?"

Angelica's breath stopped and she couldn't feel her arm. *It was all real.* Not just the memory of staying here for six months in that attic room, but the dream about what happened to the couple after she'd left. The black-clothed man that had plagued her dreams, following them from one place to another, killing the man who'd lived here. He'd liked to whittle boats—canoes especially. Had always had a knife and block of wood in his hands. The woman before her had baked delicious cherry pies that she'd placed on the counters to cool. Did she do that now or had her life stopped when her husband's had?

Angelica's heart pounded against her rib cage. Why had she not known it was real? "I was only seven."

The woman's voice was iron. "You have Custos blood in you, and we remember everything. You chose to forget, and that's unacceptable. You need to go now."

The words stung as if she'd slapped her. Angelica stepped back. "I just want to know what happened."

The woman stood and attempted to straighten her stooped shoulders. "Then remember it."

The woman shuffled toward her back screen door. She fumbled with the latch, and then shut herself away from Angelica.

Angelica stood a moment, unsure that it had just happened. She'd wanted to know… had felt compelled to discover the truth. Well it had been real, all of it.

What did that mean though? What else had she tucked away as just a bad dream? And how could she be the person who'd so convincingly lie to herself? She made her living on lying. Shouldn't she at least be able to tell the truth to herself?

She shook her head and made her way back to the rental car she'd parked at the curb of the subdivision.

Her mother, Lily, had done all of this when Angelica was a girl and the only part she had left of the woman was this old journal.

I've found a home- safety, love, and freedom in New Orleans.

Was there more for her to find there? How far did the truth go back? And what did it mean to be Custos? It was a word that kept reappearing in the journal and now uttered by this woman—a word she'd never heard of before three weeks ago. At least that she remembered.

Angelica had to know. She needed to know what had happened all those years ago that had made it so easy for her to convince herself it was a dream.

Then New Orleans was her next stop. She had no choice.

Three

New Orleans

Cain leaned further into the coolness of the shadows of Pere Antoine Alley. The Wednesday night Bourbon Street crowd was lighter than usual which was good for tonight's mission, but bad for business in the Quarter. It probably had something to do with the young girl's body being staked to the doors of a shop near the St. Louis Cathedral last night, but his assignment didn't involve worrying about that tonight, and Cain had learned long ago to follow orders at all costs.

A rustle in a doorway fifty feet away drew his attention toward Echo's looming shadow on the brick alley. Contempt grew in his gut for his teammate. The soldier completely lacked stealth. How he'd moved up the ranks to his position he couldn't fathom, and it was Cain's misfortune to have him assigned to his team.

Footsteps approached, growing louder in the stillness. Cain focused on the approaching brain waves, slipping in like a subliminal message. He came and went from others' heads so quickly now that he didn't notice the transition anymore. He reached past layers of fear and into the rambling thoughts of his target.

The thoughts were skittish, darting around like a squirrel. *He didn't want to be involved in Vindica business. His wife was gone ten years now. He wanted to pretend the Custos line didn't exist.*

His slight, stooped frame limped past Cain at an inconsistent pace with his thoughts. Echo fell out of the doorway seconds before he should have. Cain's anger flared briefly. He'd be sure to reteach him these covert skills later in training, the hard way. For now he'd have to deal with his bumbling inadequacy.

At the ally exit, his third teammate Falcon noticed the glitch and compensated by closing the gap. Cain stepped out of his doorway, relieved that his father's lackey had at least assigned one competent member to his team.

The target whirled around in a circle gawking at the three of them, and the warmth of satisfaction pumped through Cain. His missions inspired fear, which offered further proof to him that this archaic Vindica organization, a hybrid of human and Custos people, was on its last shallow breath. They couldn't even muster a last bit of courage when faced with extinction. It was time to bury the Vindica not resuscitate it. His father was wrong about his plans, and that satisfied Cain even more.

Cain honed in on the target. Tonight's mission was information retrieval, and that meant a little use of mentalism. "Do you know what we want?"

The target's whole body trembled. "I… I don't know anything."

His eyes widened behind his bifocals and his lips trembled. His name—Lewis— slipped into Cain's conscious. He'd tried not to associate the man he'd sat across from at dinner with his target. It kept things uncomplicated.

Cain cringed. These missions were pointless and made them cowards. Lewis had no Vindica abilities… he was just a friend of the organization. A defenseless man who'd provide no new information, but it made their leader feel as if he was doing something. Cain had become uneasy following orders these days with the new methods adopted as some invisible clock counted down to the end of the "world as they knew it." Whatever that meant these days.

Echo grunted. "We'll decide that."

Cain glared down at him until he looked away. His instructions were to remain quiet. He was there for physical presence not his abilities. Cain returned to Lewis whose face had grown deathly pale. "What does John Landon know about Valor?"

"Who?" He chocked out.

Cain cracked his knuckles and Lewis fell to his knees, yelping in agony. Cain winced. Lewis didn't even have the basic defenses to fight against the abilities of the Custos people. Usually friends were taught a few protections. He'd need to be careful not to kill him accidently.

"I'm sorry." Lewis forced out between ragged breaths. "I really don't know anything."

Cain delved further into Lewis's mind, his skin crawling with Lewis's fear. *I'm going to die, how can I warn John, we don't know who Valor is. Why are they targeting me? I don't know anything.*

Pointless.

Cain nodded once. Falcon and Echo stepped closer and within seconds Lewis was suspended in the air above them. Cain listened closely to the surrounding area. This ability could give them away to the general public, and secrecy was the main priority of all Custos. There could be no witnesses.

Cain stepped under Lewis, inches from his face, maintaining awareness of his surroundings. "What does John Landon know about Valor?"

Cain probed Lewis's thoughts as his speech left him in fear. *How did this Dark Soldier know he was in John's confidence? How did he know that he'd be there tonight; he hadn't come in months.*

Cain smiled, swallowing a laugh. The Vindica organization was dying; it wasn't stupid. Even in his fear, Lewis's thoughts could go in the right direction. These missions could backfire if they weren't careful.

"What does he know about the prophecy?"

The prophecy's time is here. The Reckoning approaches. War comes. How will he know who Valor is? Is Valor responsible for starting it? How will John stop an unstoppable war?

Cain alone possessed telepathy among his teammates. No one else could hear this internal conversation. Falcon and Echo couldn't go back to the Dark Soldier organization. It would be so simple to not report it, to simply let it happen as it was predicted. War could be the distraction he needed to stop following orders.

Cain whispered. "Do you want to be here for the Reckoning?"

Lewis's lips trembled as his eyes watered. "It's not my war. I'm not one of you. Please…"

Cain stepped back from Lewis's face. "No one will escape. It's prophesized that the war will change the entire world, not just the Custos people."

Cain flipped his wrist and the hovering Lewis whirled in slow motion. Echo and Falcon joined in and he spun faster. His face blurred until Cain couldn't see the fear shinning in his eyes. Cain flipped his wrist again, and he flung Lewis toward the cathedral's gates.

A flick of Echo's wrist snapped Cain's attention, but he was a millisecond too late to catch Lewis crashing down on the posts, being impaled on two spikes.

Heat pumped through Cain, slowing his heart rate. "What did you do that for?" Cain yelled. He felt Lewis's heart stop. It was too late.

Echo faltered. "Dark Knight said no witnesses."

Cain growled, pacing to burn off the white-hot anger that burned through him. "We didn't have any. He didn't know who we were."

Echo's voice trembled. "I thought he meant to kill him."

"You didn't think. Sheep, all of you. No one ever does. We can't get information from a dead man. If you kill everyone who can tell you something, you can't learn anything."

Falcon cleared his throat. "We need to get out of here before there are witnesses." He'd maintained vigilance of the area, scanning the alley continuously. Nice that all his father's men weren't idiots.

Cain unclenched his fists and stretched his fingers out. Disgust ran rampart through him. The organization couldn't die quick enough.

Four

With a blinding flash of silver, Angelica's eyes fluttered open under the sweltering sunlight pouring in from the taxi window. For a moment, panic seized her middle as she passed unfamiliar two and three story dwellings. It took a few seconds for her downtown New Orleans destination to fire through her brain and the panic to ease. She looked through the front windshield and caught the cab driver's eyes in the rear view mirror staring her down with a strange glint in his deep eyes.

Geez, why did she have to be tired enough to fall asleep in this creep's cab?

Of course, she was beyond tired. She couldn't remember the last night she'd slept well without the reoccurring nightmare. It was probably before her grandmother's funeral three weeks ago. Back when she'd been a typical unhappy college student marching her way toward graduation and headed for a career she didn't want. In three weeks time, she's chasing clues from Georgia to New Orleans trying to figure out her mother's secret.

She must be mad. It was the only explanation she had besides from the instinct that she was headed toward something. She had no idea what that something was and she could be rushing blindly to the edge of a cliff. Mad, she knew, but she couldn't seem to help herself from heading toward it.

Out the window she noticed they were down a busy city street. Groups of people bustled along the noisy French Quarter sidewalks on either side of the cab on this hot October afternoon. Two dark-skinned, young boys tap-danced while spinning a bicycle tire on their heads in front of a small antique shop. The only prop was a tilted cardboard box containing several coins and bills. Up ahead at the corner a painted silver mime posed on top of the same shade color box as a few onlookers attempted to distract him, while a father took his daughter's picture standing in front of the Royal Street corner sign.

It felt touristy and exotic all at once, like a fever overtaking her. She had the compulsion to walk down the street and get lost in the crowd.

The taxi braked past the tap dancing act and pulled at an angle to the curb. Bystanders turned to look as Angelica hurried out of the white taxi and inhaled the exotic and not so appetizing smell of the quarter. It wasn't the stiff manor of her grandmother's old antebellum house in Georgia. Much looser, older, and charming. She glanced down to make sure she wasn't rumpled. She wouldn't pass military inspection, but she was good enough for the laissez-faire attitude of New Orleans if what she'd heard was true.

A bum staggered toward her from an open doorway and she looked around the cracked limestone sidewalk, hoping someone else was his target. With her telepathy, she could see that the army salvation coat covered the brittle bones of a man who'd lived on the streets for a long time with only the cheap whisky hid in his torn inside jacket pocket to warm him.

With images like these, it was no wonder she turned her abilities "off" most of the time.

His lips parted to reveal a toothless smile and he drenched her in a whisky stench. "You 'ave 'mazin eyes. I see myself witchim."

Her friend Michael from a different life had told her that her eyes were Caribbean pools, a rare color that she'd looked for in others but rarely found.

Several bystanders returned their attention to them and she began to feel like she needed to escape.

"Angelica, up here!" The call came clear over the cacophony of noise on the street.

Angelica looked up where a woman leaned over the second floor balcony. The blunt midnight black pixie cut disguised the round faced, formally blond, high school friend she'd come to see. Angelica would bet that Denise had changed more of that nice girl persona she'd perfected throughout school. Angelica had always been able to recognize others pretending to be who they weren't. It was an ability she'd honed that had nothing to do with Custos blood, as far as she could tell at least.

The voice rang through again from her pierced lip. "I'll meet you in the art shop."

Angelica grabbed the handle of her suitcase and gave an uneasy smile to the homeless man before entering the tall open doorway of the shop.

Paintings protruded from shelves, wooden bins, and three deep on the wall racks. A long-haired man with a goatee stood in back of a cash register examining a painting of a dirt lined quarter street with a middle-aged woman. They were the only occupants in the cluttered but clean shop.

A heavy white door in the back of the shop swung open, and Denise waltzed out with a smug smile playing on her plum lips. Heavy eyeliner and an eyebrow stud drew her away from the smile. Angelica had enough time to notice a navel ring before she was seized into a tight, uncomfortable hug.

"It's so great to see you." Denise pulled back. "You haven't changed a bit."

Angelica laughed, glad that Denise was unable to read her thoughts. "I can't believe I'm here."

For a moment, Angelica caught the expression of the former varsity cheerleader she'd known- the one that had charmed the student body. "We have so much to catch up on. I'm so glad you're here. The entrance of the apartment is the next door from where you came in. I'll give you a key later. We can go up this way though. Leave your suitcase, Rodney will bring it up."

There wasn't even a breath until she finished.

No matter how much she'd changed— some might say destroyed her former image— Denise was still Denise. She talked too fast, loved attention, and bounced with energy.

Angelica's hand lingered a moment over her suitcase as she looked again at Rodney holding the painting for the woman. His small eyes watched her and his thick lips didn't smile. Angelica's flesh prickled. His burliness and glare weren't what you'd want to meet on a deserted street at night, but Denise had managed to stay alive this long with him. Angelica could protect herself if it came down to it. Famous last words, she knew. But she was mad these days.

Through the doors, the courtyard was small, but the greenery and angel statue were beautiful touches. The iron stairs cascaded up the brick and added to the romantic nature of the scene. Angelica could like this city. Beautiful without being uppity.

Upstairs in the second floor apartment, Angelica's eyes swept across the large open room with wood plank flooring and intricate plaster ceiling. Throughout the room candles and incense burners cast eerie shadows against the white walls before they were absorbed by the sloppily painted celestial stars. Nice touch. She'd dated a real estate agent a few months ago and he'd yammered on and on about property values. She didn't think this would add to the property value of the place.

She'd guess that the stars were Denise's contribution as an art student at the local university. Denise's childhood home had crystal chandeliers in every formal room, along with stiff Victorian furniture crowding the spaces. Afternoon tea was served at four o'clock with all the respectable women in the neighborhood as attendees, including Angelica's grandmother. Angelica would assume that Denise's mother hadn't visited this place or she'd seriously mellowed out in the last four years.

Denise twirled around, arms waving around the hollowness of the space. "Home sweet home. You're going to love staying in the quarter."

A temporary home maybe. She'd thought staying here might be a good idea, but she wasn't feeling assured of her choice at the moment.

Angelica took in the sparse furniture and noticed a man propped up in a recliner watching the small television on a table pushed up against a wall. His face held a two-day stubble, and his clothing was little more than rags with paint splatters.

The thought occurred to her that she should have asked how many people shared the apartment that Denise had boasted about during yesterday's phone conversation. "Who lives here?"

Denise threw herself down on a rolling chair. "Rodney and I live here. David here lives upstairs. Rodney and David are cousins, so he forgets he's upstairs with his own roommates."

David pulled himself from the whale documentary and looked up at her. *Damn, she's hot. Nice tits.*

Angelica slammed the door closed and blocked his thoughts. She didn't know if it was because she was tired or this personal quest was bringing down her defenses, but she needed to be more careful.

He nodded with a goofy smile. "The famous Angelica. I thought you were a figment of Denise's overactive imagination, but what do you know."

Angelica smiled politely before looking away. "It's always difficult to live up to Denise's stories."

She could feel David's gaze bore into her, but she wouldn't give him more of a moment's glance. He removed his bare feet from the ottoman and leaned forward to get her attention. She cringed. "Denise says you've known each other a long time."

The chair rolled back as Denise stood and walked toward the front balcony. The French doors were open and the white sheers snapped in the wind. She glanced back at David, and gave Angelica a little smile. Always the dramatic flare. "Angelica came into Ms. Mission's second grade class, and the girls immediately hated her because Jeremy thought she was the prettiest girl in school. She of course became the coolest girl after Jenny Patterson floated to the ceiling during a game of light as a feather, stiff as a board. The whole school thought Angelica was a witch after."

Angelica noticed the smile twitching on Denise's lips and a twinkle of humor in her eyes. Angelica recalled the floating incident differently. There'd been a group of hysterical preteens convincing themselves that they weren't holding Jenny up. Denise had greatly embellished... then and now.

David chuckled. "So what brings you to New Orleans? Looking to study voodoo?"

"Maybe so." The coy smile rose easily to her lips. Instincts died hard. Charm was an instant switch when you were conning someone, and Angelica had honed these instincts the last three years.

Denise's laugh interrupted her. "Angelica's come to solve the mystery of her mother who abandoned her."

Angelica's heart stopped a moment. Instincts vanished. When she'd decided that Denise was worth the cheap room, she'd forgotten how fascinated Denise had been by Angelica's missing parents when they were children.

She forced her head to tilt and a smile to come to her lips all while her heart restarted at a sprint. "I'm just enjoying my recent freedom. No purpose. Just a little fun."

Denise's expression didn't change. She wasn't convinced. A loud bang behind Angelica caused her shoulders to jump. She looked behind her to see Rodney towering in the doorway with her suitcase at his feet. "Not much fun these days with murder. You need to be careful here."

Angelica held her smile, but her chest trembled three times before she calmed it. Rodney scowled down at her like a ferocious bear. She stood still under his glare.

Denise threw herself into the chair. "Everyone's afraid now that the retired professor was impaled by the gates behind the cathedral. There was some girl before that they aren't saying much about either."

Angelica gripped the back of the sofa as she flashed back to a dream. Gray tweed, a flash of silver as blood dripped. She bit down hard on her bottom lip as bile rose in her throat. She'd never succeeded in turning off the ability to see. She didn't even know how.

Denise stared at her, making her feel self-conscious that her pulse had increased and heat had flushed through her. "It's baffled the police and they can't even say for certain if it was murder, suicide, or Mother Nature."

Rodney's long strides closed up the space as he scooped Denise into an embrace, swallowing her petite body. "Some crazy stuff out there is all I'm saying. You gotta stay vigilant."

"Don't scare Angelica her first night." Denise swatted at him playfully. "I'll show you where you'll be staying, let you freshen up. You look like crap."

Eager for a moment away from everyone, she grabbed her suitcase and followed Denise through a large arch. There was a door to her right and left, and Denise turned right. This arrangement may have to be rethought but for now a moment alone was enticing enough to have her follow.

The bedroom held an old canopy bed with matching mahogany plank flooring. An old, rose velvet Victorian settee was crammed into the corner and a scuffed armoire stood on the opposite wall. Above the settee was the canvas silhouette of a woman standing naked on a balcony looking out to the French Quarter scene below. Angelica was stunned by how normal it looked in terms of décor. It was a room that would meet Denise's mother's approval and probably had at some point. The nude picture was probably Denise's way of slipping in a go-to-hell, Mom.

Denise walked around the room not looking at her, which was unusual for Denise. "It's too bad about Grams."

Angelica sighed. Her feelings about her grandmother's death were complicated, and she felt too exhausted to think about them very less deal with them. "She was in the kitchen when it happened."

Denise looked her way. "Still have that same faded gold cherry wallpaper?"

Angelica laughed as an image of the kitchen popped into her head. "Yep, I don't think she would've changed anything in that house. I suppose Cousin Linda will have plenty work now that it belongs to her."

She didn't feel the bitterness this time. Grams had not left her anything but a few trinkets from her mother's room. The will hadn't been read, but she'd seen a preview of it. She'd left before the reading with a wide range of emotions fueling her mission to discover the truth. Many she didn't want to deal with at the moment, especially with Denise watching her.

Denise opened the French door leading to the balcony. "I don't suppose you miss her too much." Her voice had caught and blown into the outside air and for a moment Angelica had to question if she'd heard correctly.

"Why would you say that?"

Denise shrugged, studying the noisy street below. "She thought you were crazy and controlled your life even now as an adult. I thought you'd be happy to be in the driver's seat finally. I mean you haven't ever changed. There has to be something you have your own thoughts on."

That had stung a bit. Not because she was wrong. Grandmother Angel had taken every opportunity to have a psychiatrist pronounce her insane. Angel believed that an evil spirit possessed her. If her mother hadn't taught her how to lie as a child, she wouldn't have survived Gram's house. She certainly would make no claims to have flourished. Too complicated for thinking about so instead she'd become obsessed with this madness.

Angelica shrugged. "She was the only family I had left."

Denise grunted as she walked toward the door. "Family's overrated."

The bitterness slipped into her voice as if it were personal. She'd have to remember to ask about Denise's mom. "Thanks for letting me stay here."

Denise turned at the doorframe and smiled. A natural one, not her dramatic cover. "Wouldn't want you to get in trouble."

Angelica smiled as she left the room. When she was gone, she released a slow breath through her mouth. What Denise had said about her not changing wasn't the truth. True, she'd walked Gram's line, but in college she'd pushed her limits with a few cons- nothing serious at least until that last mess three months ago. She'd learned to manipulate, and it seemed it came too natural these days. The trouble was she didn't want to be Gram's angel or the campus hustler. What was left though?

Angelica lifted the heavy suitcase on top of the chenille white bed spread and unzipped it. A brown unwrapped package rested on top of clothes, hair dryer, several leather bound books, and various shoes. Angelica grabbed the package and flapped the suitcase lid closed. The bed creaked as she sank into the feather mattress and the snapping ecru sheers drew her attention.

Angelica shivered, spooking herself with thoughts of someone standing within the folds of the sheers.

She untied the package, revealing a worn brown journal. The softness of the leather caused a tingle from her fingertip up her arm. Whatever spirit was haunting Angelica had come with the finding of this diary: her mother's sixteen-year-old journal when she'd run away from Grandmother Angel's house, never to return. At sixteen, Lily's father had died in a car accident, and Angel had turned on her because of her abilities. Angel had tolerated it for sixteen years because of her husband, but with him gone, she'd promised Lily she'd rip her abilities out of her with every religious method she could find a priest to try. And she'd tried several before Lily had escaped.

The surprise was that Lily had left Angelica on Angel's porch steps at seven-years-old, thirteen years after vowing she'd never return.

The memory of that night was scarred into Angelica's memory no matter how often she tried to forget. It easily surfaced at the scent of night Jasmine or the chirp of a cricket.

They'd stood on the sidewalk under a dim street light and a quarter moon. Lily's auburn hair had cascaded around her tear streaked, but set face. "You must take care of yourself. It won't be easy here, but you'll be safe."

Angelica had reached out and pushed Lily's damp hair out of her bluish green eyes so that she could see into them. They'd always calmed her before. What she saw there made her tremble and her fear to escalate. "I want to come with you."

Tears had tumbled down Lily's face faster. "It's not safe anymore; you know this more than anyone." Angelica had struggled with a breath, her chest heaving with the weight. "Are you wearing your charm?"

Angelica clutched the black onyx stone between her shaking fingers. *Why had she told her mother about the last vision?* "I haven't taken it off."

Lily's index finger had gently stroked her cheek. "Do not ever take it off. Keep it close to your heart where I will always be. The blood stone protects you when I'm not here."

Angelica had choked, a pain throbbing merciless in her chest. "Please don't go Mommy."

Mommy. The word had felt strange on her lips. She'd called her Lily always, but she'd needed to say the word that night. To know that it was true.

Lily had tucked the journal under Angelica's arm and had encouraged Angelica to walk up the steps to ring the doorbell alone. When Grams had opened the door on the third ring, Angelica had turned around and Lily was gone.

A trickle of laughter and shouting drifted up through the balcony and dragged her back to the present. How could fourteen years melt away so quickly and leave an aching in her chest as if the sadness was yesterday? She rolled off her bed and walked onto the balcony. She breathed in lavender, chicory, and something she couldn't identify.

Grams had turned on her two months after she'd arrived. It was the night she'd shrieked out in terror as she'd watched Lily die. Angelica watched those eyes turn off like the fading sun. Grams had tried to be nice until then. She'd baked cookies and tucked her in bed, and Angelica had pretended to be normal. But through Angelica's sobs after the nightmare, she'd hardened, pulled away. There'd been no more cookies or good nights.

She inhaled deeply, releasing the sadness balled in her chest. What had she needed protecting against? Why had Lily left her with a woman who'd tried to destroy her? All questions that Angelica had never answered. They hadn't taken up too much of her teenage thoughts as she'd focused on being normal instead of her abilities. But Angel's death had stirred it all, left her feeling as though she needed the answers.

Grams told everyone that Lily had died in a car accident. They'd held a memorial service without a body. Angelica had stood near the empty casket in her black frock wondering where Lily's body was. But she'd shed all her tears the night Lily had died and had been unable to muster anything for an empty shell.

Angelica opened the yellowing pages of the journal to a marked page near the end. She'd studied this page every day for three weeks. Puzzled over it; tried to recall if she'd heard it before and had forgotten it.

Those who walk upon the land
With powers that exist within their hands
Will suffer endlessly at the will
Of those who do not hold their powers still
The Valor of the Vindica will rise
The gifts of five no longer in disguise
Those who've suffered will be avenged
When Valor of the Vindica seeks revenge

She couldn't remember it no matter how many times she read it through. She'd concluded it wasn't her mother's handwriting. But this was all she was certain about.

A shiver ran over her flesh as it did each time.

There was something there. She knew it. Something in the words that she was supposed to remember.

The city below her should be able to help. It's where Lily had found herself when she'd run away, not unlike what Angelica was doing now. Maybe. But maybe she was running toward something, and that's the idea she clung to as she chased this obsession.

Five

Reximortum glanced up from his newspaper as Tom entered the smoking room. Tom's silent footsteps had not disturbed the stillness of the house and announced his arrival. This pleased Rex, who'd trained him long ago but could not have predicted his good fortune in the training turning out so well.

"Sir, you have a call from New Orleans."

Rex nodded as he looked toward the grandfather clock. He'd been waiting for a call for over an hour. Waiting for anything brought displeasure, but for one of his generals to keep him waiting was unacceptable.

He picked up and waited for the connection.

Dark Knight's deep, pompous voice rang through. "Lord Reximortum, I apologize for the late hour. My contacts took longer to reach than I expected."

Rex forced even breaths. There would be time enough for punishment later. He'd grown tired of Dark Knight's incompetence, but his other generals were in necessary strategic positions. Though New Orleans was important, Rex could put an unintelligent fool as general there because he owned the city.

"What is the latest report?"

A nervous laugh crackled in the phone line and his voice whined.

"All of our contacts agree that the events will begin with the full moon. There are conflicting reports, but many also agree that it will be the naming of Valor that sets everything in motion."

Ah, so the rumors had gone through everyone now. Was it fear driving the predictions or truth? It was too rampant to tell anymore. He'd known long ago about this coming time from a more reliable source, but he also knew from experience how time changes circumstances. He'd need to be prepared either way. "I will be returning to New Orleans in the morning. You should prepare for my arrival."

A sharp intake of air crackled in Rex's ear. "You believe it will occur here?"

"Yes."

Rex returned the phone to its base and reclined back in his chair. He'd waited over twenty years for this opportunity, but what the Custos were good at was waiting. They'd existed long before *homo sapien* man and would likely exist long after if he got his way. But it felt like the right time now.

Of course, he'd thought twenty-one years ago that it was the right time as well.

Rosemary, the old crone, had destroyed that dream in one swift motion of the ax of fate that still caused anger to bubble in his veins.

He'd walked in on her in his sitting room of his Louisiana plantation where she'd been bowed over a book. He remembered thinking that Rosemary was old. Her discolored skin held the wrinkles of an untold number of years, but her eyes radiated the crystal blue of youth.

She'd snapped the book closed, the sound echoing in the quiet plantation home where they'd lived, and a scratching noise started in her chest and escaped her lips as she exhaled. "I have foreseen the future of the Vindica and yourself in a dream."

Rex had inwardly groaned, thinking he'd have to hear another prediction of his demise. He'd grown tired of warnings from those who feared him and those who lacked his vision. He'd been young and arrogant then. Ah, how time had taught him these difficult lessons. "What have you seen this time?"

Rosemary had laughed. He'd fought lunging at her, his temper quick to boil then. "You skepticism will decide your fate."

Rex had run his fingers across the black velvet bag in his pocket. A simple fix, so easy to dispose of his detractors. Rosemary had been loyal to him until his wife had begun working against him. Her abilities would be a loss, but her disobedience and annoyance outweighed her abilities.

She'd squinted at him, a strange look he'd never seen before in her eyes. He'd always seen a quiet sadness instead of this. "Great power was born today. Power you will never grasp. The power will be protected for the next twenty-one years, and then the Custos will face reckoning."

Tom had entered the room at that moment, and Rex had looked away from Rosemary. Tom had set the silver-plated tray with tea down near him, and Rex slipped Tom the velvet bag. Tom had offered Rosemary the laced cup before bowing low and exiting the room.

Rex had returned his attention to her, anticipating her sip and how long it would take to run through her. "What exactly did you see in your dream?"

Rosemary's eyes were that rare shade of blue and clear all at once. In that library as a young man, he hadn't learned the origin of those eyes. Her life would have been spared if he had.

"It truly was a vision." Her thin lips had smiled. "Abigail, one of the original Vindica founders, came to me. Her words were gentle and true. The Reckoning events have been set in motion with the birth of Valor. You are too late."

Rex had crossed to the fireplace not allowing his agitation to show. The Vindica organization held many superstitions and the belief that the end of the Custos would come, the Reckoning, was the one that caused a once powerful organization to decline. He'd wanted so much more for the organization. He wanted to make it powerful, return it to its full capabilities, but at each turn he met outdated beliefs and superstitions.

He'd spoken quietly, masking his anger. "You've warned me often of the Vindica in the recent past. I question your loyalty."

He'd felt Rosemary's eyes on his back. "I'm loyal to my people, our race. They must survive."

Rex had gripped the mantle tightly. He'd fought the urge to stop her heartbeat with his own ability. To reach inside her chest and feel the artery pumping from her chest and clench down on it and feel it shutter as he stuffed it out. He'd held back for some small sentiment for his teacher and mentor.

"Have you seen your own death?"

She'd leaned back and smiled wistfully, her eyes never leaving his. "My death will come in moments. I will not attempt to change my fate, for I die with purpose. We all play our role in destiny, and I have done mine."

Rex's anger had surged through him and he'd yelled. "I'm not superstitious. Seeing the future is for fools. We make our own destiny. No one will know what you have seen therefore no one will make it happen."

Rosemary's blue eyes had twinkled and she'd laughed at him. "My book holds my visions, and it will preserve my tellings. Every one of our kind will know what is to come."

"The book will be destroyed upon your death."

Rosemary's breathing became shallow. "I've sent my book to a place you daren't step foot in to be preserved for the one who'll destroy you. The prophecy will happen. The question is where will you fall after the Revelation."

Rex had yelled. "I will not fear a prophecy."

Rosemary had blinked rapidly. Her hands had clenched the chair as her eyes rolled back. "Your fear of failure will be enough."

Rex had smashed the tea tray, and it had clattered against the terra cotta tiles.

She'd found a way to prevent his dream from happening no matter how much his arrogance at the time had believed differently. The Custos line did believe that the Reckoning was coming, that its time was now. The Reckoning had been prophesized early on at the beginning of the Vindica organization. Their people would war—the different factions would fight for control. As the leader of the Dark Soldiers, the prophecy said he would lose. The savior of the Vindica would be Valor, a name given because the prophecy did not give specifics about who this person would be. He still believed that he made his own destiny, but he would have learned nothing from the past if he didn't admit to the fear that rested in his heart. He didn't fear death or the end though. As Rosemary had said, he feared failure. His desire was to be the leader of all the Custos line, and he did not want to die failing. He'd never let it happen.

Rex picked up the phone on his desk again and punched in the number that had taken years to procure. Years of searching for a way to get around destiny had brought knowledge that no one else possessed and had prepared him for what was to come.

"Yes?"

The voice on the other line was rich and grave. The man behind that voice was fear incarnate. "I'm requesting you meet me in New Orleans. I have a job for you."

A long silence followed. Rex breathed deeply to keep his heartbeat even. Only the coming events would make him make a deal with the devil.

"My kind does not work for you."

Rex taped his fingers on the desk. He'd expected this response. "You and I have a common goal that together can be reached."

Another long pause followed, and Rex waited. "I'm listening."

Rex exhaled. "I know you know about the prophecy. If we destroy the girl, we will find the book and we both win."

"You have identified this Valor?"

"No, I have a list of young women who will be twenty-one near the full moon that are possibilities. I don't care if we destroy them all, I guarantee we will find the book."

Another silence followed.

"Do you understand that I will destroy you if any deceit is involved?"

Rex inhaled slowly. "Yes."

A grunt followed by silence, his only response. He'd hung up.

Rex sank into his chair and allowed only a brief moment of doubt before shaking it off. Seven years ago when he'd discovered this individual, he'd begun planning for this moment. He didn't like giving up any of his control, but with time drawing to a close, his options had waned.

He'd make this work because he would not fail.

Six

The sun was a sliver behind the French Quarter horizon as the street lamps flickered. Angelica turned down Orleans Street, leaving behind the revelry of Bourbon Street. She'd wandered the streets for the last few hours alone, trying to get lost in the old world architecture and street entertainment. A calmness and relaxation had descended upon her with each street, and she knew she was falling in love with this city.

Her mother had written in her journal about this city as if it were her first lover. The words seemed strange in context, but Angelica understood as she wandered through the streets. It was beautiful, old world magical with its music filtering through, and the people's laissez faire attitude.

Lily's teenage scrawl babbled about friends and places she'd found on these streets when she'd lived here. Angelica wandered around looking for signs of those places. The people would come later, but she searched the places from twenty-six years ago that could offer some connection to her mother.

She stopped abruptly before a crumbling gray brick building with its weathered wooden sign scorched with the words *Gris Gris*. In the dull window of the deep green door, a plastic "help wanted" sign hung crookedly, and a faded open sign hung next to it. Menacing hand carved wooden masks and religious figures hung in the cloudy picture window.

Angelica searched for the carved initials on the door panel, and she found them near a carved triangle. *L.V.* This was it. The place her mother, Lily, had worked while living here.

A bell jangled as she pushed the door open. Tables of wooden carvings, bins of crystals, shelves of candles and incense, and a glass case with labeled potions filled the tiny shop. A strange herbal smell mingled with the smell of old. A rather tall, spiky haired gentleman stood behind the counter discussing a glossy paperback book with a loud intoxicated woman wearing a black and silver feather boa around her neck.

He was quite striking with his dark hair and deep bluish-green eyes. Angelica was studying the arch of his eyebrows and the beautiful long lashes when his eyes met hers. She looked away and bit down on her lip to hide her embarrassed smile.

She turned from him and pressed her fingers along the edge of a display table. She wanted to see those eyes again, but she straightened her spine and forced her gaze at the labeled minerals in tiny bins on the table.

She reached the end of the table and noticed the books lining the back wall. She ran her fingers over the spines of witchcraft, vampire, and voodoo books, conscious of the signs that read only touch the books if you're buying. She pulled a large, heavy book from the shelf and peeked back toward the counter.

His eyes met hers and she'd swear his lip twitched with a smile. He probably thought she was flirting instead of just giving into her eye obsession. Eyes fascinated her, and she looked for eyes like her own—unique, one of a kind, on stranger's faces. He certainly was handsome enough to flirt with though. *Not now, Angelica.* Angelica glanced away and looked down at the book she held with both hands.

The title, *Book of Shadows*, burned deep black into the blue leather. Something about that title caused memories to shift inside her head. She waited while an image struggled to the surface.

There'd been blinding flashes of white. Lily had worn a long white cotton dress with her hair pulled back in braids. She'd sat in a field intertwining long stemmed dried flowers around a midnight stone. A book had lain in her lap with yellowing pages. It was open to a picture of…something that had scared her. She'd looked away quickly.

Angelica's eyes sprang open and the image faded.

"Are you planning to buy that book?"

Angelica jumped as the store clerk stared down at her, a curious expression crossed his face and Angelica wondered what he was thinking. She could easily peek, but she didn't want to ruin this moment where she could just wonder and it could be anything.

He grinned. "I didn't mean to startle you. Can I help you with that book?"

Angelica laughed, recovering from her shock. She could feel her face form its expression. The expression she used to lure people in, to make them believe they were the center of her attention.

She hated that it came natural; she hated that she had to think not to fall into it. "I'm sorry," Angelica glanced down at the book. She *needed* to buy this. She felt it stir in her abdomen. "I'll take this book."

His eyes sparked with a grayish light. She nearly let her guard down and listened to his thoughts. It was such a strange reaction from a stranger.

He turned toward the register and she followed him. "Where are you from?" He asked glancing back toward her.

A skinny, dark-haired woman walked into the store and drew his attention from Angelica. The woman moved behind the counter and straightened an eclectic arrangement of objects on the counter.

Anywhere. Nowhere. Places she didn't remember. "Georgia, I'm visiting with a friend."

He smiled at the woman while he punched numbers into an antique register. His eyes didn't light the same way as earlier. A co-worker then? Not a girlfriend. What was she thinking anyway? She'd come to find answers not a love interest. "Roxy here means my shift is over for the evening. By the way, I'm Lysander. I'm a transplant."

Angelica watched him place her receipt inside the book. She reached out to take the bag and brushed his fingers before he jerked his hand away. The shiver up her arm was unexpected. "I haven't eaten since before I boarded a plane this morning. You wouldn't have a recommendation for me, would you?"

Lysander laughed, a nice relaxed sound easy on the ears. "There's a great place on St. Peter's to get good fried shrimp."

Angelica smiled coyly. "I'm afraid all the streets seem the same to me. Would it be too much trouble for you to show me since you're getting off? I'd really appreciate it."

Roxy snorted. "Mr. Cheap is not going to buy your lunch, darlin'."

Lysander glared at Roxy, reproachful.

Angelica smiled, focusing her attention on him. Rule six of getting what you wanted was making your mark feel as if he was the only one in the room. She inwardly cringed at her own thoughts. "How about a free meal in exchange for all those places I need to see while I'm in the city. I'd be eternally grateful if you did." She tilted her head for good measure.

Their eyes met and her face began to heat. That was new. Normally she felt nothing, only the intoxication of success.

He grinned. "Who could refuse an offer like that?"

She was good at pretending. She'd learned at the feet of Lily, her mother. She didn't even know what to call the woman who'd given birth to her because of all the lies that had been so convincing.

Fifteen minutes later after an awkward, but exhilarating walk, she and Lysander sat at a corner booth with red and white check tablecloth in the back of a small, noisy restaurant chasing fried shrimp po-boys with a cup of café au lait. Darkness had swallowed the streets moments after their entrance. People had come and gone at a fast pace through the small closet of a restaurant.

Angelica set her cup down and peeked at him below her eyelashes. She'd noticed he was studying her as much as she studied him. They'd gotten past pleasantries, but he seemed to be holding back. People didn't do that normally. "Have you worked at *Gris Gris* long?"

"Four or five years." He studied her with his arm resting on the back of the booth.

She suspected he was working his own charms, which felt ridiculous, but possible she supposed.

"Are there many people that work at the shop?"

"Roxy and I are it right now, except for the owner. We're looking for help, you interested?"

Angelica laughed as she leaned forward. "My resume says psychology school drop out."

Dead end with him, as she expected of course. Lily would have worked there long before he or Roxy. She could have gotten lucky and he could have been the son or grandson of the owner, but it had been a long shot. The owner may be a connection though.

"Is it one of those family tradition businesses, you know kept in the family for a century?"

"Nah." Lysander shook his head. "Mr. Roeneaux has only owned it for nine, maybe ten years. I think it was a distant relative that owned it before, but I'm not certain."

She'd have to try elsewhere. She studied the tawny liquid in her cup to hide her disappointment. It wasn't as if she'd expected to find the connection the first night. She hadn't expected it to be easy, but she'd been hopeful for some lead. She didn't have many places to look that were mentioned in the journal, and she needed to find something so that she didn't feel crazy for embarking on this search. She shook herself. Maybe it wasn't a complete loss. "So what else do you do besides the voodoo shop?"

"My band has a standing gig three nights a week, and I work for this parapsychologist. Really boring work."

Angelica traced the top of the cup with her finger. Her back stiffened and the hairs on the back of her neck rose. "I'd think chasing the paranormal would at least be interesting."

"Sometimes seeing is believing if you know what I mean. There's not much to see, and I'm just not the enthusiastic type."

Angelica's eyes didn't meet his. She breathed slowly to lower her pulse. "Sometimes people looking for the paranormal are overly enthusiastic."

She'd been harassed for three years of high school by an overly enthusiastic parapsychologist. He'd had constant video of her and had attempted to out her with various set ups that had resulted in more than one precarious situation. He'd even tried to trick Grams into signing over guardianship of her that last year. It'd been the first time she'd used a certain ability of hers she pretended didn't exist. She still didn't like to think about it- any of it.

She pulled herself out of the past and felt Lysander's eyes on her. Angelica checked her defenses and the walls were drawn tight. Being the paranoid she typically was with strangers, she couldn't believe she hadn't checked yet. She briefly lowered them and peeked into his thoughts, but she heard nothing. No random thoughts, no white noise. That was odd in itself, but she was being ridiculous. The statistics of meeting another psychic randomly couldn't be very high.

"I hate to end our conversation." He smiled, a dimple in his right cheek appearing. "But I must get ready for tonight's gig."

Angelica tucked her hair back behind her ear. She wouldn't call this evening a success, and she wasn't sure why her tricks hadn't worked on him. "I suppose I should get back to my friend who may have a search party out for me by now."

They stood up at the same time, and there was an awkward moment of smiling and staring. Angelica smiled as he allowed her to walk first and consoled herself with the thought that at least she didn't have to see him again.

At the open doorway of the restaurant, Lysander towered over her 5'4" frame. "It was nice meeting you. I hope we run into each other again."

She tilted her head as she touched his arm, not that her charms had worked on him. "I'm sure New Orleans isn't so big that we won't stumble upon each other again."

She slid her hand away, and his eyes darkened. "I play at Luther's Cross if you ever want to stumble in that direction."

"Maybe," Angelica said as she turned toward Bourbon. "Goodbye, Lysander Daniels."

She could feel his eyes on her with each step. Finally, at the corner of Bourbon, she looked back and smiled. He waved and then walked in the other direction.

Maybe it hadn't gone as poorly as she initially thought. Exhilaration returned to her as the street lamps glowed. She didn't want to return to Denise's and ruin this feeling.

She took a right instead of a left on Bourbon, avoiding the heavy crowd that had thickened since her first walk. The night air sparked with electricity and she wanted to feel it moments longer. Her mother had been here and loved it. It was nearly twenty-six years ago but she felt the connection as tangible as if it were the journal.

She'd walked about a block or two when she saw a small house set back from the three-story buildings. It conjured images of the Wizard of Oz and houses falling from the sky. The tornado had even dropped the front stairs down while all the other building's doors opened onto the street.

In the grimy window, a cardboard sign read help wanted.

It was a perfect analogy to how she felt. Her grandmother's death had dropped her into a world unfamiliar to her, and she could use a yellow brick road to point her in the right direction.

She walked up the stairs. It felt right, and maybe it was because she was like Dorothy. *Toto, she wasn't in Georgia anymore.*

Seven

Cain tightened his jacket around his middle and ducked away from the crowds. The buildings loomed overhead and draped the city streets in shadows. Not a place to lurk late at night as the news had reported continuously the last few days. The locals gossiped about Lewis's death and dead bolted their doors at dusk. Only their kind braved the streets knowing they were what the people feared. But it made it difficult for him to disappear on an empty street.

His double life was exhausting him, and with the addition of a third identity, he was having trouble keeping it all straight these days. It was a necessary evil to reach his final goal. His independence would all be worth it.

He turned left at Royal Street from St. Philip. He casually glanced behind him, for any signs of a tag-along. He didn't even know anymore who he didn't want tracking him, so it was better to just be alert. Performing a quick sweep of the area, he gathered no one hid in the corners.

The Cornstalk house on his left caught his attention as it always did. The house was a mention on the carriage tours, a tourist attraction. Everyone heard about the fence that Judge Francois Xavier Martin had imported for his young wife who missed her native Iowa. No one looked further than that. There were other cornstalk fences around the Quarters. White Street and Thalia Street both held a cornstalk fence, but people spoke about this one only.

He knew this city, the stories of the city. His father couldn't show up and assert his control over a city he'd abandoned long ago. It angered him, and he didn't want it to. It meant his father still had power over him, and that had to end.

He stopped walking at a rundown building on the corner of Domaine. He scanned the area once again, not hearing any sound of human brain waves, so he approached the shop. He peered into the dusty beveled glass window and saw her behind the counter.

Her mocha curls were pulled tightly behind her head, and her beaded earrings framed her delicate neck. As she reached overhead to pull a bottle down from a shelf, her shirt rose revealing the delicate, sensuous flesh of her concave belly.

Cain peered in with his telepathy, and heard only her humming. Her father was gone for the afternoon, hence the humming.

Cain entered quietly into the voodoo shop, holding the door against the jangle of the bell. He slipped behind the rack of woodcarvings and watched her as she moved around the shelves, collecting supplies as she hummed. Her movements were fluid as a dance, in and out of the jars and trays.

The dance ended and she stood behind a small table bent over her supplies. He crept around the shelves toward her. He'd been trained to move without sound, to breath unheard, and take someone by surprise before they realized they weren't alone. He moved in on her without hesitation.

Her heartbeat emanated through him as he came up behind her, and he nearly melted into her.

"I told you not to do that again." She continued working, only her hands moving. Cain leaned toward her, wrapped his arms around her middle, and breathed in deeply from the crook of her neck.

Vanilla and lavender lotion mingled with the ginger of her concoction and a spicy smell he couldn't identify.

Intoxicating. He placed his lips on the delicate crook of her latte neck.

"You need to tell me your secret."

She turned, her lips a crooked smile. "Never. Then I would not know when ya were 'ere."

Cain tenderly ran his finger down her arm, and his pulse quickened as she shivered under his touch. The feel of her nestled against him, the passion in her expression, even the accent all weighed on him tugging up a moan.

She reached up and brushed his face with her fingertips. "What am I going to do with ya?"

He lifted her easily by her derriere and molded her into him. She snuggled her head into his neck and delicately worked her lips on him. He groaned as the warmth traveled downward. He edged them around a display of glass bottles and made it to the back room before her nibbling on his neck rippled to the point where he took her in her father's front storeroom.

Muted candlelight illuminated the back room casting seductive shadows against the walls. She'd known he was coming. This only heightened his anticipation and his body heat increased. He was so lucky to have found her. He lay her down on the fuzzy white rug that she'd added months ago after they'd made it back here. As he straightened up, she arched her back toward him and pulled him back down.

She whispered into his ears as she caressed his neck with her lips. "Don't worry about da door. No one will come."

He pushed her skirt up and gripped her hips as he rubbed her against him. She fumbled with his pants, and he nearly leapt out of them as she slowly eased them off.

He grabbed her roughly, but she returned the roughness by rolling herself on top of him.

He looked up into her needy emerald eyes, and couldn't imagine her not being his. She came down on him hard, and he groaned as she worked him inside of her.

He allowed her to work slowly until he couldn't resist anymore, and then he yanked her below him, gripped her tightly and worked her until her eyes warmed, and she groaned with pleasure.

He placed her on top of his chest and sighed. She snuggled into him, running her hand along his chest.

"My Dark Soul always comes to please me."

He inhaled perfumed bath cream mingled with her flesh. He ran his finger down her arm feeling her body respond to his touch.

"I want to see more of you. It's never enough."

She sighed as she spread kisses across his chest. "Everything will fall as it will."

He looked into her guarded face. Her eyes did not look up into his own. She wasn't one to shy away or be intimidated. She was a category five hurricane, fearless and destructive.

"For us?"

She snuggled closer into his chest and didn't answer. His gut clenched tightly as he breathed in uneasy. She was the only one he trusted. The only one who truly knew him—all sides of him and she didn't run or try to change him. As a powerful seer, he counted on her to have the answers. Pauses meant to worry.

"De future is not certain, but I will be 'ere for you until you don't want me to be."

He gripped her tighter, a little of the uneasiness unclenching. "Then you will be mine forever. I've told you this. This plan will work, I promise."

There were no other options. It had to work because he needed to escape his father, and this was the only way.

She looked up at him, her eyes hopeful. She shifted herself and crawled over him until her face was even with his, before resting back on top of him.

"Ya future is 'appening now. You will get what ya want. I'm certain."

The rest of the uneasiness uncoiled. "No doubts, nothing you aren't telling me?"

She kissed him; her lips searching his.

"Priestess Madame Lulu says so, and she's never wrong."

A brief moment of intoxication flooded him. Relief. Satisfaction.

He'd be successful. He'd finally get what he wanted. Madame Lulu was a powerful Voodoo priestess and Simone's grandmother. Simone had trained under her, but Lulu was a force not to be screwed with. And thankfully for Cain, she was on his side- most of the time.

He pulled her closer, feeling her warm, soft flesh against his own. "You know I want you right there with me, right?"

She nodded and rubbed her fingers through his hair. His body responded again.

Eight

Angelica glanced up the street once again toward the cathedral and then back down at the row of colorful analogous looking buildings. This was the place. Lily had sketched a picture of the house with its thin poles and second floor ironwork on a page of the journal with the words "First Home" across the top in pencil shaded letters.

The house appeared normal. Its yellow was faded only a shade or two, and the door appeared to have been repainted its evergreen shade recently. Its three stories rose above her from her place across the street and no sign of life appeared in any of its many windows.

The journal ended with Lily living happily ever after here, but Angelica knew that the story had gone on after the fairytale ending. And the true end wouldn't be found in a fairytale book, only Brother Grimm's version.

Angelica crossed the narrow street and walked right up to the door and knocked before she changed her mind.

A tall, dark-haired gentleman swung the door open after a spell. His intense blue eyes stared her down, and Angelica squirmed and glanced back to her safe spot across the street that was now blocked by a white van crawling down the pavement.

"Can I help you?"

The door opened wider and Lysander stood to the stranger's left.

Angelica, taken back, lost her composure a moment. She recognized the panic seizing her and exhaled to release some of it.

Lysander's eyebrows dipped into confusion. "How did you find me?"

Angelica swallowed and forced her lips into "the smile" as she referred to it. "Don't flatter yourself. I've come to see a Mr. John Landon."

There was a flicker through his blue-green eyes. A flicker of anger, maybe? She couldn't tell, but a moment later his face relaxed and he grinned.

"Now you've embarrassed me. Sorry for my rudeness, come on in."

The two gentlemen exchanged a look but stepped aside for her to enter a grand foyer. She brushed up against Lysander, hesitating in the middle of the move. Her brain said stop it. No conning here, just a simple search for information.

She exhaled in an attempt to relax. "Is Mr. Landon busy?"

The foyer's twelve-foot ceilings were trimmed with intricately carved wooden moldings. The wood staircase rose before her with rounded banisters, and elaborately framed doorways lining either side of the sweeping ground floor of the stairs. A massive oil painting hung from the wall to her right. According to his hairstyle, spectacles, and suit, it was an older portrait, some ancestor too long ago to be living now. A vase of fragrant white magnolias was placed on a table to her left.

She couldn't see how this grand house was much different than Gram's Georgia manor. What had made the place so comfortable for Lily?

The stranger glanced at Lysander with a frown. "We're actually all working on something right now. Was John expecting you?"

It was the look that passed between the two that was telling. That steely edge to his voice backed it up. Her instant assessment was that his suspicions had been aroused. Suspicious people needed more convincing—a full-blown cover story that was bullet proof. She didn't have that yet. Better to go with Plan B.

"If this is an inconvenient time, I could come back later."

Lysander stepped forward, his eyes on her. She kept the smile. "If you want to wait, I don't mind waiting with you."

A shorter gentleman with a whitish blonde receding hairline approached from the far corner of the house. "Wait with whom?"

Lysander gave the gentleman a quick glance as though he weren't important. "Griffen Jones meet Angelica, I'm sorry, I didn't get a last name?"

Angelica reached her hand out to meet his already outstretched one. "Angelica Acacia."

She turned to the stranger who was studying her still, his eyes like lasers. He hesitated, but then reached out. "Mark Bryant."

Griffen glanced in Lysander's direction before returning his kind eye toward her. "How did you come to know Lysander?"

She laughed, feeling the pressure of Mark's eyes boring into her. "I met him at *Gris Gris*. He's the friendliest face I've met since arriving yesterday."

A loud thump against a wooden surface erupted from a room to the left. The doorway was at a far angle so she couldn't see what had made the noise. How many people were in this house? She hadn't prepared for a large audience. The panic crept under her cool exterior shell and she could feel herself becoming jumpy.

Mark pointed towards an opposite doorway. "How about we move this party into the study until Landon's available?"

At this, the three men glanced toward the doorway. Griffen's face was the only one that didn't wear a poker face expression, and his look of fear sent a sharp stab of heat through her center. What was in that room?

Griffen motioned his arm toward the study. His freckles all seemed to scream that something was wrong. "Shall we, Angelica?"

Angelica smiled, not at all confident in her ability to get out of this one. She was confident that she could open the door when she needed it, but not without giving herself away. "This is an amazing old home. I've heard it was once a hotel."

When in doubt, small talk always worked. As they all shuffled toward the study, Angelica peeked at the other doorway.

She froze as the scene unwound, registering bit by bit in her conscious.

A blonde girl stared at a floating vase. She'd never seen anyone else do this, and this caused a rampage of emotions to surge through her.

Angelica's protections evaporated and behind the blonde's glare, Angelica felt anger ignite.

Angelica glanced up at Mark as she felt him brush up against her back. A shock ran through her as she felt the pop of a firecracker as the woman's anger boiled over.

She looked back into the room to see the vase hurtling toward her.

Everyone froze. The vase grew larger and larger.

She heard someone yell but sound would not be distinguished through the tunnel she found herself in.

Angelica could nearly feel the vase before she lifted her hand and froze it in mid flight.

She released a breath of relief as it hung inches from her face. Her senses began to awaken, and she felt all their eyes on her.

Her body began to tremble as she was watched in fear. Alarm bells vibrated through her as the room full of witnesses came into focus. Lysander looked down at her, expectantly.

The tremors coursed through her. Lessons of her childhood

screamed at her from her conscious. This ability was to be hidden at all times. It could be seen. The trembling reached her hands and panic seized control of her body. Who would they tell? Fear tore through her like a runaway car.

The vase exploded spewing shards of glass everywhere. Hands flew up around the room in protection, and they tucked their heads under. Angelica sprinted toward the door, repelling the shards away from her.

She waved the front oak door open with a switch of her wrist and darted out into the street. She ran breathlessly down Charters and ducked around the corner of St. Ann's before slowing down.

What had she done?

Lily's first rule of not getting caught was to never reveal an ability to strangers.

Angelica forced herself to a walk at Royal, and she blended in with the small groups strolling down the street.

She breathed deeply, her mind raced, and she scanned the area for followers. A balding man watched her from his lean to against a brick building.

He didn't glance away when their eyes met.

Angelica continued walking, watching to see if he would follow her.

He continued to lean against the building, but his eyes never moved from her. He wore a wrinkled suit and a black tie as if he were out of some bad spy movie.

He didn't follow her as she turned left down Royal. Just some curious tourist she supposed. She must be imagining it.

It was the witnesses she'd left on Charters street that she needed to worry about.

Nine

The metal warehouse doors shuddered and announced Cain's late arrival. He hardened himself and waited as Dark Knight approached him.

The ceremonial candles lit the room as if spotlights erupted from the wicks, and Cain could see the twelve cloaked figures gathered in neat military style rows.

They were the last to arrive of the New Orleans unit that had dwindled in the last five years. His father's doing to be sure, as he'd scattered men to the far corners to enact some top-secret plan that no one gave any indication of knowing the details.

Dark Knight stopped before him and crossed his arms against the red sash around his waist. "Discipline, Dark Soul Cain. You must learn the lesson of punctuality."

Cain gritted his teeth. He hated when this man, who's real name was Kevin, spoke like some ancient Chinese philosopher. As a soldier, he understood discipline, but it was the archaic rituals, the robes, the candles, the chants, that he took issue with. They were a militia. That's all. No one believed in the rituals anymore. It was their abilities that brought results, not some mumbo jumbo muttered above candlelight.

"Our situation presents a problem at times. We do what we can.

If punctuality is more important than our cover, please advise us as such."

Dark Knight stared down at him a moment, dislike evident in his blank eyes. Finally, he lifted a black glove and motioned for them to take their places in the lineup. Cain moved forward as well as the two behind him who'd remained quiet.

The chanting began as they lined up, and Cain used the opportunity to look around the room. To escape his father, he'd need an army. A much smaller army than the hundred plus soldiers his father led as head of the Dark Soldiers, but he couldn't be a threat to his father alone. He didn't need to out number, he just needed to be smarter.

Unfortunately, intelligence is what these sheep lacked. He'd narrowed his list down to two possibilities amongst this crowd by the time the chanting had ceased.

With a wave of his hand, Dark Knight called the men to order.

He barked out "Status updates" and the room silenced.

"What have we learned about this Serena Landon, Cain?"

Cain focused on the black stain on the concrete in front of him. "I believe she will be declared Valor due to circumstance. I don't feel she's powerful enough to be a threat."

"Still, she is a young woman of the age. Lord Reximortum will decide how to proceed. What of the other young woman?"

Cain flinched. "She's unknown. The threat has not been assessed yet."

Dark Knight's eyes filled with fear like a balloon. Not surprising. He'd only heard the word threat.

"Is she a threat to our plans?"

"It is too early to speak with certainty."

Water dripped in the distance from within the warehouse as Dark Knight's thoughts tick-tocked through his brain. With Reximortum's visit, Dark Knight would need to prove his usefulness. It was the same with all the leaders, the appearance of action counted for more than meaningful action. Cain could feel gears clicking into place in his mind.

"We will assign someone to gather intelligence."

Cain turned as the robed figure to his left cleared his throat. "I volunteer for the assignment, Sir."

"Falcon, you have not reached full Dark Soul status yet. Are you ready for this assignment?"

Falcon's head remained lowered, his face untouched by the licking flames. "I've learned much from our best men. I'm ready to prove myself."

Dark Knight studied him. Falcon did not twitch under the scrutiny. "Very well. Your assignment is to monitor the young lady and submit regular status reports."

Cain's mind drifted as other status reports began. His father would return after two years away; an absence Cain hadn't minded.

Forgiveness was not something he'd allowed his father, and his father had come to hate the reminder that stood between them.

Rex had taken away his mother, and he couldn't bring himself to forgive the man responsible, his own father.

At eleven years old he'd discovered a woman locked in the back building of their compound while hiding from Tom. Cain had taunted her for weeks: throwing rocks at the wood, pretending to unlock the door, and even dropping her food in the dirt. The woman hadn't yelled or cried, although he'd tried real hard to make her do both. She'd look at him in this certain way that twisted his insides like the rocket ride he'd ridden at the festival. Within weeks, that guilt that gurgled in his belly had led to him swiping bread and grapes from the kitchen to annoy Tom. He'd listened to her talk about Gandhi and finding a better way. He'd asked her if she was trying to be like the old philosopher. Sadness had tugged at the corners of her smile.

He didn't know who she was. She hadn't told him, and he hadn't bothered to ask since there was always some prisoner.

At a Dark Soldiers' gathering, he'd hidden himself under a linen draped table within hearing distance. His greatest wish at the time was to be allowed to attend. He'd been thrilled when his father had stopped to have a conversation near his spot.

A balding man had mumbled. "Have you taken care of the matter with your wife yet?"

A silence had answered. Cain thought Rex was looking around for eavesdroppers, so he'd held extra still, holding his breath.

Rex's voice was low and detached. "She's been captured and is being contained on the grounds. I'll deal with her shortly."

"Good, good. We must be cautious if our aim is to be reached."

His entire body had frozen as his thoughts raced to grasp and hold onto those words. His father had only one wife. He'd badgered many tutors attempting to find out if his father had been honest about her abandonment. Only one woman was on the grounds that night.

He'd had to wait an hour to escape the table. An hour where his own thoughts tortured him. After everyone had moved to the altar, he'd torn off down the property, his desperation for answers driving him. The guards hadn't crossed his consumed mind.

He'd reached her first though.

The word mom had leapt from his throat from some deep place within. He'd thrown off the padlock, as she'd burst into tears. He'd landed upon her, and she'd cried harder. His heart had hurt in a way he'd never known it could.

The guard had yanked them apart, but not before her words had seared through him.

I have always loved you, my baby. I never wanted to hurt you. I wish I'd been given another choice. Please forgive me.

With those words and her death, all the hatred that had built inside of him settled onto the man responsible.

A shudder echoed throughout the building as the warehouse doors closed, and Cain pulled himself back to the present.

The man now approached. He was a slight man, with thinning black hair. His crystal blue eyes cut into everyone as he assessed each robed figure. Cain's fist clenched again as his father's eyes slid over him barely registering his presence.

"Dark Knight, I'd appreciate an update."

Dark Knight faltered a moment. His fear wrinkling his forehead, but he then motioned for everyone to rise. "Meeting is dismissed." His eyes met Cain's and a sadistic spark lit them. "Would you like an update with your son as well?"

Rex's attention passed him over again. "No, I'll discuss matters with him later. Our situation here is more immediate."

Rex and Dark Knight walked toward the door.

Nothing had changed. He'd been dismissed long ago.

Everyone was quiet as the two walked toward a back office area. The tension was so thick it draped the room like a thick New Orleans' fog.

As their backs disappeared behind the doors, a collective sigh went up around the room.

"Did you know he was coming?" Alfred, a gentleman older than his father, asked.

Cain shook his head. "I'm just a soldier."

Alfred regarded him in disbelief for a moment but then nodded concession.

"Does that mean it's going to happen here?" Echo asked with too much eagerness in his voice.

No one responded, each concealing his own thoughts. None of them were thinking this was a good thing. The full moon was in a week, and the New Orleans Dark Soldiers weren't ready for any kind of attack.

"We should be chasing the book down not some legendary person we don't even know exists." Falcon's tone indicated his disapproval. He'd need to watch that. This group wasn't to be trusted.

"Nonsense." Alfred glared at him down his long nose. "You young people know nothing."

Echo chimed in enthusiastically. "Then tell us."

"It isn't my place." Alfred shook his head. "But I will say, the book throughout time has found its way to Valor."

"Throughout history?" Cain asked. "There has been more than one Valor?"

Alfred shushed him. Cain coiled back as if he'd lashed out at him the sound had been so forceful. "We don't speak of these things. I've said too much. Let us disperse before we get into dangerous territory."

With that, he walked away.

Cain and Falcon exchanged a look but neither said anything. Cain stored that tidbit of information with everything else he'd gathered and could use to go up against his father.

Ten

She didn't belong with them. Kline lurked in the shadows, darkness his cover. He watched from afar, but it didn't matter. He could hear all their thoughts.

She stumbled in those five-inch heels and a string of profanity ran through her mind, but not past her lips.

Control. Good.

The hairy one laughed. "She can't hold her liquor. I told you not to give her that last one."

"Shut up," the strange looking one called Denise replied. "She's fine."

"It's just those fucking heels you dressed her in." The speaker was the one that Kline disliked. He was too close to her, touching and brushing against her each chance he had. It caused an uneasiness in him and he wasn't sure why. He'd never spoken to her, but he'd watched her from afar for days. He'd noticed the way she bit her bottom lip when she was deep in thought, and the way her entire demeanor changed when she was talking to people as if she were putting on a show.

Her appearance still startled him after days. Her long hair fell perfectly into place no matter what she was doing, and although her eyes hadn't met his own, the clear blueness of them had mesmerized him through glass and a few mirrors. Her heart shaped face was delicate, but her thoughts were tough. Such a strange contradiction that stirred him and intensified his fascination.

I'm not drunk you idiots. Oldest trick in the book. Dump it in a glass when you aren't looking.

Her thoughts were strange. Kline knew these were what humans called friends, but she didn't hold them in high esteem.

She stumbled again, but he could tell it was forced this time. "I think I just need to sleep."

"Come on, one more stop," Denise whined. "We always get a night cap at Trace's."

David's hand came to the small of Angelica's back. "I can take her home."

Kline tensed and his vision darkened. David's thoughts licked in and out with alcohol, but they involved thoughts of what he could do to her as he tucked her into bed.

As if. Not going to happen, jackass.

Kline chuckled to himself to retain his silence. She could read Kline's thoughts as well. This had caught him off guard the first time he'd watched her. He'd only been told that she was one of the targets, not what abilities she possessed. She was a strong telepath. She closed herself off, and still the thoughts around her filtered in. He had to remain a safe distance so his own thoughts didn't transmit.

Denise stopped in the middle of the street. "No." She placed her hands on Angelica's shoulders. "You are in New Orleans, the party capital of the world as far as I'm concerned." She grabbed Angelica's chin. "Wake up!"

Angelica gritted her teeth and that smile Kline had come to know appeared on her lips. It was fake. Her real smile was more natural and slightly lopsided.

I'd like to wake you up with a swift kick to your tiny ass.

"Okay, one more drink. But I'm doing this under protest."

Denise released Angelica's chin and twirled in the street. Kline stepped further into the darkness as Rodney scanned the street. They were the only ones on it right now, and Kline hid only thirty feet away.

A car door slammed and drew his attention toward Toulouse Street. Kline could have sworn that he'd been spotted, but no they all began to move forward.

Angelica looked back though and Kline stilled his heart. Instinct. Custos could hear heartbeats like the inching forward of the second hand on a clock. She couldn't do it though. The humans only had drops of Custos blood inside them. It gave them the abilities, but not the senses on steroids effect.

She tilted her head though and listened.

What is that? Something pounding?

I must be imagining it.

She shook her head and followed the group.

The ramifications of her thoughts jolted through him. That wasn't possible. She shouldn't hear anything. None of the humans could. It had been part of his guard studies. Lucilius would believe she was the one.

He'd kill her.

A strange emotion flooded through him as he stood in the dark watching them walk away. Was that panic? He wasn't even sure.

He could wait though. He could watch her more before he reported it to Lucilius. He could keep this to himself. It would be real simple since Gint was caged for the night. It was Kline's job to watch the women and assess the danger before Gint did his duty.

Gint the sadist. The man who brought death; controlled by Lucilius, who thought nothing of killing these women, but wanted as much information from them before he allowed Gint to torture and kill them.

Yes, he could keep this to himself for now.

A slight shuffling nearby drew him from his thoughts. A tall figure wearing a hoodie strolled down the street with his hands tucked into his jean's pockets. He looked like a local just passing through, but something made Kline pay closer attention.

He walked slowly, trailing the group by twenty yards. He kept pace with the group though. Kline thought he might be imagining but then he slowed again as they slowed.

Under a dim street lamp, his face fell out of the shadows of his hoodie, Kline recognized him. Dark Soldier Falcon.

He had another name as well. The one he used when he pretended to be a Vindica member instead of a Dark Soldier. Kline had yet to learn it.

So whom was he watching her for? The Vindica or the Dark Soldiers?

This could be problematic for his plans. This guy had just moved himself to the top of Kline's need to identify list.

Eleven

Angelica sifted through the bins of crystals, studying their small black printed labels. Gregory, another employee, had mentioned that they had healing properties. They looked pretty, but she wasn't certain about this healing business.

The tiny bell jingled over the door and Angelica straightened up as a young woman entered. The blonde hesitated at the antique dolls to her left and city souvenirs to her right. Angelica had suffered the same reaction. The shop hadn't decided its identity yet.

The woman tucked her arms close to her chest and eyed the dolls with mistrust.

"Can I help you?"

Angelica smiled, but the woman's gaze didn't shift from the porcelain faces.

"I have an appointment."

"Oh." Angelica nodded, understanding her discomfort. "He's finishing up with the last appointment now. You can wait by the door or you can browse the store."

"Thanks," she said finally looking to Angelica, her lips twitching. "I've never done this before. My friend made the appointment and then had an emergency. Is he any good?"

Angelica smiled. *He's cheating on you. He has been for months. He plans on leaving you next week.* "He's better than most."

Angelica cringed. Gregory was the worst of the three psychics that worked out the back room. He was a complete fraud, and Angelica hadn't seen him do a correct reading yet. Gregory insisted that the psychic energy of the Quarters spoke to him. Yep, strange one. Annabel at least had people instincts, and could read body language. Madame Regina, the owner, seemed to be the only one of the three with any psychic ability. Even she didn't get a connection every time like Gregory claimed to have.

The couple that had entered earlier pushed their way through the beaded doorway. His face was stiff, his eyebrows were furrowed in a cross sort of way, and his eyes stormed with anger. The woman's lips trembled and her eyes glistened with unshed tears.

Angelica sighed. Gregory had told her that she'd never have a baby. They'd been trying for four years.

A tremble ran through Angelica. The woman was pregnant now. Five weeks. There'd been a party with a few drinks. They'd relaxed. Angelica stopped the vision there.

The woman looked back toward the curtain as the other woman disappeared behind the wooden beads.

The woman ran a hand over her flat belly. "He could be wrong."

The man snarled. "I'm more psychic than he is. Let's go get a drink at that bar we saw earlier."

The woman turned and met Angelica's eyes. Angelica smiled.

You know you're pregnant. They'll have a test at that store you passed earlier. You don't have to wait to find out.

The woman's eyes cleared. "I need to get something at that store we passed earlier."

"Fine, let's get out of here."

Angelica returned to her crystal gazing, a smile plastered on her lips. That had felt good. It was rare for her to feel good about using that particular ability. It usually felt dirty to dip into someone else's mind. She didn't usually implant positive thoughts; hence the guilt.

The bell jangled again, and Angelica turned to meet the new customers, feeling rather pleased with herself.

Lysander's tall, brooding figure erased the smile from her face.

"How did you find me?" It popped out before her thoughts could organize themselves.

He smiled. "I didn't. I came to have a reading."

Had he really? It sounded like a line, but maybe Annabel, Gregory, or Madame Regina belonged to the Vindica. Angelica had found herself suspicious of everyone since the vase exploded.

"Our psychic on duty is not very psychic, but I have a feeling you know that."

He moved closer to her, and her body tingled.

"Couldn't you help me with a reading?"

His eyes seared through her and her temperature raised a notch... or two.

Angelica licked her lips. "What would you like to know?"

He grinned, revealing his perfect teeth. Damn. She wasn't some doe-eyed schoolgirl with a crush. It was too dangerous to get involved with him after what she'd learned.

"Why didn't you tell me when we first met?"

"Do you tell strange women something like that?"

"What?" He stepped closer. "It's my best pick up line."

Angelica laughed, and she felt the tension ease. "You wouldn't use it as a pick up line if those white jackets had tried putting you away."

His face contorted and his tone was sharp. "You weren't protected by your guardian?"

Angelica struggled to breath as his strong, manly protective emotions consumed her. Pulling the threads tighter around that wall separating his thoughts from hers, she tried not to allow his urges to intoxicate her. "My Grams was the one who tried to commit me."

He stepped closer and she could feel his breathing. She wanted to touch his chest and feel it rise and fall beneath her palm. He must be doing something to her because this was so unlike her.

"John would like to speak to you."

And there it was. Reality crashing down on her shoulders. "How do I know if I can trust all of you?"

His fingers reached out and trailed down her arm. She steadied herself against the chill. It was too intimate for work and a blush heated her. "Your abilities will not lie to you. Trust them."

Her instincts were crap when he was around.

The back curtain parted noisily and the woman emerged smiling and relaxed.

Gregory had told her that the scuzz bag boyfriend was going to propose to her next week.

What a shock it will be when she finds him in bed with his coworker.

Angelica sighed. Ms. Soon-to-be-Scorned was on her own for this one. No whispering in her head could put a positive spin on that mess.

Gregory stood between the strings of beads evaluating his fingernails and jutting out his chin. "You can go now, Angelica. Annabel should be here in fifteen minutes and I have no more appointments."

Angelica wasted no time grabbing her knapsack and heading toward the door.

Lysander followed her. "Do you mind if I walk you home?"

Manners or a hidden agenda? She grappled back and forth between the two. He had to have some flaw.

"I suppose," Angelica said smiling. "I'm not inviting you up though. I don't think we've progressed to the stage of you meeting my friends."

"Two dates isn't enough?"

Angelica looked sideways at him. Two dates? Since when did this count as a date. "I don't think I'll even let my future husband meet these friends."

He laughed, soft and deep. She enjoyed the sound of its softness. They took St. Ann Street to Royal. Angelica didn't notice the darkness of the hour until they left the bright lights of Bourbon Street.

"Isn't the city beautiful at night? Almost like it was a hundred years ago." She could imagine the horses and carriages instead of the parked cars. Dirt instead of black top.

He nodded. "Dangerous, too."

But couldn't they take care of themselves? She must admit that safety didn't play too often in her thoughts. She'd always assumed she could take care of any threats. But if he said it was dangerous, what did he believe to be out there?

When they reached Royal Street, Angelica spotted a woman in a neglected store doorway. Beneath mounds of curly coffee hair, intense brown eyes scrutinized her. The woman's gypsy skirt and big bosom peasant top appeared normal, but the high cheekbones, flawless tawny complexion, and bottomless eyes caused Angelica's flesh to prick.

"You shouldn't be out at night." Her rich deep voice rang out.

The chill vibrated through her and increased as Lysander stepped closer. "Lady, go away."

The woman's scrutiny burned through her. "People like you are killed when they are out late at night."

Angelica shuddered and Lysander draped his arm around her shoulder and squeezed. "I've got it under control."

Angelica felt as though everything in her head opened to this strange woman. The walls neglected.

Her eyes gazed into Angelica's own. "Fate is the devil and will not be ignored forever. War and darkness will descend upon your people. You will answer its call."

Angelica allowed Lysander to pull her away. "Don't the crazies get hospital care?"

Lysander continued the brisk pace. "Not all the street psychics are insane."

And there it was. That panic fluttering in her middle. Did she really want to get involved with whatever this was? A few weeks ago her biggest issue was convincing Trevor to stop planning con jobs. The weight of what this place could be scared her. She'd come here for answers, but the possibilities were beginning to send warning signs that leaving may be her best option.

At the door to the apartment staircase, she turned to Lysander to say good night. She wondered what it would be like to kiss him. To really kiss him, not just because she was conning him.

She couldn't though. He and Landon House came as a package deal, and she wasn't certain about the package yet.

He smiled. "Shall I see you tomorrow at Landon House then?"

"No restraints or tests?"

"I promise." He laughed. "Maybe later though."

She didn't want to go. Everything in her screamed that it was against what she'd been taught. But if she didn't go, she'd need to give up on ever knowing about her mother Lily. She couldn't make that choice. It wasn't in her. "I'll be there tomorrow."

"Good night, Angelica Acacia."

Her mouth opened to correct him. To add that last name that she'd dropped long ago on those front steps of Grandmother Angel's house. But her instructions were to never use it. A part of her to remain hidden, along with everything else.

She closed her mouth and unlocked the door and disappeared

into the courtyard without a backwards glance.

This is what they meant when they said playing with fire. She could feel the embers igniting and the whole charade going up in flames.

Twelve

Reximortum assessed his accommodations with a quick scan. His study had gone untouched, though this wasn't even his home anymore.

"Sir, you mentioned that the event will occur here. Is there someone specific we should be watching?"

Rex signed. Dark Knight's anxiousness wore on his nerves, which were already tense.

"Who have you examined so far?"

Dark Knight jostled about, jarring furniture as he moved around the room. "Serena Landon, John Landon's adopted daughter has been assigned someone." He paused, and Rex took that as a sign that he needed to pay attention. "There's a new prospective. An Angelica Acacia. Nothing is known about her yet, but I've assigned someone to find out though."

Rex nodded. "Don't waste your energy on Serena Landon. Keep me updated on the new one."

"You believe it to be the new girl and not Serena Landon?"

"No." Rex shook his head. "Serena is not powerful enough to be a threat. This new one may be."

Tom entered the room. Rex had noticed his step was slower, and his messages suffering. He was nearing seventy and maybe he'd like to retire. Rex couldn't imagine not having him around, but he'd been loyal and deserved the opportunity. He'd broach it after the coming weeks.

Tom nodded. "He's here, Sir."

Rex felt a jolt in his chest. "Send him in. Thanks, Tom."

"Who's here?" Dark Night looked to him expectantly.

"I'm sorry, Dark Knight." Rex straightened his tie. "This is a private meeting that I've gone to great lengths to arrange. You'll have to excuse me."

Dark Knight stuttered. "Of course, I'll just be in my own study down the hall if you need me."

He rose, stood for a moment flabbergasted, and then exited the room with his quick shuffle.

Rex gave the room a quick scan, and then waited as he heard footsteps down the corridor. He was nervous. Though he'd never admit it to anyone else—weakness shouldn't be worn on one's sleeve— he believed in acknowledging his feelings. This philosophy had prevented him from irrational actions over the last several years. A lesson he'd learned in painful ways during his youth.

The door opened and Tom showed his guest inside and closed the door behind him. Rex knew that Tom would be waiting on the other side of that door when the meeting concluded.

His guest filled the room with his near seven-foot height. His pale complexion was milky, but what drew his attention were his eyes. He had the blue eyes of a Custos, a shade they called sky.

Lucilius snarled. "Let's get this straight. I'm not working for you. This is a partnership. That book belongs to me."

Rex studied him. Rex had been twenty-six when he'd first learned that pureblooded Custos still existed. Pureblooded. Not the hybrid mix of human DNA and Custos DNA that existed in Rex's people, but the direct descendants of the originals that had existed thousands of years before *Homo Sapiens*. He'd stumbled across it by accident while searching for the book and had come close to losing his life in that crossing. Lucilius was the only one he'd ever met, and he'd never said if there were others. Rex assumed there was, but he wasn't certain.

"I believe we can both get what we want."

Lucilius glared at him. "It's a girl who's supposed to have it? Which one?"

Rex smiled. "I don't know which one, but I have a method to discover that information."

"A method?" Lucilius regarded him suspiciously. "I thought you knew she was here. I'm not going to chase one of your hunches."

"She is here." Rex shifted. He could feel Lucilius scanning his thoughts. Although Rex was the most powerful he'd ever known, it was impossible to block out a pure blooded Custos. "I have three women whose birthdays all fall within the window. I want you to kill them."

"Is it one of them?"

Rex would have liked to lie, but he knew that it was impossible. "No, but their murders will cause the Vindica to face what it has avoided. They will name Valor, leading us to her."

Lucilius contemplated his words, before drawing a breath. "Sounds like a waste of life, but it makes me no matter. How do you know this will work?"

Rex nodded. "This person knows who she is and will realize that if she comes forward no one else will die. Protecting the innocent is a weakness of the Vindica."

Lucilius grunted. "I will know if you cross me. Remember that your tricks don't work on me."

Rex nodded, and then Lucilius was gone.

Dooming girls to die was really the Vindica's fault. The original prophecy didn't specifically say that the savior would be female or male. The organization had made that assumption a few hundred years ago, and then it had become part of the myth, part of the facts. Reximortum rather thought this was limiting in a search, but when one wants to force an organization to act, one must play into its fears.

Tom entered the study and closed the door. "I hope you know what you are doing, my Lord."

Rex smiled. He heard the strains of worry. "I've had years to plan, and I've learned from past mistakes. What have you learned about that matter we discussed?"

Tom nodded. "It's as you suspected. Cain does not obey Dark Knight's orders well. From what I gather, he hasn't gone against orders yet, but he pushes it to that point."

Rex sat down at his desk chair. "Good, Tom. I grow tired of Dark Knight, but they all attempt to hide things from me."

"They fear you, Sir, as they should, but they need lessons in loyalty."

Rex laughed. "Where do I find more men like you?"

Thirteen

Angelica shifted from one foot to the other as she stared at the yellow brick building. Images of those green doors thrusting open and close had plagued her dreams last night. Nothing else— only doors and dread and a pounding heart jerking her awake, countless times.

A general rule she'd clung to involved not walking into anything her wits couldn't charm her way out. She couldn't shake this feeling of being sucked into those green doors and not having a way to back out safely. That thing that she'd been running aimlessly toward felt as if it were tightening its grip.

She was drowning in secrets. Lily and Grams had made keeping them easy with their constant reminders to hold her tongue. Truth had always been her natural instinct though.

Stepping inside those green doors, she'd need to lie, play the con once again as she had her entire life. She desired nothing more than to be able to tell the truth, but Lily had taught her well. People couldn't be trusted, especially people who had the same abilities as her. After all, she knew exactly what she could do with hers.

Angelica reached and touched the doorbell before courage failed her.

After moments, the heavy door swung open, and Angelica had to look up nearly five inches to meet the russet eyes of a thin, blonde haired woman near her age.

"Good morning." Angelica smiled. "I've come to see John Landon. I believe he's expecting me."

A grin spread, but her eyes did a nervous twitch. A lack of confidence, maybe? Something to hide. Angelica's nerves were jumpy. "Why hello. You must be Angelica Accacia, right? I'm Gabney."

They stood there a moment both smiling. Angelica could feel a thick fog of awkwardness rising.

A vein at Gabney's temple twitched. "I'm sorry. Why don't you come right in?"

Angelica stepped pass Gabney into the foyer. The glass shards had been swept away, but her flesh pricked with an electrical current bouncing off the ruby walls and towering ceilings.

"I don't recall seeing you last time I was here."

"I was in a class at UNO. I don't actually train here." Gabney's eyes focused on a large portrait on the wall. "Just an ordinary civilian."

She laughed nervously, her eyes meeting Angelica's before shifting away.

Interesting. Not everyone here had abilities. Was that something new or had Lily been the only one with abilities when she was here? Angelica wasn't sure how to get those answers without asking the questions directly. Not yet, anyway.

"It must be an interesting place to live."

Gabney's natural smile lit up her face. *Innocent.* She'd been trying to put a description to Gabney in her head and that was the correct speculation "You wouldn't believe. Uncle John is like a second father to me, so I totally respect what they do here."

"Is Mr. Landon here now?"

Gabney nodded, nibbling on her bottom lip. "He's in his library. I'll just let him know you arrived."

Gabney pivoted and glided toward the doorway on the right,

disappearing behind a cherry door in the back of a sparsely furnished sitting area.

The house creaked in its farthest corners. Angelica could feel the enormity of the space, and its vastness allowed for silence to bounce around and ring in her ears.

A creaking door snapped her back to attention, and she watched Gabney emerge.

"He'll see you now." She motioned to the small sitting area. "I'll be in the tea room if you need anything."

Angelica entered through the cherry door, her heart galloping ahead of her. In a brown leather chair, a stoop-shouldered, white haired man gripped a brown leather book. His side part fell as haphazardly as the odd objects and books that overwhelmed the room. Several chairs were pushed into corners creating odd seating arrangements around the large room, but a chair strategically sat opposite Mr. Landon's massive wingback chair.

A loud vibration cleared his throat. "Why don't you have a seat right here? I'm afraid I don't move around as well as I once did."

She moved toward the chair, assessing his stance, his sagging eyelids, his shaking fingers. "I'm Angelica Acacia. I don't believe we were able to meet the other day."

Acacia tugged in her throat. Lie number one.

His small kind eyes studied her. "I apologize that the incident wasn't handled better. You startled our residents, I'm afraid."

"I apologize as well. I was always taught to hide my abilities, so I panicked."

Landon's fingers rubbed the top of a carved wooden cane. Its pecan stain was a lighter brown beneath his fingertips from wear. "My home is a place for people with abilities not unlike your own so they don't have to hide them. Tell me, how did you hear about me?"

"As a teenager a psychologist mentioned it during a meeting."

Lie number two. Acid bubbled beneath her skin. Her instincts told her to tell the truth, but she couldn't trust her instincts. Lily had proved that to her.

"Acacia is an unusual last name."

His gaze bore into her. She wasn't fooling him.

"Acacia is my middle name. My mother left me at my Grandmother's house when I was a baby, and neither one bothered to give me a last name."

His thoughts were less critical of her answer. Probably because it was as close to the truth as she could get without giving a full confession.

"Did they tell you from whom you inherited your abilities?"

Angelica shrugged. "My mother, I suppose. Grams is a definite no, and I have no other family."

He nodded. It was a you-passed-round-one nod. She wasn't sure if she was ready for another round. "Did you have a purpose for wanting to see me?"

Yes. She wanted to scream. Lily had left her with so many unanswered questions, and he was the first one who probably had the answers. She pried at the walls around his thoughts, but they were relentless. He'd protected himself from her intrusion. How'd he do this with no physic energy?

She stood abruptly to give herself a moment to think.

"I just want to know."

Lily's face stared at her from among a collage of photos on the mantelpiece. A young version with blond hair in braids. Damn Lily. What was she supposed to do?

"As a girl, I dreamed of my mother's murder. No one would believe me, but I knew it was real. I've read her journal over and over, but it doesn't tell me why."

"You saw it in a dream? You have visions of the future?"

His alarm vibrated through her bones. Angelica turned to see it in his eyes. "Why does that scare you? I thought you said the people here have abilities."

His heart rate increased. "You read people's thoughts too?"

She shuddered under his fear, and she reconstructed her wall to keep his anxiety out. "I try not to use it. It made me feel like I was going to go crazy when I was younger."

Landon's fingers trembled against his cane. "Have you ever told anyone about your abilities?"

Angelica countered. "Have you?"

Landon cleared his throat. "We keep what goes on here quiet."

"Is there a reason?" Angelica sank into the seat. "I mean people have claimed to have physic abilities before."

"The people in here are not street fortune tellers. I assume you've kept your abilities quiet for the same reason we have."

"Because you don't want the men in the white lab coats studying you?"

Landon laughed, but then stopped abruptly. "I'm sorry, I haven't had the opportunity to laugh in recent weeks. But no, it's not about the men in lab coats. Your abilities have a history. A long and complex history that means we need to protect ourselves."

Angelica leaned back in her chair. "Do I get to hear this history or is there some kind of ritual involving giving up my soul first?"

Landon laughed until it died out naturally this time. His chest heaved under it. "No such rituals here. Just the magic of trust."

They assessed each other. His eyes were warm but guarded. He didn't expect her to tell him more after meeting him ten minutes ago.

"How about I give you the basics until we've had time to get to know each other better."

Angelica smiled. He knew how to read people, too. "I've waited twenty years. I have a little longer."

Not much though. She could feel something getting closer. Better to be gone before it arrived.

"Have you ever heard of the Custos?"

That mysterious word. Custos. It rolled from her tongue and teased at a memory. "Is it a family name? I've heard it mentioned but I can't place it."

He leaned back in his chair. "The Custos are a man. To be exact, they aren't human as you know humans. They are a different evolutionary man. In other words, *homo sapien* is one man; *homo custos* is another."

A sharp burst of laughter burst from Angelica's throat. "Are you serious? So you're saying I'm not human?"

"Of course you are." Landon frowned. "You are a hybrid Custos/Human DNA mixture. The abilities come from Custos man."

Angelica swallowed. His words felt stuck in her throat unable to go down. "So if there is another species of man walking around, why haven't we heard about it? I can't imagine that is easy to hide."

Landon smiled. "In 1584, our records show that the last of two pure Custos mixed with two humans and five children were born. They became known as the Vindica five. Each had abilities ranging from telekinesis, clairvoyance, telepathy, psychic healing, and mind walking."

"So the abilities were passed down through some large family tree?"

"Ah, yes. Legends are tricky business. Some stories suggest magic was involved, but others stick to the science of evolution. Like all legends, most of it is guess work and you have to believe what you can."

"I feel like I'm on some hidden camera, you've been pranked show. It doesn't sound real." Angelica paused. "And yet, I feel as though there is more."

Landon smiled. "Well, as in all the best legends, the Vindica has tales of a prophecy."

"A prophecy? As in something bad is going to happen?"

Landon shrugged. "Stories say that in 1591 Mennigas, a very strong mind walker, abused his gift and began harming innocent people out of greed. Abigail, the healer, cast a spell calling for the birth of someone who would possess all five gifts to put an end to the evil among the growing family. The prophecy grew as the family enlarged over time. Legend dictates that one day someone will be born with all the abilities and will unite the Custos once again."

"That was four hundred years ago. Was anyone ever born?"

Landon's fingers tapped the top of his cane. "Actually, we shall find out. The people who know say that it will happen by the full moon."

"What if I had all five abilities?"

Landon's fingers stopped the rhythmic tapping. "Do you?"

She'd never tried to heal someone. Did four out of five count? She wasn't even sure how healing was supposed to work.

"What if I didn't want to be this person?"

John released a deep breath. His fingers gripped the cane tightly. "The Vindica's name for this person is Valor, for the quality that the lives of others are more important than her own. It requires choice." He paused. "Legends only have power if you believe."

Risk her life for others? "Wait, are there still people to fight against like in the past?"

"Always. Just like in stories, where there is good, there is evil. We call them Dark Soldiers. We must all be careful of them."

"How do you know I'm Custos? I could be an ordinary street psychic."

He smiled and his eyes sparked with a mischievous light. He enjoyed the challenge of her questions. This told her that no one asked him questions anymore and he liked it. These were the things that she used to con people. When would she stop thinking this way?

"Have you ever seen anyone with eyes your color?"

The flesh on her arms rose. Her obsession. "Maybe once. Why?"

"That color blue is a Custos genetic trait marker. The only way to achieve that shade is to have Custos DNA, and a very high degree of it, I might add."

"There's no other way? Aren't humans born with all shades of eye color?"

He shook his head, a smile tugging at the corners of his lips. "Afraid not. The Vindica has geneticists who study these things. In the last few years they've achieved unimaginable breakthroughs, so I knew you were part of the Vindica upon seeing you, as will others."

"You mean those Dark Soldiers, don't you?"

He frowned. "I'm afraid so."

The cherry door creaked open and Gabney's head popped inside. "I thought I'd give Angelica a break and show her around a bit."

Landon nodded. "Good idea, Gabney. Gabney's in my training so to speak. We don't have your abilities, but we do enjoy a good story."

Gabney laughed, her voice cracking and her eyes twitching. "Our abilities are just different."

Angelica followed Gabney out because she was expected to do so, but her head swarmed with questions. She'd discovered nothing about her mother.

She glanced back at Landon, but he'd closed his eyes to the room.

Back in the foyer, Gabney twitched. "I'm sorry to cut it short. Uncle John hasn't been feeling well lately."

A fear jolted through her. Lily's pictures sat on his mantle; he was her connection. "Is something wrong with him?"

"I don't think so." Gabney frowned, her eyes losing focus as though she were considering it, but then she shrugged it off. "He's just had a difficult time with the Vindica Council lately."

"There's a Vindica Council?"

"Every ancient society has to have some bureaucratic old people telling it what to do." Gabney laughed. "The council doesn't want to name Valor although the prophecy calls for it to be happening like yesterday. Uncle John keeps trying to reason with them. Reasoning with a cabbage would be easier."

Gabney's cheeks pinkened. She'd rambled and she knew it. Her thoughts were wide open with no shields or guards. "You know most of what goes on in the Vindica, don't you?"

Gabney stared at the floor. "Uncle John says I will become Vindica historian one day. I don't believe it likely since no one accepts me but him."

Angelica laughed. "They can be a side act in a circus show, but they don't accept you?"

Gabney grumbled. "Let's see how you feel after you meet them. I promised to bring you to the back courtyard."

Angelica sucked in air. "Today?"

"Right now." Gabney laughed, tugging on Angelica's arm.

Angelica felt like she was the new kid in middle school. She tried to remind herself that she'd be twenty-one in a week, but nope the nervousness still flipped in her stomach.

Angelica stole quick glances into several open doorways. They passed a curious room with old looking weapons hanging on the walls and even a piano in a far off room. The journey ended as they skidded into a large kitchen with a massive green door in the rear. A chef turned to glare at them, but Gabney only giggled and pushed her toward the door.

Bright rays of sunshine glared down on them as Gabney pushed the door open, and Angelica blinked to adjust. Gray patio stones held several chairs framed by vines crawling up wrought iron work. A decaying building rose up beyond, blocking the area from street traffic.

Eyes turned to stare at them, and Angelica inhaled sharply. She hadn't expected so many.

Lysander and a group of five men stood tossing a football beyond the edge of the patio, and four sets of eyes greeted her from iron patio chairs.

Vase thrower glared at her from one of the chairs. Her long blond hair hung limply over her shoulders, taunt skin stretched across her high cheekbones, and a long thin nose added to her gaunt look. Those same honey eyes that had concentrated on the vase to move it, narrowed and seared through her now.

Gabney stepped between them.

"Angelica, I believe you've met Griffen Jones."

Griffen stood from one of the chairs and extended his hand. "I'm so pleased you've decided to return after our bad reactions."

Angelica smiled and shook his hand. He squeezed but not in a power struggle, more of an assurance that he was harmless.

Gabney smiled and slight pinkness rose in her cheek before she looked away from Griffen to another seated onlooker. "This is Jack Coefield, a teacher here."

Jack Coefield brought his hands together as if he were going to pray. "I assume John Landon has met with you and deemed you legitimate." He paused, glancing toward the others. Angelica was aware that the football toss had ceased and the men had moved closer. "However, don't believe your trials are over. Griffen and I are both experts in our fields, and we don't trust as easily as John Landon does."

Okay, first impressions weren't always accurate, but then again, sometimes a pompous ass was just what it looked like.

Her head throbbed. She felt Serena yanking at the walls she had erected to block her thoughts. She hadn't experienced that feeling in a long time.

Jack Coefield glanced at Serena and a small grin curved the corner of her lips. She was enjoying this.

Everyone waited for her reply. Indignation swelled in her chest. She hated bullies. "John Landon and I have reached an understanding, but it doesn't concern you. I don't see why I'd need your trust, and I don't need confirmation of my abilities."

Serena blinked as Angelica kicked her out of her mind. "Breaking a vase doesn't confirm your abilities unless you are showing us you are weak."

Angelica's cheeks flushed. Anger surged through her. She pictured their chairs rising, and in an instant they were in the air, shrieking in fear and a little delight.

A laugh bubbled inside her. Control slipped like sugar through her fingers and felt just as sweet. She'd never allowed herself to slip. It was intoxicating.

Angelica waved the chairs down. Griffen Jones sprang from his seat. "That was unbelievable! I've never seen such concentration, such strength before. You must give another demonstration."

Serena glared at Angelica before storming into the house, nearly knocking Gabney out of the way.

Jack Coefield's face burned hibiscus red. He lurched upward and gaped at Angelica. His lips moved fluidly, but words did not escape.

Griffen frowned. "Jack, you can't be angry. This is great!"

Jack stammered. "Our kind doesn't use our gifts against each other. Dark Soldiers do. I must have a word with John Landon."

He swished past Gabney and Angelica muttering about being in danger as if she couldn't hear him. The adrenaline may be intoxicating, but the worry nestled at its core had a sobering effect.

The dark haired woman from the other chair stood up and studied Angelica with her Custos eyes. Her hand on hip tough stance revealed toned bared arms.

"I'm Roxy Decambre. I'm sure we'll get to know each other well, but first I'll go smooth things over."

Those Custos blues were icicles. She'd said Decambre—one of the seven families from Lily's trail of death. At least seven that she remembered from reoccurring dreams.

What were the chances of her being from that Decambre family? From the glare in her eyes, pretty high. Would she expose Angelica? Did she remember her even? At first glance, she appeared to be around Angelica's age.

Griffen waited for Roxy to leave. Angelica felt his mind racing over Zener tests and performance tests he could conduct. "I'd love to work with you tomorrow. I know you don't want to, but really I only study what people do."

He only wanted someone willing to work with him. He wasn't like them—like her. He and Gabney were both denied because they were human not Custos. It was all so much for Angelica to wrap her head around.

"I'll give it a try."

She reasoned that she needed an opportunity to return, and she didn't know when another invitation would come along. She still needed a connection to Lily.

Lysander smiled at her from the group of men at the edge of the patio. Seeing him again would be an added perk.

Fourteen

Cain's anger simmered in his gut, rising into his throat at intervals when he couldn't distract himself. Not only had he had to make an appointment to see his own father, but he'd also had to give a reason as to why he'd needed any of his father's valuable time when his father was so busy. Typical dysfunctional father-son bonding happening.

After his mother's execution, Cain had rebelled in major ways. In his inexperience and youth, he hadn't learned to focus his anger in a way he'd actually hurt the man. So he'd set fire to the outbuildings. He'd destroyed several books, and he'd gone as far as to try and poison Tom. He'd been unable to follow through with it, and that's when he'd lost his father's respect.

He'd been sent away for "training." Considering that all the training occurred at Rex's compound at that time so Rex could keep a close eye on any future potential threat, no one had believed that excuse. Rumors had spread through Rex's men; many of them contained bits of the truth.

His private trainers had decided that torture was the way to enforce discipline. At twenty-three he'd become the youngest member to reach Dark Soul status. Cain had breezed through the two weeks of required torture that was part of the testing regimen. It had been easy after the years of torture at his trainer's hand.

Tom's slight form emerged from the darkness of the house. "He'll see you now, young master."

Cain grunted, and then dived into the darkness. He'd known every corner of this house during his training here, and he'd used many to hide. He wasn't hiding today.

His father sat among rolled parchments and opened documents. His reading glasses rested on his nose in a delicate way, but he removed them as Cain entered.

"Ah, what was of such importance that you needed to see me at this time, Son?"

Cain forced the sneer from his lips. "I've been offered a job at the law firm we discussed, and I'd like to take it."

Rex was silent, and Cain hoped that meant he was considering it. "This would mean you'd be away from your post at Landon House, am I correct?"

Cain nodded.

"Then no," Rex said frowning. "I can't afford that loss at this time."

"Don't you think it'll be suspicious that a nearly twenty-five year old law graduate still hasn't taken a job?"

Rex waved it away. "The economy is bad, and you'll handle any suspicions, I'm confident. Do you have anything to report from the house?"

Fury roared inside him, but he'd come a long way from youth and inexperience.

"The woman, Angelica, is a stronger telekinetic than even you."

"Impossible." Cain glimpsed the wrinkles deepen on his forehead though.

"She lifted four people in the air today, held them for nearly a minute, and then set them down."

Rex stared at him, and Cain glared back, unblinking.

His father sighed. "I hear you didn't wish to sacrifice Lewis."

"He could have proven useful in the future."

"Unwillingness to kill is seen as a weakness with our people. Going against orders shows disloyalty."

Cain clinched his fists and pumped them hard at his side. Control of his temper remained elusive around his father. "I have a problem with ignorance. We will never achieve what you want with the people you have placed in charge."

Rex stood. "A soldier does not question a leader. That is a high form of disloyalty."

"We both know I'm not a leader yet because I'm your son. I'm more intelligent than most of your men."

Rex shook his head. "Your intelligence is hampered by your rashness, your emotions, and your temper."

Cain's fury burned through him, and he knew nothing else would come from this conversation but a loss of his temper. "If you have nothing more, I'll take my leave now. I will not, however, agree to stay at my post indefinitely. I've sacrificed enough of my life for your quest, and it is apparent I will never move further in our group."

Rex sighed. "Don't be dramatic."

"Good evening, Rex."

Cain exited and moved toward the outside door in the dark. As he passed the den, he noticed someone else waiting.

His milk flesh and size startled Cain a moment, but it was his eyes that made him stop in his steps.

They were the blueness of the shallow waters of Mexico or of the clear blue sky. Custos blue.

Apparently, his father was keeping secrets, too.

Cain forced himself to move toward the door, only missing a step, but his mind raced over the possibilities.

Fifteen

Lucilius was agitated. Kline could tell by the tense set of his jaw and the unconscious tapping of his thumb against the railing. Kline remained quiet, hands crossed in front of him, waiting.

"He's lying," Lucilius mumbled and tapped his thumb harder.

Kline listened without a word. Lucilius didn't like to be interrupted, especially when he was thinking.

"But I can't do anything about that yet. I need his inside information." He shook his head. "Need is a strong word though. I could kill him and get my information elsewhere."

He looked back at Kline, and Kline continued his poker face, unflinching.

"But this is the quicker route, correct?" His eyes bore into Kline. He was working himself up and something would be destroyed soon. No one would witness the cruelty from his temper though. Lucilius kept his loss of control discreet.

"Both, Sir." Kline said, gauging his reaction closely. The vein in his temple didn't throb, so he continued. "You need information from him, but you should also look elsewhere to keep a level playing field."

Lucilius stared him down, his expression giving nothing away. He looked back out onto the street after an intense moment. "But who?"

He shrugged. "Rex doesn't keep confidences with anyone. He's smarter than that."

"One of his men will notice something. We always notice. You need to find one who isn't loyal."

Lucilius regarded Kline with that deep glare that penetrated all the way to the bone. Kline controlled his thoughts, knowing that they'd be fully exposed to Lucilius. He thought of Bileka, one of the few Custos young women who was available and would be mated off soon. She was good-looking in a pale, wispy way. The other guards all wanted her as their life partner, so Kline knew with his family connections he was not going to be a candidate. He hadn't really thought much about how the male Custos outnumbered the female three to one until he'd reached the age that mates were chosen. He knew with his grandfather and father's ruined name, he was on the bottom of the hierarchy, so he assumed he wouldn't be paired.

Lucilius finally looked away, and Kline felt the release of tension all the way to his toes. It had worked.

"I need you to find someone for me." Lucilius thumped his thumb against the balcony again. "You've been watching these people; find me someone who I can use."

Lucilius dismissed him with a nod and Kline stepped out into the hall.

Kline took the stairs two at a time and was in the downstairs command room before he allowed any thoughts to enter his mind.

He could care less about the Custos women, but he did need to keep his real thoughts to himself.

The wallboard in the room was filled with snapshots, many of them labeled with names and details. He'd only brushed the surface of New Orleans Vindica members though. The list that Lucilius had provided for him was extensive and many were out of the city.

His gaze immediately went to Angelica's picture. He'd snapped it as she'd been leaning over the balcony of her bedroom. She'd been lost in thought and her eyes were unfocused.

She was the key. He'd figured it out as he watched her. She could undo it all, with a little help. He'd have to find a mole for Lucilius, but she would be what Kline had been waiting for.

It didn't matter whether she was this mythical Valor or not. His family had been biding their time and he'd believed he'd finally found a way.

His gut twinged. Although he shouldn't be worried about it, he'd be placing her at risk. They'd never spoken, but he'd watched her. No, he'd studied her.

And he wanted her even though he shouldn't. It was against the Custos laws to mix. It had happened before, of course. But the punishment was death.

He was getting ahead of himself, considering the consequences of actions he had not taken. But he needed her for his plan, and she'd need a little training to insure his plan followed through to his end goal. He could start there.

Sixteen

Angelica pursed her lips around the straw of some fruity drink as Lysander gazed into her eyes. Her body flushed against his intense stare following the movement of her lips.

A jiggle from behind brought the crowded bar back into focus, and she dropped her eyes down to her fingertips to gain some control. Her intoxication with him was fueled by attraction and a little bit of not having to hide her abilities. It could be reversed though; she could be intoxicated more by not having to hide, and this caused her to want to slow it down. Way down.

"Do you do this often?" Angelica squirmed, feeling his hidden laugh.

Lysander's fingertips brushed her bare arm. "We used to come out every weekend. Not so often lately."

She attempted to push a calming breath through her body, but his crooked grin broke her concentration.

Angelica looked away. "Have you known everyone long?"

"I've known Mark and some of the others for years. Belonging to a Vindica family means you know everyone."

Angelica smiled, deciding to focus on conversation instead of his nearness. "Are they like the family members you don't want to claim?

Lysander chuckled. "Definitely intense. Parties can be treacherous, but I'd like for you to stick around to find out first hand."

She sipped the fruity concoction for relief and dragged her eyes away from his. The crowded bar had people brushing against each other. Not her favorite scene, but Gabney had begged for her to join them. Angelica had relented since it was Gabney's twenty-first birthday, but the large group had splintered as soon as they'd entered the bar.

Serena glared at her from a corner table. Mark distracted her often, but Angelica continued to feel the distrust and dislike shooting her way. Mark's frustration bounced around them as he sipped a long neck beer. Bruce Meek, another resident at Landon House, was failing miserably with a tanning booth, perfect complexion amazon. Roxy was behind the bar, and Angelica had caught her suspicious glares each time their eyes had met.

Gabney leaned against a wall near the door, hands tucked inside her jacket pockets. Loneliness wilted her eyes, her face, and her shoulders. Her thoughts broadcasted across the room, screaming among the various naughty thoughts of the bar's patrons. She'd thought they'd spend a fun night out, and everyone had turned from her, as usual.

Gabney's thoughts drifted. Uncle John worried over her safety. Did she know too much? Did she even know anything important?

Angelica peeked at others to see if anyone was listening. Gabney was too easy to read and open to anyone who cared to tune in.

Lysander's hand stroked her arm, and chills traveled up her arm. "Gabney feels left out."

Angelica smiled. Finding out his abilities would have to be on her priority list. She wasn't big on surprises. "I agree. I think I'll go see if she wants to go back to the house since I'm not really into large crowds."

"I know what you mean. Maybe we can find a more intimate setting for our next date."

Angelica grinned. "Maybe next time you can ask me out if you want to call it a date."

She left him, feeling his eyes follow the sway of her hips, hearing the smoldering thoughts he broadcasted as he drank it up. She'd never known that this particular talent could drive her this kind of crazy.

Gabney watched her approach with suspicious thoughts bouncing around her head.

"So birthday girl, you're not having a good time?"

"I don't seem to have your luck. You and Lysander seem to have hit it off."

"No sharp fangs or dead bodies lurking in his pockets. That's a win for me. But tonight was about you."

"I'm okay." Gabney frowned as tears drowned her eyes. "My dad was supposed to be here, but he couldn't make it. He's never missed before."

"How about we go back to your room and do something girlie like manicures. Just because you're twenty-one doesn't mean we can't have a birthday, slumber party style."

"You don't want to stay with Lysander?"

Angelica shrugged. "I don't really like crowds, and the guy needs to learn to ask for a date."

"Well," Gabney said, looking around, "what are we waiting for?"

Angelica shivered as the night air swallowed them at the door. Apparently, October weather changed daily in New Orleans.

The street crowd was sparse for a Thursday night, but the building's old world charms were distorted under neon lights. Its charm still hid in the shadows of the unlit buildings. She couldn't help feeling drawn to the city. Blurring her vision she could imagine the houses before they became weighed down from years of harsh revelry. The streets felt more welcoming than the cold, gray of Gram's home.

The sound of a distant drum pricked her ears. A strange evenly measured sound. She strained to hear it closer, but it hid in the distance. A soft murmur began in the back of Angelica's skull.

They turned from Bourbon Street onto St. Ann Street leaving the light buzz of voices behind. The drum increased in volume as though it moved closer. Angelica scanned the empty street but the murmur of warning moved into full alarm. There were two more blocks before they reached Charters Street, and the darkness pushed at them.

Gabney stopped, the darkness causing panic inside of her. "Do you think we should go back and get the others?"

Gabney's thoughts flooded through her. Uncle John confided in her. They killed for knowledge. He'd warned her to be careful. Not to be alone.

Angelica squeezed Gabney's arm as a queasiness boiled in her stomach. She shouldn't have walked with Gabney alone. Since being around these people, her survival instincts seemed to have been put on off-duty status. "Don't think. They may be able to read your thoughts."

A brief surge of embarrassment flushed through Gabney's mind, but her rambling thoughts ceased. Angelica listened to the silence with all of her senses. The same slow drum echoed in her head. Angelica's mind whirled. She knew someone approached, but she'd never experienced this drumming sound before. It was a sound of recognition she registered somewhere deep in her unconscious.

"If I say to run, just go. Don't look back."

Cold panic surged through Gabney's body. Angelica released her grip on her arm to avoid absorbing more panic; enough was already eating its way through her.

Angelica moved to step forward as a tall figure stepped out from a parked car. The drum pounded a slow beat of a tribal ceremony from under the cloak. The sound vibrated through her, making it hard for her to concentrate.

She shook herself and reached further, feeling through strange thick layers.

The slow measured beat was his heart.

What? How could she hear his heartbeat? That was new, not to mention a little disgusting.

A covered arm flung forward, and Angelica felt rushing air before she smashed against a brick wall. Pain tore through her shoulder and tears burned her eyelids. Ouch. She attempted to push herself up and tremors of pain shot up her side. What the hell was this? Wasn't she supposed to be strong?

Gruff measured words droned from the darkness of the cloak. "I want to know where the book is located. Your life depends on your answer."

Ignoring the shooting pain up her back, Angelica reached out her arm and flung him against the car. The alarm shrilled in her ears. He rose, turning toward her. She couldn't see his face except for the whiteness of his eyes.

He was surprised, but the reception broadcasted muffled. He was hard to read with only fragments making it through, but he hadn't sensed that she was gifted until she retaliated.

Angelica screamed. "Run! Gabney, Run!"

Gabney gawked at the stranger, frozen.

Angelica felt his intrusion into her mind. Her walls crumbled like landslides. Her mind opened without warning and everything from her first dance to Lily's eyes rose to the surface.

She counter attacked with her own intrusion but darkness abounded. His thoughts were like falling through a well. A well dripping in red. Blood.

Gabney gawked, statuesque. If Angelica failed, Gabney would be helpless against him.

Angelica pushed forward, every muscle straining with the effort and aching where bruises were already forming.

"To hell with this," she muttered to herself.

Angelica thrust forward, kicking his robe in the middle. Without hesitation, she delivered a second kick to his ankles, and then came down on his back as he went down with both elbows. He sprawled to the ground before her.

Angelica reached into Gabney's shocked mind and yelled at her to run. Gabney looked around as Angelica yanked her arm nearly from her shoulder and pulled her forward at a run.

Angelica's insides twisted as she shrugged off the residue of Gabney's mind. Pain shot through her bruised shoulder, and she was afraid to look back.

They were breathless as they reached the welcoming door of Landon House. Before they could propel themselves inside, Gabney fumbled with the lock and shut the door behind them. They each collapsed on the foyer's floor. Angelica rubbed her shoulder and waited for her heart to slow.

Footsteps vibrated from within, and in moments John Landon and Jack were in the foyer.

John rushed to a trembling Gabney. "What's happened? You're shaking and breathless."

A fumbling at the door increased Angelica's heart rate, and a whimper escaped from Gabney.

What if they were followed?

Lysander and the others walked in.

Mark glanced from Gabney to Angelica. "What happened? We left when we couldn't find you two. Lysander said y'all wanted to come home."

Tears streaked down Gabney's cheeks. Angelica could feel Gabney's disgust with herself for giving into tears. Angelica wished she could afford them because they were burning in her throat. Fear.

She trembled with it and bile rose in her throat at the emotion.

Landon put his arm around Gabney and helped her up. "Let's go into the den and find out exactly what happened tonight."

Lysander came to help Angelica up, but pain jarred through her when he touched her arm.

"Jack, get Barbara to get some first aid supplies. Angelica's injured."

Angelica's cheeks burned with shame as the others turned to stare. She gritted her teeth. "I'll be fine. Make sure Gabney's okay."

Roxy narrowed her eyes and peered at her, but Angelica couldn't figure out what she had said that had caused the glare to subside for a moment.

Angelica followed the others into the den, but within moments Barbara was beside her with bandages and peroxide. Once Angelica caught a glimpse of the bloody bruised flesh of her arm and shoulder, she clinched her teeth tightly together and attempted to focus on Gabney's words describing the ordeal instead of Barbara's fiddling with bandages.

A collective awe traveled through the room by the end of the tale. Someone was more curious than awed, but Angelica was too exhausted to distinguish the brainwaves.

John squeezed Gabney's hand. "I suppose Angelica's gifts will no longer be our secret, but your lives are worth losing that advantage."

Serena sat next to Mark, stroking a large gray cat. "Angelica didn't win with her gifts though. How did you learn to defend yourself like a common street thug?"

Angelica glared at her, feeling the sneer within her thoughts. The curiousness wasn't coming from her.

Gabney grinned a goofy grin at Angelica. Angelica could feel Gabney's bravery returning. "Angelica was spectacular. She knew someone was coming before he stepped out. If it weren't for her, I'd be dead."

Jack sipped his tea. "It's obvious the man wouldn't have been after you if it weren't for Angelica."

Angelica felt his distrust, as well as his dislike. She hadn't made a friend there. "He was after Gabney, and he was surprised by my abilities. He thought Gabney had knowledge of a book. What book?"

Landon sighed. Angelica felt pride mingled with fear. "Angelica's right. Everyone who's been targeted recently holds knowledge. I believe they are searching for that book again."

Mark shifted and glanced at Angelica. "They want the *Book of Shadow Souls*."

Jack snorted. "It doesn't exist. Rosemary destroyed it if it ever did exist. I've always believed it was a myth really."

Landon frowned. "Whether it exists or not, doesn't matter. They believe it does, and they are willing to kill for it."

Angelica's shoulder burned, and she'd like to be alone so she could look at it, cry about it, or something other than pretend she didn't mind it.

"What is this book?"

Mark leaned forward. "It's actually one of five books that are supposed to contain all the practices, beliefs, rituals, everything really of our ancestors."

Angelica tried to focus. "Where are the others then?"

Roxy was back glaring at her. No surprise there. "The Vindica has two of them. No one knows where the other two are, but Reximortum had the *Book of Shadow Souls* until twenty-one years ago when Rosemary is believed to have destroyed it."

Angelica bit down on her lip. "So why is this one important?"

Mark picked up his head. "What?"

Angelica sighed. Exhaustion had settled into her bones. "Why do they want this one and not the others? What makes this one something to kill for?"

Landon's pride swelled, and Roxy again had that puzzled expression on her face. Angelica was too tired to consider why.

"And who is Reximortum?"

The room grew quiet and eyes studied the floor.

John stood. "How about you and I discuss these things tomorrow. I believe we all need some sleep, and your arm will feel better after some rest."

Angelica followed Gabney up the stairs. No one would look at her as they climbed the stairs, but she figured tomorrow would be a nice day to start using some of her people skills and winning them over with her charming personality.

"Angelica, did you ever tell me to run? It was so strange."

Angelica stared at the banister beneath her fingers. "I yelled, but you were in shock. I'm sure tomorrow it will be clearer."

Angelica could feel Gabney's doubt. They'd neglected to train her to defend herself, but they'd made her knowledgeable of dangerous information. Angelica saw that as neglect. At least Lily had believed they should hide themselves among people who could protect themselves. Angelica wondered why these people were unable to see their own faults. Angelica had always seen hers clearly.

Seventeen

Cain knocked on the third door of the night as he lowered his hood and scanned his surroundings. He waited as he felt the movement stir slowly in the bowels of the house.

Moments later, the door eased open a small distance.

"Yes?"

"Reginald, it's I, Dark Soul Cain."

Cain bowed.

"It's four o'clock in the morning. Has something happened?"

"There was an attack tonight, and we are inquiring if it were a Dark Soldier attack."

"Are you saying you're not sure?"

"We are uncertain," Cain paused, considering how to phrase it to cause his desired effect. "We are the foot soldiers, and we were not sent. We are unsure if there is a new threat."

"My family is not responsible," he grumbled. "I will certainly make my own inquires."

"Sorry to have disturbed your sleep; we believe our inquiry to be of high importance at this pressing time."

"No matter, Dark Soul. We don't want any unforeseen obstacles at this pivotal moment. Carry on your inquiry. I will add my calls to it at first light."

"Good evening, Reginald."

Cain stepped away and slipped into the darkness. He kept to the shadows and made his way to Pere Antoine Alley.

His inquiry had turned up nothing, and he needed to find out if the others had experienced the same. His father was up to something, and Cain didn't like not knowing. He did not find pleasure with the idea of a more powerful Reximortum. Hope at escaping his father's command would diminish if Rex found that book first.

Rumors had flown twenty-one years ago that Rosemary had destroyed the book. Rex had found a torn, burnt page in a pile of ashes. For a time, Cain had thought Rex believed it had been destroyed. Six years ago however Reximortum had decided that the book did exist and that Rosemary had sent it to someone to hide. As usual, he didn't explain his source for his change of mind.

That was when Cain had been sent to Landon House as a spy.

The problem that Rex had not foreseen is that Cain enjoyed living there. He liked the group of people who weren't chained to the command of one. He had choices at Landon House, and he even liked John Landon, his father's enemy.

Rex could not comprehend this.

Cain reached the alley and spotted the others near the abandoned doorway.

"Any confirmation?"

Echo shook his hood. "No, no one acknowledged sending him."

"He's gone outside the soldiers, I know it."

Echo squirmed. "Aren't we going to get in trouble for asking questions?"

"No," Cain said. "Everyone will be talking about it. We will say that we were concerned there was a new player, which we are."

"Who do you think this new player is?"

Cain looked to Falcon, though he was a new Dark Soldier, he was close to Cain's equal. Although fiercely competitive, Cain respected him.

"I don't think he's human. I saw him, and I think he's something else."

Echo drew in a sharp breath. Echo, on the other hand, needed to be cut from his team.

Cain glared at Echo a moment, and he squirmed. "How are you going to find out?"

Cain looked toward the looming buildings beyond. "I'm going to see someone."

Eighteen

Angelica sat up in bed for the fifth time. Sleep eluded her and these fluorescent white, glow in the dark walls weren't helping. A gallon of paint would do wonders for the place. As a guest room it worked, she supposed. It wasn't as if it was her room to decorate, and after tonight's injury, she wasn't planning a decorating theme just yet.

She ran her fingers over the rough texture of her shoulder. The stinging had dulled a bit, but it was the conversation that was keeping her mind from rest.

Her courage had failed when it came to digging into Lily's past, but it felt negligent not to know what was going on with these people if she was going to put herself in between them and trouble, especially if her body would need to be stopped with any more brick walls.

She couldn't lay awake in this bed any longer. Anxiety crawled across her flesh like ants.

Angelica padded down the hall barefoot. At Gabney's door, she stopped, but Gabney needed to sleep and forget about her ordeal.

During the conversion of this old hotel into a home, the floor plan wasn't altered much. Angelica passed three bedrooms on each side before she made it to the staircase. Her breath caught as she stepped onto the wooden stair, hoping it wouldn't creak under her weight. Her movement down the staircase went unannounced.

Downstairs darkness swallowed her before her eyes picked up a faint glow in the direction of the sitting room that led to Landon's library.

Angelica followed the glow, her eyes adjusting to the darkness. All she needed was to walk into furniture and wake up the entire house.

She knocked softly on Landon's library door, glancing toward the foyer, wondering if anyone else was awake in the house.

She nudged the door open at a muffled greeting.

John sat behind his massive desk, which was now piled with open books. Reading glasses rested on his nose, and he had notepaper spread on top of the books.

His eyelids were heavy, and his face was pale. Angelica would guess he hadn't gone to bed tonight. "You couldn't sleep?"

Angelica closed the door behind her. "Certain things were bothering me and keeping me awake."

Landon waved his hand over the pile of books. "Something you said got me to thinking, so that left two of us awake tonight."

"What did I say?"

Angelica yearned to walk around and peer over his shoulder at the books, but they hadn't reached that comfort level. She had the impression that no one reached that comfort level with Landon, ever.

"Why is that book more important than the others. You see, we've had two for centuries and no one has attempted to use them. The council won't even allow me to open the covers to peer inside. Why has this book caused so many deaths? Why does the Dark Soldiers want this book? More importantly, what does it contain that they would want so desperately." He motioned to the pile again. "As you can see, I've worked myself into quite a frenzy."

"Any answers?"

"No." He frowned. "A few leads though. What has you awake at this hour?"

"Questions without answers, like who is this Reximortum?"

"Oh." Landon reached and pulled his glasses down, setting them vicariously on top of the books. "It's difficult for the others to listen to stories about him. I didn't put you off to avoid the question."

Angelica nodded. She recalled the downcast eyes of the group, and it made sense. "He's not one of those super hero good guys, is he?"

"'fraid not." Landon sighed. "He's been the leader of the Dark Soldiers for about twenty-six years now. He's the worst in the last hundred or so years. I'm afraid he's killed many family members of our residents. Roxy's father, Serena's mother, the list goes on."

"Can't he be arrested for murder or something?"

"Oh, your abilities don't leave evidence as lay people would put it." Landon smiled. "No, I'm afraid historically, it takes someone more powerful to come along and kill the other. Unfortunately, we don't have anyone who qualifies at the present."

"Do you think it was him tonight?"

Landon studied her, and Angelica stilled. Even without abilities, it felt like he could see inside her. "What do you think?"

"I know this is going to sound crazy, but I mean coming after the things you told me, I guess I shouldn't feel like that..." Angelica stopped and gathered herself before she continued rambling. "Are there other things besides humans out there?"

He laughed, a hearty chuckle, and Angelica waited.

"You know." Landon straightened his shoulders, leaning back into his chair. "People have been here for years and have never asked the questions you've asked in just a few days."

Angelica's breathing ceased, unsure if he'd confirmed her question or acknowledged she was crazy.

The humor left his face. "I apologize, but actually your answer is yes. Many of the myths are true, but they do not cross paths with the

Custos line. They abide by their own laws, so although they exist, it would not have been some supernatural creature."

Angelica released a deep breath. It wasn't relief that filled her though, more of a heightened sense of fear. If he was human, then why was the drumming heartbeat so strange? She wouldn't even begin to think about what Landon had just said about supernatural creatures tonight. Her head might explode.

"What made you think it wasn't human?"

"I could hear this heartbeat, the sound of a ritual drum. Slow and steady."

"You've never done this before?"

"Never."

"Interesting." Landon wrote a long, loopy note on the notepaper in front of him. "Something more for me to look up."

"Would it…" Angelica paused. "Would it be okay if I helped? I don't like not knowing what's going on here."

Landon stood, his chair creaking at the release. "That's certainly a good idea, but I believe I'm finally ready to go to sleep. So perhaps later on today would be more suitable." Landon paused. "You know, what you do need to do is train. I'm afraid being near the Vindica is dangerous."

"I know how to use my abilities." The words chocked out more defensively than she intended.

"Using your abilities against an untrained person is quite different than using them in an engagement with someone who is trained. Just something to consider. Mark is our best fight trainer here. I'm sure he'd appreciate a fresh pupil."

"I'll consider it." Angelica nodded. "You know though, I think Gabney needs to be trained in some basics. It's dangerous for her as well."

"Touché." Landon nodded. "You two can become pupils together."

Angelica watched him swing a bookcase open to reveal a small elevator.

He winked at her. "When I designed this room, I enjoyed myself with the hiding spaces. Please shut the door behind you and leave the light on."

Angelica watched him disappear behind a thin door before exiting the library. Eccentric came to mind, but he was growing on her. Thoughts of leaving New Orleans occurred less and less, and tonight's incident didn't leave her feeling certain with the change of direction of her thoughts.

Nineteen

The soft murmur of voices crept through the tombs like fog. Cain stepped further into the shadows and waited. St. Louis Cemetery Number 1, normally closed to the public after three o'clock, played host to a certain group of people tonight who were tapping into the energy of the dead.

Cain was not part of this group.

The voices emerged from the shadows of the barred gate and the shapes of three large individuals took shape.

"I don't like it none." A loud voice boomed through the silence. "I don't like it none at all."

"Uh, um… the dead telling us to run isn't a good sign, Cherie."

Madame Lulu's deep alto voice soothed like warm honey. "We are made of stronger stuff than that. The dead only said it was going to be bad, not that it was impossible. We must have faith."

She straightened her large bosom up and looked around, peering into the dark. Cain released a shallow breath. She'd sensed him.

"Let's meet and discuss this tomorrow. The dawn will bring a new view of the day."

The other two nodded and trudged off to an old, rust orange truck.

Madame Lulu stood watching the engine turn and then waved as they pulled onto the street.

"Why have you come?"

Cain stepped out of the shadows and toward her. Madame Lulu's turban made her head rise above his own. She was a heavy-set woman with a belt cinching her hourglass waist. In all her softness and curves, fear still struck him within her presence.

Cain nodded. "There has been a development. I think there is another player."

Madame Lulu's whites of her eyes stared through him. The shadows made it difficult to see the tight set of her lips that he knew was there. "Didn't I ask you to keep this away from my people?"

"You and I both know we come from the same people."

Approaching her, those cocoa eyes studied him a moment, and he couldn't deny that there was a certain amount of fear mingling in his resolve. The woman had power, a power he didn't understand, and anyone with intelligence feared her abilities. Even Reximortum didn't meddle in her affairs, which was all the more reason to have her on Cain's side.

"Maybe." Her large bosom heaved upward and then fell. "But what we decided to do with our abilities has made all the difference."

Cain nodded his agreement. The Anihi branch of the Custos, although small, didn't spend their time fighting and killing each other off. They hid in the shadows of the Vindica, blending with humans as Voodoo practitioners, although their practices were vastly different. Madame Lulu acted as a leader of the Anihi, similar to their Vindica council but much more powerful. If a person had heard of Madame Lulu, they were aware of her ability to see the future. Her reputation typically preceded her.

"I have seen what you will face." Her strong voice faltered for a moment.

A tremor rose from his feet. "Is it human?"

Silence swallowed them as she simply stared at him. The anxiety tore through him. Madame Lulu was scared, something he'd never known her to be.

"We aren't human," Madame Lulu heaved, "but we have humanity. This abomination has no humanity."

"What is it then?"

Madame Lulu's turban shook side to side. "Don't know. He's not human in the way we are though. When I get glimpses of him in my visions, it's a darkness, a lurking shadow."

"I think he's working for my father."

"That's not all." Madame Lulu stepped closer, her eyes scanning the area.

Cain's heart lurched forward and then stopped as he waited.

"This creature isn't alone. There are others. The others are more familiar."

"What do you mean?"

"I mean, I believe they are Custos."

"So they are like us?"

Cain felt a sense of relief. He could handle Custos.

"If I wouldn't know better, I'd say they were pure."

Nonsense, Cain thought. Custos had been gone for over four hundred years and very rare even then. He must be dealing with a purer bloodline of Custos than the Vindica. Occasionally, it had occurred due to interbreeding between families. Genetics hadn't been something he understood the details, but he'd received the gist of the lecture in training.

But he'd seen that man at his father's house, and he'd felt something strange there. He'd felt the possibility. Yet, he couldn't believe it to be true for so many reasons.

"Does this change the outcome you saw?"

Madame Lulu turned toward an old Chevrolet. "Nothing is decided young man. The paths are all laid out. Each decision we make leads us to our destiny."

"But Simone said…."

"My granddaughter should learn to keep things to herself for her own safety." Madame Lulu's voice was curt. She heaved a deep breath out through her wide nose before speaking in a much calmer voice. "But having said that, I believe you can succeed at what you wish."

Relief. He hadn't realized how much he'd put into her assurance of his success until it flooded through him.

"But I worry about the cost."

"What cost?"

"That remains to be seen." Madame Lulu opened the car door. "Don't get my granddaughter involved, Cain. I warn you."

"How do I find out what this creature is?"

Madame Lulu paused. "Allow Simone to see for you, but leave her behind the scenes where she is safe."

"I plan to, Ma'am."

Madame Lulu disappeared into the car.

Cain began the long walk back to Charters Street.

Simone would be able to help. He needed to know what he was up against as this new threat distressed him. He'd need to be stronger than his opponent, so identifying him was of the utmost importance. His independence and freedom depended on it.

Twenty

"I can't believe you've been here for nearly a week and you haven't tried beignets yet," Gabney continued on. "You are going to love them."

Angelica only smiled this time. Gabney had mentioned this fact five times in the last ten minutes. After a good night's sleep, Gabney's energy had returned and her incessant chatter was exhausting Angelica beyond the three hours of sleep she'd managed.

"My dad has come down for every birthday since I've been in New Orleans. Tradition says we go to Café Du Monde the morning after."

Angelica followed Gabney down the staircase. "And why couldn't he make it down this year?"

Gabney shrugged. "Something about some pressing research that couldn't wait. He's supposed to visit soon though."

As they approached the bottom of the staircase, a small man emerged from the sitting area doorway. Thin wire glasses framed his grey eyes, which were brightened by the splash of gray hair circling his ears, not to mention a spot on top.

"Dad!"

Gabney flew down the stairs and at her father. She towered a good six inches above the gentleman in khaki slacks and a white button shirt. She must look like her mom because Angelica didn't see any resemblance between the two.

Gabney pulled back. "How are you here?"

He frowned, a crease forming on each side of his mouth. "I had a call last night from Uncle John, so I caught the early flight out this morning."

"I'm so happy that you are here."

"I can see that." He smiled and glanced up at Angelica as she reached the bottom of the staircase. "And you must be Angelica, the one I need to thank for saving my Gabney."

Angelica smiled and clasped the out reached hand. He had cold hands. "Nice to meet you."

"We were on our way to get beignets like birthday tradition calls for."

Griffen entered from the back hallway and Gabney turned her smile on him.

"Are we now?" Griffen walked up to Mr. White and shook his hand. "Nice to see you again, Sir."

"Likewise," Mr. White responded. "How about I get to know Angelica and hear all about last night as we cover ourselves in powdered sugar."

"Griffen, will you come with us?" Gabney's warm eyes searched his. Excitement had made her bold. Angelica hid her smile and looked away from the two. Watching the two dance around their attraction felt like something she should be doing from behind a curtain.

Griffen nodded. "Of course."

The walk to Café Du Monde on the river was a short one as it wasn't but a few blocks from Landon House. Gabney chatted the whole way about everything from her psychology professor to her grad school applications. Her father stood much more reserved in his questions, allowing Gabney to fill the air. Griffen followed behind Gabney, listening to every word.

Distracted by every passerby, Angelica trailed behind, weaving in and out of the conversation, catching bits here and bits there. Her attention was absorbed by the guy with the grey hoodie leaning against the building and the silver haired tourist with a camera hanging from his neck. She listened for that strange heartbeat within every chest they passed, including a fellow who tried to read their palms.

She wanted to know the cause of that sound and she dreaded knowing at the same time.

In a crowded corner table over warm fried dough and mounds of fluffy powdered sugar, Gabney recalled the details of last night's incident, and Angelica again searched the faces of the café's patrons for that quickened heartbeat.

"It sounds like," Mr. White wiped his mouth, "that you two need to be more careful in the future. You got lucky this time."

Griffen nodded. "I agree. We are all in danger right now."

"I don't think it was human," Angelica said, joining the conversation and leaving the tourists' minds alone.

"Oh?" Mr. White said.

"I could hear its heartbeat." Angelica shrugged. "It wasn't a human heart beat."

"Is that even possible?" Griffen asked. His tone indicated that Gabney's dad would know the answer. Wasn't he a doctor or something like that? Angelica vaguely recalled that information among Gabney's incessant chatter. Maybe he did know the answer.

Mr. White's head tilted to one side. "A few Vindica members in the last two hundred years were supposed to have the ability to do this. It's all legend, of course, since they are gone and the VRA can't investigate it or prove it."

Angelica asked, "What's the VRA?"

Gabney grinned with a spot of powdered sugar on her cheek. "It's my dad's special project."

Griffen nodded. "Stands for Vindica Research Agency. They have done a wonderful job in the last five years at filling in the gaps."

"What does it do exactly?" Angelica asked, looking towards Mr. White.

He fiddled with the napkin dispenser. "At the agency we are tracing the genetics of the Vindica and connecting the family tree so to speak."

"How do you reach back through time when so many are dead?"

"There are ways that I can show you while I'm down if you like. I will be working from our New Orleans lab for a week or so."

"Sure, I'd love to see it."

Griffen nodded. "It's fascinating stuff. Even Gabney is on the tree."

Gabney blushed. "Only because of my family. I don't belong there."

"Most families have had the same issue," Mr. White responded. "Even I, a healer, only have the ability to know what is wrong with someone. I must use my medical training to save my patients."

Gabney said, "Angelica's abilities are amazing though. It hasn't happened to her branch of the family tree for sure."

Mr. White nodded. "Perhaps we can see where she falls on that tree."

Angelica looked into his eyes. They weren't threatening or sinister. He wasn't trying to make her uncomfortable. It was the idea of where she'd fall in that family tree that was causing this nauseous feeling in the pit of her stomach. Was Lily on that family tree? If she was, then they would discover her secret.

Twenty One

Cain slipped into the shop without allowing the bell to jingle. Today his stealth was for a different reason. Simone's father was in a back storeroom where he worked on the books twice a month.

Simone smiled at a customer as she handed the elderly woman her purchases. Cain watched her make small talk with the woman, enjoying the ease of Simone's smile, the rise of her shoulders, and the flow of her banter.

Cain waited until the woman had left the shop and the little bell signaled her departure before he stepped out from behind the display.

Her lips fell into that straight line as her eyebrows straightened. Damn. She was still sexy when she was angry. "What are you doing 'ere? My father 'es in the back."

Cain nodded, waiting for her to approach him, which took her only moments to sweep toward him with her skirt swooshing against her quick movements.

"You know I wouldn't have come if I could have helped it."

She nodded and then melted into his arms. His blood heated, and he stroked her back.

"I don't know who he is, but I saw him."

Cain sighed. "What can you tell me?"

She pulled back. "I don't think e's human. Something strange about 'em. He's old, way too old, but doesn't look it. Every reading is blurred, but 'e changes things. I don't like it."

He pulled her closer. "How can I be certain?"

"You must find the girl who is part of the Vindica, but doesn't associate. She lives near a Bayou, and though she is not stronger than me, she shares the blood, so there is a connection."

"Will she be able to tell me who he is?"

Simone shook her head. "She will help you find the book. You must find it before this man or your plans will be ruined."

He leaned down and inhaled the scent of lavender and closed his eyes. "You're coming with me when I have the book."

She laughed, a deep throat laugh. "Do you promise?"

"Simone," a deep, booming voice echoed from the back of the store. "What are you doing?"

"I'm sorry, Sir. I was just leaving." Cain bowed his head as Simone stepped away.

"Yes, you are. I told you, your kind is not welcome here." He looked toward Simone. "I told you to leave this man alone. Go to the back and retrieve the new vials."

"Father, I told ya I will see whom I choose." Simone rattled on, but she walked toward the storeroom anyway. "Be safe, my *animus*."

Cain nodded to her father one last time and slipped out the door.

The bayou. Cain knew one person from the country, and he'd have to hope for luck to be on his side that it would be the right bayou of the hundreds in Louisiana.

Twenty-Two

Reximortum swooped into the dank shop, wondering how the ancient documents crowded on the shelves didn't mold in this humidity. He'd forgotten how he hated the weather shifts in New Orleans, but the Vindica seemed to enjoy being entrenched in this city.

He returned to his purpose as he searched the miniscule shop for its owner. The owner sat hunched over his workstation, repairing the binding of a fraying volume. His spectacles hung precariously from his nose and his large fingers moved smoothly over the binding. His white hair frayed in many directions around his hair, and his thinning flesh showed lines of veins crisscrossing his face under the bright lights.

"Joseph Respichin, I've come for knowledge."

Joseph rose, startled, and only showed his distaste for a mere second. No matter to Rex. Men like Joseph hated to be afraid, and Rex remained someone to be feared.

"Knowledge is contained within books, Rex." He walked around his workspace. "Have you brought me a book?"

Rex pulled a parchment from the folds of his coat. "Very delicate and quite painful to track down. We're having difficulties with a translation."

Joseph grunted. "Don't you have a man, I believe Andorne, for that?"

"We do, we do." Rex offered a pleasant smile. "He's having difficulties about making a decision. We thought we'd ask for a second opinion."

Joseph unrolled it slowly, and his beady eyes sifted through the words. "The Latin is easy enough, but some of the words are out of context."

Rex nodded. "It's a letter written from Abigail to Mennigas. The early Vindica manipulated their personal writings to avoid the inquisition."

"Ahh." Joseph scanned the document again, his eyes lingering over phrases.

Rex waited. Mennigas was the creator of the *Book of Shadow Souls*, the book he'd only held for mere weeks before Rosemary had stolen it from him. He'd barely scratched the surface of the book before he'd believed it destroyed. Obtaining that book again was the key to all that he wanted. He could wait for an answer.

Joseph's forehead crinkled. "Mennigas and Abigail were married?"

"No." Rex shook his head. "They were lovers."

"Doesn't the legend say that she created the prophecy to stop him?"

"Do you know what happens as a legend is passed down in families for five centuries?"

Joseph nodded, returning to the document. Rex could feel the gears clinking in his head as he turned phrases over.

"Mennigas was a Custos," Joseph released the words with awe.

"That's the little matter needing to be cleared up."

Joseph delved further into the letter. "She tells him that his *animus*, soul, contains too many of their secrets, but her *viscus*, heart, holds the key."

Rex waited as he analyzed the phrasing, not just the translation. The order of the words, the capitalization, the delicate balance of syntax.

He looked up from his document. "You need both books."

Rex nodded. "That was our conclusion. Of course, you work much faster. I might consider replacing Andorne."

He handed Rex the letter back. "I prefer repairing my books, but thank you."

Rex smiled. "I know, Joseph, but I consider you a man that I can trust and respect."

"My secret." Joseph nodded. "How will you get both books? No one has heard a whisper about the *Book of Heart* in centuries."

"I believe it was kept in the family, but I prefer to focus on one book at a time."

"Is there anything I can do?"

"You can let it be known that I'm looking for old documents. That should stir up some interest."

Joseph nodded.

Rex slipped back out the door and eyed his surroundings before heading toward his St. Charles residence.

Rex felt him move in before he felt him at his side, but he continued to keep his pace. Without abilities, he didn't ripple a threat through Rex's radar.

"Sir, I have a proposition I'd like to introduce."

Rex would like to show him why he shouldn't approach him, but the crowd wasn't thick enough for them to go unnoticed. Too much was riding on timing right now for him to risk it. Once, in his youth, he would have made the man drop dead from a heart attack.

"I know who you are, and I'm not crazy." The man continued, quickening his pace to keep up. "The name's Ronald White, and I've been studying your kind for most of my career in the FBI, and now that I work for a private company, I've figured out a way to use gene therapy to make humans have your abilities."

Rex stopped walking and studied Mr. White's receding hairline, his sweating forehead, and nervous twitching in his temple. At least he had the wits to be nervous. "I do not conduct business meetings on the street. Send me a proposition, and I'll let you know if I wish to meet with you."

His face spread into a smile.

Rex frowned. "The next time, do this in an appropriate manner or I won't spare you."

Rex continued walking, leaving him behind. It was an interesting concept, and Rex would not lie to himself that when he'd heard his words, he hadn't thought about having more power for himself and his soldiers. It wasn't a priority in the next week, but an idea to research in the future.

This week was about a book. As far as he was concerned, a race was on. It didn't matter if the other side knew it or not.

Twenty-Three

The wrinkled man in the rocking chair on the porch steeped in shadows watched Kline approach the front porch. The black dog at his feet picked his head up as he stepped onto the first step.

Kline paused. "I'm here to see Magis."

The whites of his eyes didn't blink. A dog howled from somewhere down the street. Finally, his head bobbed in a stiff nod.

Kline stepped tentatively onto the next step, watching the thick dog's head move his. At the screen door, Kline rapped his knuckles against the blue wood. A voice croaked from inside, and the door squeaked loudly as he pulled it open.

Dim overhead lighting and candles glowed, but it was the intoxicating smell of frankincense that overpowered him and made the room fuzzy.

"Magis?" Kline called into the room, blinking against the haziness overcasting the overstuffed room.

A small rumple of fabric moved. "You shouldn't have come."

"My father said you would help me."

Silence answered him.

A small hunched figure emerged from the shadows. "What can I do for you?"

"I need to get word to him to warn him."

Her round, wrinkled face didn't reveal any emotion, wiry gray hair shot crazily in all directions giving her eyes a steely iron appearance.

"The young are sometimes foolish. The old sometimes too as your grandfather learned."

Kline felt the scorn she felt for them, his kind. He delved deeper, smelling the acidity of her blood. Anihi. *Dark one.*

Why had his father made a pact with an Anihi?

"Foolishness is only perceived as such when it fails. I won't fail."

"Humph." She shifted, pulling herself up with much effort. "I've foreseen your plan. It depends on a young woman. Foolishness."

Kline tensed. "Have you foreseen failure?"

The shaky hand paused over a bowl. "The future is undetermined in this moment. Too many people with plans hoping to change destiny. Some plans will fail, some will succeed. It is too early to tell."

Kline watched as her fingers moved over containers of black roots and dried incense. She stuffed them into a tiny satchel before pulling it tightly closed and handing it to him.

"What is this for?"

"Put it under where she sleeps," Magis said, shuffling back into the shadows of the room. "It will open her to your plan when it is time."

"What about my father?" Kline asked, stuffing the satchel in his pocket. "I need him aware in case... I need him to know I'm planning something."

"It takes three days for news to make the journey. Lucilius monitors all other communication."

Kline nodded. "Thank you."

"Don't thank me. This could be your death sentence." She sighed in the darkness, layers of fabric ruffling. "Your grandfather would be proud though. He never was one to sit by and let others have their way."

Kline nodded, unable to speak. He turned and pushed the screen door behind him and entered the clear blackness of a moonlit sky. The dog lifted his nose in Kline's direction, but the old man didn't blink.

Kline bounded off the porch in one step and headed back toward the Quarter. By the look of the moon, he had a full hour before his surveillance time for the night ended. If he hurried, he could get to Angelica and place it under her bed before he had to report back.

Trickery had not been part of his plan. He was sure he could convince her to help him on his own, but his father still had two years left of a fifty-year slavery sentence for the deed of his grandfather. If Kail failed, his sentence would be upped to life since Kail had no children to pay for his transgressions. Kail couldn't take any chances.

Beneath Angelica's balcony, Kail sensed her asleep. Scanning the area with all his senses, he felt the desertedness of the street. He floated himself to the balcony, landing softly on his feet, careful to remain still a moment in case he'd been heard. Custos couldn't fly, but telekinesis could be used on yourself to a certain extent. Hybrids weren't strong enough to do this, so no human had ever seen another human flying. Custos wanted it to remain this way. He pushed the door gently that she'd left a small opening to allow the night air and slipped inside.

Surrounded by pillows, it wasn't difficult to see why his grandfather had fallen for her ancestor. The delicate features of a human woman and the strength of a Custos mixed in a mesmerizing body. Angelica's abilities didn't speak of hybrid though. Kline hoped to use this in his favor, but it also marked her. She'd need to be strong enough to withstand it all.

Kline pulled out the satchel. He didn't want to go against her will, but once his grandfather had attempted to merge the Vindica with the Custos, to bring the branches back together. He'd believed it was time, but Lucilius had made sure he paid for that political move with his position, his reputation, his life, and Kline's father's life.

Kline's oath to his grandfather on his deathbed had been to return their family back to their former place among the Custos council and unite the clan once again. Lucilius would have to be removed from his position in order for this to happen.

Kline tossed the satchel under the bed. Angelica stirred in her sleep, gripping the pillow tighter. He backed out the door slowly. He'd stayed too long. His presence, his heartbeat had begun to summon her awake.

He must get back. Duplicity, the name of this game they were all playing.

Twenty-Four

Angelica bolted upright in bed, her heart pounding in her chest and perspiration beading on her clammy body. Residual fear from her dream still coursed through her, and she shuddered as the images pounded against her skull.

In her dream, she'd walked down a deserted street after leaving a small bar after five A.M. It had been a long night on her feet behind the bar. Angelica knew she didn't work at a bar, couldn't even apply until a few days, but it had felt real in her dream.

Home had been right around the corner when she'd heard him behind her. Weirdly, she had felt him but the girl in her dream had not, almost as if she were split in two.

She'd been lifted into the air and floated there, grasping at the wind, staring down way too far below at the cracked cement sidewalk.

He'd wanted that book. Those same gravely words spoken to Gabney before he'd sent pain ripping through her body, burning through her until blackness had overcome the white streetlights.

Angelica groaned. What were the chances of it being just a nightmare?

She turned and glanced at the clock on the nightstand. 5:22 A.M.

Angelica pulled the pillow over her head and attempted to relax her mind enough to return to sleep.

She awoke again some time later to the sound of laughter and sunlight pouring into the window. She strained to see the clock without moving, and it was now 10:00. She must have drifted to sleep, finally.

Laughter drifted through her closed door again and stillness washed over her. She recognized that laugh, but it couldn't be.

Angelica rose and hastily grabbed some clothes. She'd left clothes at Landon House, but she hadn't brought much with her so the pickings were slim. Her things remained in storage, but she still hadn't made plans to move them here.

She was still pulling her hair back when she stepped into the small living area where Denise was curled up on a chair and Trevor was spread out against the sofa.

Angelica felt as though she'd stepped into another dream. "What are you doing here?"

"Is that a way to greet your best friend?" Trevor said, a goofy grin giving him a caricature appearance.

Angelica looked from Denise to Trevor. "You're supposed to be in school."

"So are you."

"I quit… well took some time off."

He grinned. "I was given some time off, too."

"What did you do?"

"Just a little trouble now. I'm only suspended for two weeks. It'll be all good when I go back though."

"I've only been gone a month Trevor." Angelica groaned. "How did you find me?"

She flung herself down on the sofa, but stood right back up. Nerves wouldn't allow her to keep still.

"Your cousin gave me the address. Figured I'd come check it out since I don't want the parents to know I'm on vacation."

Denise was being quiet, and Angelica noticed that she hadn't looked at her since she'd walked into the room.

"Why didn't you come wake me?"

Denise shrugged. "Figured I'd find out what you've been up to the last three years since you haven't been too forthcoming."

"You've been holding out." Trevor chuckled and his wide shoulders shook with it.

Denise turned on her with flashing eyes, which wasn't a good effect on Denise. It usually meant anger or evilness depending on what was going on. "I wasn't sure if he was even describing the same person. He's had some interesting stories to tell."

Angelica turned on Trevor. "What have you been telling her?"

"Oh." Denise inched up higher in her chair. "Just about the criminal you've become. How you've tricked people out of gifts and money and expensive items. That's sure a change from Ms. Virginal high morals in high school."

Angelica sighed and glared at Trevor. She imagined this is what it felt like for two worlds to collide; a strange numbness mixed with a sprinkling of panic.

"We didn't do anything illegal. Trevor is exaggerating."

Trevor laughed deeply, and Denise rolled her eyes.

Trevor quieted. "What are you doing here, Angelica?"

Denise grunted. "She's spending time with these people that she won't talk about."

Trevor bobbed his head up and down. It was a conspiracy: high school best friend ganging up with college best friend to analyze Angelica's every bad decision. Next thing they'd be talking about that low cut homecoming dress incident.

Trevor turned to her with a big goofy grin. "You're hustling them."

"No, I'm not."

The doorbell rang. Angelica's body temperature rose. She was becoming flustered and that hadn't happened to her since she was five.

When she'd get jittery, her mother would buy her a chocolate doughnut with sprinkles and milk. Lily would practice her story with her. My name is Sarah. I've five. My name is Jennifer. I'm six. He killed my mother, and Lily is taking care of me. I'm an orphan.

She'd never forget her story, and there was always another doughnut and milk treat the next time they moved on to a new story.

She'd never been nervous or flustered because she'd absorbed her story and made it her truth.

She didn't know what her truth was anymore. But that wasn't true either. She felt more and more that she was where she belonged, and Trevor and Denise's version were only stories.

The doorbell rang again.

Angelica cringed. "I'll get it."

On the other side of the door, Lysander leaned against the railing in an easy slouch with his brooding eyes blinking in the morning sun.

"Who is it?" Denise called from within the apartment.

"Someone for me." Angelica answered before going out onto the stair platform and closing the door behind her.

Lysander grinned. "I don't get to meet the friends yet?"

Angelica smiled, still feeling flushed. "Right now I'm rethinking the friendship."

He nodded. "Gabney says you work tonight."

Did he come to ask her on a date? She wondered what the calling in sick policy was at work. Probably not a good idea after only a few days.

Angelica smiled. "Until eleven o'clock."

"John wants me to escort you to the house tonight."

"Oh." Angelica tried to hide the disappointment and managed to keep her face from reflecting it. "Any reason why?"

His eyes flickered and his lip twitched. "There was a murder this morning. He doesn't want you out alone, and Mark thought you'd like to attend training tomorrow morning."

Angelica breathed in calmly, though her heart picked up its pace. "Who was murdered?"

"Megan Cicero. She made twenty-one two days ago. She trained at Landon House sometimes."

Light-headedness descended. "Dark hair, blue eyes, worked at a bar?"

Lysander tilted his head and looked at her puzzled. "How did you know?"

"I saw her death at 5:22 this morning."

"Oh, I'm sorry." Lysander reached out and stroked her arm. "The Vindica isn't usually like this. It's just that stupid prophecy about the full moon this month."

"You don't believe in the prophecy?"

Lysander shrugged. "I'm not really superstitious. I believe what is proven to me."

"But you believe in our abilities?"

He grinned. "What can I say? I'm a contradiction."

Angelica noticed he hadn't removed his hand from her arm, and she began to grow warm again. "I suppose I will see you after work tonight then."

"I will be there. Do I call this a date?"

Angelica laughed. "A walk home? You haven't dated much have you?"

"What we are, what we're about, I don't want to pass it on."

"Oh." Angelica paused, trying to get the part of her brain that came up with witty comments to kick in, but she had nothing. "I guess I'll see you tonight."

He nodded and then took the stairs two at a time.

She groaned and slipped back inside. Trevor stood inches from the door, and Angelica jumped back startled.

"You gonna leave my first night here?"

"You were eavesdropping?" Angelica accused.

Trevor shrugged. "You never minded before."

"Trevor, I didn't invite you here. You need to go home."

"I like him," Denise called from the living room. "I'll invite you to stay. You can share a room with Angelica since she doesn't stay here often."

Angelica groaned and stomped back to her room to pack her things for the night.

Twenty-Five

The night air blew through his cloak and Cain pulled it down further around his face. He kept to the shadows of the old, run-down gas station as he listened in on the conversation inside.

A couple was inside wanting babies. Cain couldn't pick up much of the conversation. Telepathy wasn't really a developed ability of his. It was hit or miss. First, he didn't like it. Second, he just wasn't good at reading the thoughts of others, especially from this distance. It was no matter though. He didn't need to hear their conversation. He just needed to know when they left.

Finding the woman Laura had been tricky. His source had to make a few contacts before they'd found her. She did readings out of her brother's gas station and didn't advertise her services. Cain had finally pieced her history together after a few more contacts. She was the daughter of Mama Fi, a larger than life woman who'd rejected the Vindica long before her daughter was born; therefore, Laura's knowledge of the Vindica was nearly obsolete, and with Mama Fi dead, there wasn't anyone to fill her in.

So Cain had come to the right place.

Now if the couple would just leave before he froze to death.

Several minutes later the rumpled couple emerged. They walked to their car in silence and left just as quietly.

Cain slipped into the open door but didn't notice the chime until it had sounded.

"Karen, is that you?"

Cain waited for her to place the vodka bottle back into the cabinet.

"I'm here for a reading."

The beads to the back room, her workroom, clanked together as he walked through them.

"I'm sorry, but I'm closed for the night," she said and then turned toward him. Her face froze in horror and she gasped.

"I promise it won't take long, but I've come a long way for this reading."

Thoughts of a faceless man circled in her mind until Cain figured out that she must have foreseen his coming.

"I'm closed...I'd prefer...an appointment," she stumbled, grasping for the words. "I promised someone I'd be home shortly."

Her eyes scoured the room for an escape, and Cain felt the desperation building internally.

"You knew I was coming. It'd be a shame not to give me an answer."

He stepped closer, blocking escape.

"Who are you?"

"Just someone looking for an answer that I was told you could give."

She straightened up. She was gathering her courage. "If I see for you, will you allow me to go unharmed?"

"Death or freedom?" He laughed as his thumb and forefinger pinched the candle flames out. "Let's see how it goes first."

Her mind began racing over what could she tell him to get him to leave.

He hadn't traveled to this dirty bayou to be given a lie.

He flung the table in the center of the room crashing against the back wall. He held her cards in the air before her face.

"How about that reading now?"

Her hands trembled as she clasped the deck of cards. Good, fear had driven out any thoughts of lying.

"That's not how it works."

He chuckled, feeling her humiliation. "Psychometry. A need for contact shows a weakness in your family line."

Doubts and self-criticism clouded her thoughts. She'd never be as good as her mother.

"Relax," Cain said, reaching his hand out. "I've come to see you because you're the one who has the answer."

"How…how do you know?"

"A witch told me that I needed to find someone like me, but not part of our family. You qualify."

Her bottom lip trembled as she clung to her cards. "I was supposed to be safe if I stayed away from ya'll."

"Who's safe these days?"

He raised his hand out again. She hesitated and then tentatively reached out with her hand to touch his.

She jerked as his images were absorbed through her fingertips, and then she paled as they continued to flow.

After a moment, she jerked away and choked. "You've killed people."

"I've done what I've had to. Sometimes it was necessary."

She stepped back. "What you want doesn't belong to you."

"Nothing has ever belonged to me." He stepped closer to her. "Now what did you see?"

She stepped back another step. "Your mother wished to hide it from your father until the girl was ready for it. She gave the secret to the person she knew he would not harm out of loyalty to her."

Cain released a breath. "Rainy."

She stared at him.

"What girl?"

Her bottom lip trembled and she muttered, "Don't know."

He crossed the expanse between them. He could feel her fear throbbing through her now.

"Just remember, I'm only doing this to save your life."

Closing himself off from her thoughts, he jabbed the dagger through her. Her blue eyes stared into his without a word escaping through her lips.

He released her to the floor and backed out of the door. In the front he flipped the switch that turned the outside speakers on, and then he slipped out of the gas station and began jogging to the car a half-mile down the road.

He wouldn't think about her living or dying. At best, she'd be in the hospital for days and she'd escape being tortured by Rex. At worst, she'd die before they found her and still avoid being tortured by Rex.

Cain wouldn't think about it tonight. He'd think about the fact that he was one step closer to finding the book, which meant he was one step ahead of his father.

Twenty-Six

Angelica's biceps trembled. Mark pushed down on her and stabs of pain shot through her arms. He'd called this stick a jo, some kind of Japanese weapon. It was supposed to stimulate fighting with swords without the pesky problem of being sliced and diced. Angelica didn't like the hard stick any better than the sharp blade as the stick thing hurt.

Mark grinned. "You're not concentrating."

Angelica's arms wobbled, and they felt as though they would fold at any moment.

"Ahhh!" Angelica threw him backward telekinetically and slammed the stick down as she stomped toward the wall of the training room.

Mark stood. "You're not supposed to use your abilities. You need to train your muscles to fight."

"Why?" Angelica asked, attempting to clear her mind. There were too many thoughts. Apparently, physical exertion brought down her defenses.

"Dark Soldiers fight with swords. You'll need to be able to defend yourself."

Her skin began to cool as her defenses shifted back into place. "Then I'll fight them with my abilities."

"Don't be stupid," Roxy said from her place on the floor. "You need to know how to fight them with their weapons unless you plan on running away."

Angelica glanced at Roxy and met an intense glare. Angelica suspected that Roxy knew about her past, but why hadn't she said anything yet?

"Okay." Angelica nodded. "I'm ready for the replay."

"Not a replay." Mark handed her the jo. "Round seven."

Angelica groaned, but gripped the jo.

Mark's lips curled at the edges, and his grayish blue eyes flashed. He was enjoying this too much.

Her entire body vibrated on the first strike.

Click. Clank. Clink.

The fluid motion of his muscles contracting registered and her reflexes responded by instinct.

Mark swung high. She nearly missed the signal. She arched backwards and the wind tickled her face.

"You need to see my next move."

Angelica blocked him again, but not before a sharp sting vibrated up her arm upon contact.

"I can't hear your thoughts with everyone's thoughts in the room."

"You need to try harder."

Again, she lowered her defenses. A chorus of voices bombarded her mind.

Serena's elation buzzed from her corner, while a romance novel scene staring Gabney as the main character flirted through Griffin's mind. Roxy thought Angelica was going to leave when it got tough, desert them. Bruce thought pizza.

Angelica's breath caught as the stick plowed her abdomen.

Angelica threw the stick down again. "I can't do this with everyone's thoughts screaming at me."

Mark grinned. "You need to learn to master the talent of letting one person in at a time."

"You keep saying that, but you haven't told me how."

Serena stepped forward with an arrogant smile on her face. "My turn. Why don't you watch trained members fight. You may learn something."

Angelica stepped back, clinching her shoulders. She really didn't like Serena and with every biting comment, the dislike grew. How could she even be the adopted daughter of John Landon? She'd learned nothing from him.

Serena and Mark squared off. Serena blocked Mark's first strike before maneuvering herself behind him. Their fluid movements were a choreographed dance. Angelica watched as they weaved in and out, the stick never making contact against body.

Angelica hated to admit it, but they were good.

Lysander stepped closer to her, and Angelica felt his presence suck the air in around her. He leaned in and spoke low. "I wouldn't worry about it too much. I think they're so good because they're a couple."

Angelica's muscle tensed. He'd been distant last night when he'd walked her here, and he hadn't said much this morning either. There hadn't been much opportunity, but still.

"How are you at this? Am I the only one who needs preschool lessons?"

Lysander laughed. "Nah, I'm not really good at this. I don't have the ability to read minds, so Mark kicks my ass every time."

Serena bit her lip as she blocked Mark's jab. Mark grinned as his eyes crinkled at the corners.

Lysander leaned in closer, his nearness tickling her ear. "Mark usually wins, but he lets Serena win every now and then."

Gabney entered, face buried in a clipboard. Blonde tendrils escaped her neat bun, and a pencil was resting on her ear.

Angelica couldn't help but smile. Gabney's obliviousness was endearing.

"Serena, I need you to finalize the party list." Gabney looked up and stopped. "Oh, I'm sorry. I thought Angelica was training."

Serena scowled at Gabney and her thoughts of how stupid Gabney was proved she wasn't nice.

"Maybe if you ever paid attention, you wouldn't have to apologize all the time."

Gabney's cheeks colored. "Uncle John wants this done before his return. He's with the woman's family, so he couldn't finalize himself."

Serena grabbed the clipboard. "You'd think since he's my father, my twenty-first birthday would be more important than a dead stranger."

"Serena!" Mark barked, his voice echoing against the walls.

Everyone jumped. Angelica had never seen him angry, just focused.

Serena blushed. "I'm sorry. He knows how important this is to me."

Gabney crossed her arms across her chest. "She's not dead. She's in a coma."

"Whatever." Serena flipped through the pages. "I suppose I'm expected to invite her, too."

Angelica stepped back. "Invite me to what?"

"For my birthday on the eighteenth, we're performing a Vindica ritual."

Angelica's heart palpated faster. She hadn't admitted to anyone here that her birthday fell in the full moon window. "I turn twenty-one on the seventeenth. My friends may be planning something."

Serena's head snapped up from the clipboard. "Your birthday is the seventeenth of this month?"

Mark and Lysander's eyes met.

"Yes."

Serena threw the clipboard at Gabney. "Great for you. Everything's fine, Gabney."

Serena stomped out the room, and Angelica turned toward Gabney. "Did I say something wrong?"

"Um…"

Mark handed Lysander the stick. "Serena is stressed with Vindica troubles. Don't worry about it."

Gabney put her head down and escaped through the open doorway.

Angelica didn't believe that flimsy excuse. She'd lied enough in her life to recognize what it sounded like.

Lysander and Mark were squaring off, and although Angelica would like to watch, she wasn't going to miss this opportunity.

Angelica backed out of the room, aware that only Roxy paid any attention to her leaving. The others were too busy watching Lysander and Mark exchange blows.

Angelica hurried into the tearoom. Gabney sat on the sofa, sniffling and blinking back tears.

She looked away when she noticed Angelica. "I'm so stupid. I don't know why I keep trying."

Angelica sat on the other side of the small sofa. "Don't blame yourself. Just between you and me, I've never met anyone more bitchy than Serena."

A laugh escaped from Gabney. "Don't let her hear you say that or I'll have to add another war to study in my history class."

Griffin stuck his head in the door. "Everything alright?"

Gabney reddened and stared at her fingers. "We're just planning the party. Only two days left."

Griffin stared a moment longer and then moved to another room in the house.

Gabney was upset again, insulting herself for not saying something more intriguing or interesting. He'd never know she was interested that way.

Angelica grinned. "Someone has a crush."

Gabney's head popped up.

"It's all over your face."

Gabney flushed. "Does anyone else know?"

"No one pays much attention around here." Angelica gave her a smile of reassurance. "So what kind of ritual is Serena having?"

Gabney shrugged. "Some ritual to call Valor. Some of the council members will be here. There's a disagreement within the council so not everyone wants the ritual performed, hence the stress."

"Hmm." Angelica turned over the information in her thoughts rapidly. "This ritual will tell them who Valor is?"

Gabney nodded. "Something like that."

The idea flowed through her and filled her with a strange sense of nervousness and anxiety.

"I guess I need to get back to training." Angelica stood. "You know Gabney, you should come out and ask Griffin on a date. He's not real perceptive, so I think you need to make a move."

Gabney blushed again. "Really?"

"Yes." Angelica grinned. "Men in our generation need a little help."

Angelica walked back to the training room, and she realized that Gabney was the only person that she wasn't ever trying to figure out who she was supposed to be when she was with her.

Interesting.

Roxy stood next to the doorway of the training room watching her. This one she'd need to figure out soon so she could assess the threat.

Roxy raised her eyebrows at her, but Angelica just smiled and entered the training room.

Twenty-Seven

Rex waited near the lamppost as the streetlights flickered on. His gaze never flickered away from the two gentlemen at the corner table in Muriel's restaurant.

Frederick, youngest Vindica Council member, was whom he waited for tonight. The tall, sallow gentleman had arrived from France for the full moon ceremony this morning, and Rex had shadowed him, waiting for an opportunity. He didn't trust any of his men to handle this task, and he'd taken an interest in this one.

Frederick had taught Rex a valuable lesson years back. Fourteen years ago he'd believed that the only emotion the Vindica would feel after a murder was fear. Then he'd encountered two young men, Davey and Ross. They'd joined the Dark Soldiers solely to work against him. Rex had killed them, of course, after they'd made nuisances of themselves by working together to prevent certain pieces of information to reach him. He'd arrogantly assumed that it would end there.

Frederick had taught him that there were still people in the Vindica who didn't forget. Frederick had made it his life interest to avenge the death of his two best friends. Frederick's lack of fear had propelled him through the Vindica chain at such a fast pace that Rex hadn't paid much attention until Frederick had insulated himself

143

within the Vindica and had nearly become untouchable. Nearly.

His dinner partner on the other hand was the Vindica council leach, and Rex suspected he wouldn't be missed much. Larkin Luke desired to be on the council, yet he'd never reach that destination. He'd gained support among those who feared certainly, but little else. He could serve a purpose in the future, so Rex allowed him to work his oily skills among the people.

Frederick stood to leave as Larkin Luke answered his cell phone. His head was down so he didn't notice Rex standing, waiting for him, until he'd turned left in the direction of Landon House.

He stopped moving and his face darkened.

Rex grinned. "Relax, I haven't come to kill you. With your lack of attention, I could have done that already."

"Even you wouldn't dare this close to Landon House and on the street."

Rex straightened. "Risks are taken during war."

"What do you want?"

Frederick's voice was harsh and impatient, but his quick glance at the front of Landon House hinted at something else.

Rex shrugged. "I have a message to deliver. I thought you'd be the best candidate to receive it."

Frederick lit a cigarette. Rex could tell it was anger scorching through him right now. He wanted so much to inflict pain on Rex.

"Have you decided to surrender?"

Rex smiled. "No, just to let you know that if you name Valor tomorrow night, the girls will stop being killed."

Frederick's eyes narrowed, and he flicked the cigarette from his fingers. "We don't make deals with you."

Rex rocked back on his heels. Sometimes he had to remind himself that his abilities didn't help in the long run, though it would make him feel better to strangle him with just a flick of his mind.

"No deal," Rex said. "Just a fair warning between adversaries."

"Frederick," Larkin Luke called coming out the restaurant doors. "Reginald will be here."

Larkin glanced toward Rex finally and paled.

"Luke." Rex nodded. "I'm sure you'll make sure Valor is named tomorrow night. I'd hate for you to have had the opportunity to save those poor girls and not have taken it."

Luke looked to Frederick, who now glared at Rex with such fierce intensity that Rex could imagine their battle on Charters Street.

Rex tipped his head. "Good evening, gentlemen. I look forward to our next meeting."

Rex turned and rounded the corner. He felt particularly satisfied, as that had worked better than planned. It would take Frederick time to take action, but Luke would have the news around the Vindica. Fear was an excellent tool in pushing the Vindica into a decision, although some still possessed courage like Frederick.

Rex liked to respect his adversary, and Frederick was courageous and intelligent. Two great qualities that deserved recognition.

Twenty-Eight

The noise below roared as though they sat on top of an engine. Angelica pulled the cloak around her middle tighter.

"I think the Vindica could use a fashion designer."

Gabney laughed. "It's just a cloak. The inner circle wear red and the rest of us wear purple. If you're named Valor tonight, you can change the fashion."

Angelica sneaked a peek at Gabney to assess that she wasn't serious. Angelica was worried about that detail now, and she'd rather it not be spoken aloud.

"Hey, do you think Serena will be named Valor tonight?"

Gabney grimaced. "Lord, I hope not."

Angelica laughed, and Gabney's eyes widened.

"I didn't mean that... she's worked for it for the last five years. It's been her obsession. She thinks it will happen tonight. It is her birthday, after all."

"Yes, but I'm sure you meant what you said before, too."

Gabney laughed. "Don't tell her that. She may lock me in my room again or make me think my bedroom is haunted like last year."

Okay, so Serena was meaner than Angelica had given her credit for.

Lysander opened the door. "Are you two ready?"

Gabney eased out of her center seat among her books spread across her bed. "The Vindica could have scheduled this around my midterms."

"We can control the full moon?" Angelica asked, smiling.

Gabney attempted to frown but ended up laughing anyway. "I suppose not. Let's hope it's quick so I don't have to repeat this anatomy class."

Lysander reached out and grasped Angelica's arm as she passed him. "Are you sure you're ready for this?"

Angelica looked up. She tingled from the intensity of his gaze. "What? Are we dancing naked under the full moon?"

Gabney called back as she reached the stairs. "We save nudity for All Hallow's Eve."

Angelica blanched, wondering if this was true, until she heard Gabney's laughter bubbling up the stairs.

"I'm serious," Lysander said. "What will you do if the ceremony names you?"

"I'll pretend I wasn't called." Angelica grinned, but his eyes darkened. She reached out and touched his arm. "I'll do what I need to, but I'm not Valor."

The crinkles at his eyes softened. "Good, I'll meet you outside. I need to get something upstairs for Landon."

Angelica smiled and went down the stairs. She was excited about the ceremony. Witnessing an old Vindica ceremony appealed to the side of her that was searching for the truth behind this organization. The possibility of being named Valor only put a small damper on her interest.

It wasn't that she didn't think she could do the job, but a month ago her biggest problem was studying for an exam and heading into a career she didn't want. A week ago she set out to find out about her mother's past and therefore her own history. Being Valor felt like a derailment of her plan since she'd pretended to be someone else and no one had divulged any information yet.

At the bottom of the staircase, she stopped as two voices rose from the tearoom. The bottom floor had emptied. Angelica supposed they'd gone outside for the ritual.

A nasally, high pitched voice whined. "Benjamin will not allow it. We cannot name Valor tonight."

"So we watch more die." A deep, anger-filled voice replied.

Angelica eyed the corner she'd have to turn and judged weather she could make it without being spotted. The size of the opening meant probably not.

Nasal voice said, "It is only you and I here, we do not have the authority, and we do not want to give into him."

"So we'll die for him."

A gentleman hurried out the room, and Angelica's body heat raised a notch. He nodded toward her and rushed passed.

Angelica took the last step down the stairs and nearly collided with gentleman number two.

"Excuse me," she said automatically.

"I apologize." He nodded, studying her. "Why aren't you outside?"

"I was on my way." She smiled and tilted her head. "I didn't want to interrupt, but then I didn't want to eavesdrop. Quite the conundrum."

He smiled, but still studied her. "I don't believe we've met."

"Angelica Acacia," she said, holding her hand out. She didn't even flinch anymore. She'd practiced.

"John's mentioned you." He studied her. Angelica felt him trying to peer into her mind, see who she was. "We'll talk later. Right now we have a ceremony to get to."

A deep earth smell filled the room, and Angelica looked around for a source. She couldn't see any.

She stepped toward the back hall, and he followed. The nearer they came to the back door, the stronger the smell filled each cavity of her body. It must be coming from the ritual.

She opened the back door, blinking against the contrast between the heavy darkness and the shooting flame from an open fire pit.

Seven red cloaks in the center caught her attention, and the intoxicating smell from an iron bowl consumed her. A strange beating swept through her, vibrating her body, but the mumbling from the circle entranced her.

She focused in on their chanting, their faces flickering in the licking fire. She tried to make out the words, but it sounded foreign, ancient, not a language she recognized.

She came back from the chant and stared into the eyes of a hunched man in a tattered cloak. She stepped back, glancing around the inner circle where she now stood. She didn't remember walking here. Her breath caught as the man's eyes rolled white, and his jerking hand grabbed an altar knife. Angelica leaned her head back as the knife pushed against her throat.

His eyes rolled brown then white. Numbness swept through her and then a slow current twitched through her spine.

Someone was controlling him.

Strong arms wrapped around her middle, jerking her back. The brown of his eyes flickered back briefly and fear overflowed. His eyes watered as he strained his body to look around for his puppet master.

She saw it coming. She yanked against the arms restraining her as his eyes rolled white again.

His hand gripping the knife plunged into his abdomen as Angelica fought free.

Screams came from far away as deep burgundy grew across the middle of his red cloak.

His brown eyes widened, terror twitching through his arms and legs.

Angelica lunged forward, and he fell into her. Gabney appeared beside her, helping to ease him to the patio stones. Thick, stickiness clung to Angelica's hands. She avoided looking at it, knowing what clung to her flesh. His eyes stared into hers and his lips trembled. She could feel him trying to reach her, but she clung to the curtain separating their thoughts.

Others jostled her from behind, and she was pushed aside. He coughed as his lips moved without sound. Jack tended to him as Angelica closed her eyes.

She felt him slip away.

Gabney cried out, and Angelica opened her eyes, searching her face. Gabney had felt him slip away. How?

Jack turned on her, purple vein throbbing across his temple. "You are responsible for this." He raised his head high and met the eyes of the crowd. "I demand punishment for this crime."

John Landon was suddenly in the middle. "Everyone needs to remain calm until we know what occurred here."

Angelica mumbled as she looked back down at the man again, his face frozen in pain. "He was being controlled by someone here. He couldn't fight them off."

A skinny robe broke away from the circle. Angelica's insides cringed as Serena's voice scratched her ears. "This may not be Angelica's fault, but if she were Valor she'd have been able to prevent this from happening. She's a fraud at least."

Even with a man dead in front of them, Serena could still find a way to steer herself toward being Valor.

A low hum vibrated through the crowds as the crowd glared at her.

Jack met the eyes of the crowd again. "I said she was dangerous. Now one of us is dead because our mighty John Landon chooses to trust the wrong person again. When will you believe me? Must any more of us die?"

Silence swept through the crowd. Some stared unabashed, mouths open.

Jack had gone too far.

But then the mood shifted. Their thoughts became frenzied. No one knew who she was. They couldn't trust her.

Angelica began to tremble, and she felt her control loosening. Screams and pleas bubbled inside of her, threatening to suffocate her. Failure. She'd failed Lily again.

"I never claimed to be Valor." Angelica looked to Landon, whose face was purple with anger. "I never said I wanted to be. I just want to find out what happened to my mother."

Landon reached out to grip her shoulder. "We're all emotional right now. We need to handle the immediate situation and deal with this issue when we've calmed down."

"Why?" Serena asked. "Why do you keep letting her get away with things?"

Anger burst though the numbness, and she shrugged Landon's hand away. "What is wrong with you? Why must I keep defending myself to you?"

Serena sneered. "You've never proved yourself to us in the first place."

Something exploded inside Angelica's head, and Serena rose in the air before her. The crowd gasped, but they felt so far away from Angelica.

"You want what I have. It burns you with jealousy. Do you feel the death of each Vindica member? *I do*. I experience each death with them. If you want all the glory, you must also taste the suffering."

Angelica lunged out and grabbed Serena's arm. A shock ran through Angelica's arm, but she held on.

Each death traveled on a pulse through her touch. The young woman in the alley. The fortune teller's assistant. Lewis on the stakes of the courtyard, and finally Lily's death. Lily reaching out with outstretched arms to get away and then screaming in agony.

Angelica pulled back before the other deaths transferred, feeling her anger and energy draining.

"In order to be strong enough to protect them, you need to be able to watch them die. Are you ready for the real responsibility of Valor?"

Serena sobbed, putting her face in her trembling hands. "It's not fair. It's not fair."

Seven deaths, now eight. Eight deaths she'd not prevented.

Angelica searched his crumpled body. No sign of life. Eight deaths on her. *Her fault.*

Angelica stumbled backwards. She couldn't breath. Her chest squeezed in on itself. Was this what a panic attack felt like?

The crowd moved away from her as she scrambled toward the kitchen door. She needed to quiet the screams from all those deaths in her head. She needed their voices out. Her chest felt as though it would explode.

She yanked the cloak off as she made it to the front door. She discarded it onto the floor, and threw the front door open telekinetically and slammed it behind her as she emerged onto the front sidewalk.

The wind stung her face as she turned left toward the Mississippi river. The stinging gave way to numbness, and it began to travel through her, and the bad thoughts retreated.

It was reckless to walk alone at night. She knew this.

She continued her trek to the deep, muddy Mississippi.

Twenty-Nine

With a flick of his wrist, Rex silenced the bell's jangle as he pushed the door open. Even with the stealthiness of his entrance, Madame Lulu looked up from the book behind the counter and looked straight at him.

"Simone, go upstairs."

Her granddaughter emerged from the aisle. "I'm not finished the shelves yet."

"Tomorrow, Love." Madame Lulu glared at Rex. He avoided angering Madame Lulu out of past experience. She possessed different abilities, which made her an unknown threat, and she'd built a reputation around this. Still, her skills could serve some use to him, and at times like this, the risk was worth it.

Simone stared at him. Neither fear nor surprise shadowed her expression. Rex hadn't paid much attention to her, but he glimpsed the potential now in her glare. He'd remember this for later.

Her boots stomped off toward a back room, and Madame Lulu waited until a door slammed from the back before she heaved herself up from her bar stool.

"I suppose you have a real good reason for dropping in on me after I've told you to leave my family out of your business."

"Sometimes you and I have the same business."

She regarded him with an intense fierceness that had certainly been a reason for her earning her reputation as a scary lady.

She brought her arms across her chest. "What do you want with me today?"

"There are those that say we are in the middle of a prophecy. The Reckoning."

Madame Lulu nodded affirmation.

Rex grabbed a dried chicken foot from the shelf in front of him. Such odd objects to believe power could be derived. "Fear runs rampant at times like this however. People spread word based on fear instead of real visions. And even with these supposed glimpses into the future, no one knows what will cause The Reckoning. It's all speculation at this point."

"What are you getting at?" Madame Lulu's chin rose and the wrinkles at her eyes softened.

"How many times has the end of the world been foretold? The end of us? Every time the prophetic ones have been wrong. Are they wrong now?"

Madame Lulu studied him a moment, her big lips pursued tightly together. "You want to know if I've seen it?"

"That," Rex said, putting the chicken leg back into its place. "And how to stop it from coming to pass."

"Why?" Madame Lulu asked, glaring at him.

"What would be the benefit to me for war to come and end our people or end the world as we know it?"

"I figured you might have had something all planned out for when that happened."

Rex shook his head. "What I want is for our people to come together and return to the strength we once possessed. My methods may not be agreeable to all, but I have the interest of our people in mind."

"Your people aren't interested in dead girls."

Rex nodded. People seldom understood sacrifice. Sometimes achieving goals required difficult decisions.

"But still, if you could do something to stop the Reckoning, wouldn't you want to know you've done all you can?"

Madame Lulu studied him for a long time. He could feel the seconds ticking off as she contemplated what she would say, what she'd hold back. His abilities were powerless against such a powerful seer, so he must wait and depend on her generosity.

Madame Lulu walked around the counter and pulled a rolled up parchment from somewhere deep in the bowels of the counter.

"If you'd ever honed your skills of foretelling, you would know that premonition isn't that simple. Several versions of the future exist at this moment; many have disappeared as choices have been made. Because no matter what your seer has said, people still possess free will. With each decision made since fear took hold…" At this, she glared at Rex reproachfully, "a noose has tightened on the future. If you want to change Rosemary's prophecy, you need to consider carefully each decision that is made."

She handed him the parchment.

"What is this?" He asked, feeling the linen-like texture of the paper against his fingers.

"It's a letter to a Vindica scholar about how the last Reckoning was avoided. It's 1920s or so, so you shouldn't need a translator."

"How did you come to have it?"

Madame Lulu's chest heaved upward. "My mother helped. The letter never made it to that scholar due to the circumstances at the time."

Rex regarded her, his curiosity piqued. His curiosity of the history of the Anihi had never been indulged due to a lack of cooperation between the two groups. It wasn't only a lack of communication though; the Anihi detested the Vindica. He couldn't imagine them working together. He felt there was more there, but from Madame Lulu's wrinkled brow; he could tell she wouldn't be sharing.

Rex secured the parchment inside his jacket. "I've heard your granddaughter follows in your footsteps."

"Yep." Madame Lulu's jaw clamped down. "She stays away from Vindica mess, as I've warned... others."

Rex caught her hesitation. The woman didn't hesitate with her confidence. Again, he knew he'd missed something. This one could be easily remedied, as the granddaughter hadn't earned the same immunity as her grandmother.

"Do keep in touch," Rex said, nodding at her. "We would both like to see a different ending."

"Humph," Madame Lulu said.

Rex turned and left the store. He'd meant what he'd said about not wanting war, but of course, he had his own reasoning. What he'd really wanted was confirmation that Destiny had spoken and he would lose. Madame Lulu had left him with hope and reason to keep pursing his plan. Just more carefully.

Thirty

The hair on the back of her neck prickled as Angelica felt someone following her. Even with the cushioned fall of his footsteps, she felt the distance closing in between them. Even still, she didn't feel ominous vibes or sinuous thoughts vibrating through the dead calm of the cold night so she kept walking, allowing the awareness to press her from the side as she focused ahead.

As the smell of the Quarters had been absorbed by the Mississippi River, her panic had eased. The blackness of the water was a wide stretching abyss that she could get lost in forever. And at least for the moment, it could swallow her feelings of inadequacy whole.

The currents could absorb her if she wanted. Angelica shivered against the thought. So much death could be escaped. Her follower descended upon her, and Angelica turned to watch Lysander ease into her hurried pace. His smell filled Angelica, but her insides only tingled. The cold air had numbed her body and made it easier for her to deaden herself to the pain.

His hands were stuffed in his brown leather jacket and his short hair was twisted and wind blown. "I didn't want you to be alone out here."

Angelica exhaled, trying to feel the heat she'd felt between them. Her heart only gave a small tingle of interest. The numbness, the cool aloofness that had been a mark of her childhood at Gram's had returned, but the numbness blocked out everything, not just the pain.

"That didn't go as planned, I'm sure," Angelica said, managing a small smile, "or if it did, someone should have handed out a program."

"Don't blame yourself. They will find out what happened, and it will all be okay."

"That man died because I couldn't save him. I'm not Valor."

Angelica trembled, a chill rippled through her flesh again. Her failure threatened to collapse her small grasp of control.

Lysander reached out and gripped her shoulder, forcing her to stop in her tracks. "They never planned on naming Valor tonight, and they never will."

"What?" Angelica stared into his greenish-gray eyes, sure she'd heard wrong.

"In every generation there has been someone strong enough to be Valor, but the council always finds a reason not to declare this person as Valor."

Angelica tried to grasp the conversation through the sudden surge of anger trickling through. "Why would they do that?"

Lysander shrugged. "The answer depends on who you talk to. My father says because Valor is the only person who can change the Vindica, and the Vindica refuses to change. If you talk to the Council, it's because Valor has never come."

"So this was all for nothing? That man died for no reason?"

He stroked her arm tenderly. "This wasn't your fault. Serena wanted to prove Valor wasn't just a legend, but some want myths to stay in the past."

Angelica's thoughts were so scattered. Just two weeks ago she'd not known about any of this. Her lessons when she was younger had not included the politics of a centuries old organization. She'd been taught to lie, to practice self-preservation, to change whom she was and start over when danger approached. Her abilities had been honed for those purposes. She must be going mad to keep walking into this situation without the knowledge she needed. But what else was she going to do? She still felt the drive that had motivated her to come here to learn the truth.

Angelica's head ached. She didn't want to think about it anymore. She didn't want to think. She wanted to feel something other than the numbness or the pain that rested in her chest.

"Didn't you say your parent's place was near here?"

Lysander studied her, his eyes deep and piercing. "It's a little ways off of Magazine Street. They're in Colorado right now."

"All the better," Angelica said, intertwining her hand in his and walking in that direction.

He walked slowly at first, hesitant even, so she stopped and faced him. "Is something wrong? Are you not interested in me?"

He grimaced, squeezing her hand in his. "Are you ready for this? And not just because of tonight?"

Angelica tiptoed and delicately pressed her lips against the smooth curve of the side of his lip. She lingered over the softness a moment, feeling his body twitch beneath her touch, his breath becoming shallow. She moved her lips over, pressing them full against his mouth, allowing him to feel her insistence. His jaw clenched with self-control and he leaned into her.

She whispered against his lips. "Where do you live?"

He led the way, his hands touching her, caressing her palm, her fingertips.

Anticipation grew on the short walk, but the numbness threatened to dampen the moment. She tried to focus on the feeling of Lysander's hand in hers, but the dead man's face materialized in the rolling fog or a passing darkened window. The heat of Lysander's palm would send a shiver through her, but then her brain would delve into the possibilities of a family the dead man left behind; children who may not have a father anymore.

Just as the numbness inside threatened to wipe out the warmth of his touch and the words formed in her throat that she needed to go, they reached an older white Acadian with a wide sweeping porch and a mahogany door. Lysander located the hide-a-key in a frog statue near a potted fern, and Angelica propelled herself inside with the last bit of resolve left in her toes.

Facing her, Lysander began to say something, but Angelica knew small talk would give her time to back out, to allow the iciness to take over.

She placed her lips full on, allowing the feeling to tingle though her. His arms wrapped around her, and she leaned into him, embracing the heat warming through her.

He led, half-carried her to a bedroom down the hall.

His lips seared through her flesh as he moved down her neck. He lay her down on a masculine brown comforter and continued caressing her neck with kisses. He slid her shirt off with fluid hands, and she trembled under his touch. Lysander groaned as her hands roamed across his chest, feeling his smooth pecks. She finished unbuttoning his shirt, tasting his flesh with her lips.

Everything evaporated from her mind as his heat and hands consumed her, and their bodies fit together. She gave into the desire coursing through her and shut her eyes as he sent waves of pleasure through her. She'd wanted to feel so now she allowed the intenseness to wash over her, driving all other thoughts out.

As they reached a feverish high, he buried his head into her hair, and Angelica moaned with the shivers from his breathe going down her neck through her body.

She snuggled into his chest, and he kissed her.

"I'm sorry," he said. "This should have been done right. Dinner, flowers, something other than this."

She traced a small crescent shaped scar on his arm. She didn't know the story behind this indention or if there were others on his body. It struck her at how much she didn't know about him. "I didn't need flowers or dinner tonight."

He ran his finger over her shoulder gently. "I thought you wanted a date."

Angelica smiled, snuggling her face closer into his chest. "Tonight I needed this, but next time I may expect dinner and flowers."

He pulled her closer in response. She felt his taunt body beneath her, warming her, steadying her, keeping the ghosts at bay. Their restful breathing filled the space.

Content, she drifted into a light sleep.

The melody blared throughout the apartment. A stoned couple lounged back, heads resting on a thick, orange plaid sofa cushion. Angelica stared as several people thrust rail thin bodies to the song's missing beat, their bodies brushing against each other in a way that captivated her young, sleepy eyes.

The gentle tug on her hair caused her to look up into Lily's creamy oval face. Lily's dull eyes were matted with dark circles blotching her bare complexion. Angelica smiled up at Lily who grinned as her hands braided locks of hair trailing down Angelica's neck.

"I'm sorry it's so noisy at Aunt Rainy's place."

Angelica glanced at the rough edges of her fingernails. She had bit them down hiding in a tiny closet, trying to escape the noise last night. "I like Aunt Rainy. I just wish her friends would go home."

Lily gathered Angelica close in a familiar cradle hug. Angelica breathed in lavender and chamomile hugging the thin white cotton nightshirt. "Aunt Rainy is just having a hard time after losing Uncle River."

Angelica watched the stoned couple kiss and grope the thin creases of flesh under thin, cotton patterned clothing. She pulled her attention away, embarrassed but curious. "What was he like? My father, not River, what was my father like?"

Angelica could feel Lily's chest expand against her back for what felt like minutes, before she exhaled unevenly. "You remind me of him. Strong, courageous, and good."

Angelica traced her finger along her mother's hand, noticing the veins protruding through thin, pale skin. The skin felt warm and soft. "Aunt Rainy says he's a bad man."

Lily pushed her lips against Angelica's forehead. "Aunt Rainy never really knew your father. He was very brave and made it possible for you to be born."

Her insides gurgled and burned. Her breathing was labored. "Why can't we have a home? Why can't we be normal like other families?"

Lily pulled her tight. "You don't have to be normal to have a home. We'll go to the place I called home when it's safe."

"But when will it be safe?"

Lily's lips moved, but roaring silence consumed her ears as darkness fell. The warmth of Lily's chest remained, but her face faded into blackness. Aftershave drowned the smell of lavender.

Angelica's heart raced as her eyes popped open. Her bare body tensed as the shadowed room registered.

She'd fallen asleep. Lysander's warm, buff body spread out beside her.

It had been a dream. The warm lingering feel of her mother was a dream, a memory really. She wasn't six years old anymore.

She eased out of the disheveled bed, studying the unmoving figure lying naked on white sheets. She padded barefoot through the room, grabbing a shirt from the floor, alertness jolted through her as she navigated the discarded clothing.

Her breathing eased as she stepped into the hall. Following a narrow hallway, she found a French door leading to a porch area. With a gentle tug the door opened, and she gave a little wish for no alarms going off. She inhaled deeply, exhaling the strange feeling inside her.

For years she'd suppressed memories of those years with Lily, but they'd pop up randomly every now and again in dreams. The woman had said that with Custos blood she just needed to remember. Perhaps her answers were really all buried in her own memories. But the memories never came without a reason.

So why had that particular memory surfaced now?

She hadn't thought about Rainy in years, but the conversation about her father bothered her. Rainy and Lily had disagreed on little, but Angelica's father had been a source of two arguments that Angelica had overheard, and the only source of knowledge that Angelica had about her father.

One said he was evil, the other said he was good. It left Angelica with the impression that she really didn't want to know; therefore, she hadn't searched for this unknown man, preferring to allow the mystery for fear that she didn't want to know the answer.

Lysander slept inside, and she stood on a back porch, barefoot and growing numb. In psychology, she'd be a classic case of daddy issues. Having had no father figure ever in her life, she kept men at a distance. Never got too close emotionally. She had no idea what to do with Lysander. She wanted him, sure, but what do you do out of bed.

The loneliness she'd cloaked herself in was feeling like that snug, red twill jacket she'd been unwilling to out-grow at twelve. She exhaled the final stray lavender scent of her mother's memory before turning away from the preened back yard. Lysander's warm body waited without questions, and it was all she needed to know for sure in this moment.

Thirty-One

Cain crotched in the door hidden in the alley of St. Peter's Street. He'd followed Rainy to the little shop on the corner, and then he'd waited in a hidden stairway for the night to deepen and her to return into it.

Finally, she emerged, waist length auburn hair flapping in the wind. Snug, straight-legged jeans ended in strappy heels clicking along the sidewalk. She'd traded in her hippy clothes for a more modern look in the last twenty years, but her lack of awareness of her surroundings hadn't changed, as she never glanced at him as she passed his doorway.

Cain listened to her hum, an upbeat happy tune.

Her thoughts projected across the distance, and they were absorbed by old friends and memories of a time twenty-eight years ago. Happy thoughts, but he noticed the shift as soon as it happened. Anxiousness itched her skin, causing her heart to throb harder.

She'd sensed him, finally.

He emerged from his hiding spot and she turned to face him. He stared into her yellow-flecked olive eyes as she searched his face, hoping for recognition. She recognized the almond shape of his eyes as his mother's; her best friend, but it had been so long she wasn't sure.

She threw her shoulders back, head high. "Who are you?"

"You know who I am, Rainy."

She searched the empty street, a lone street lamp casting a dim glow around them. "How do you know me?"

"The same way you recognize me."

"Lily," she said breathless. She studied him closely, lingering over the face of his father, except for the eyes and the chin.

Cain smiled, clenching his jaw against the memories. "You have something I want."

Rainy cleared her mind. He could feel her body switching from offensive to defensive as she prepared herself to fight him. "What do I have that you could want so badly?"

"I want Valor's message, and you have it."

She hesitated, but only for a moment. "Which means it's not meant for you."

Cain's anger lit through him, but he buried it inside to maintain focus. "I've always had to take what I wanted. Are you sure you want to fight me?"

Rainy stepped back. "You're not going to let me go even if I tell you."

Cain nodded. "I admire intelligence. Most of our people lack that today."

She inhaled deeply, calming the momentary hopelessness that had struck her. "Your lack of intelligence is what drives you, but you will not have it. I'm not the only one standing in your way, but I can at least stand in your way."

Cain's muscles clenched. He hadn't planned to hurt her; he'd hoped to intimidate her for she had no real ability to fight him off. Stories of his mother always involved the pair in situations. Even his father avoided confronting her, which Cain had never understood since Rex seemed to have no loyalties.

"I will not fail."

Rainy's eyes flashed as she tilted her face to the moonlight, wind whipped around her. "Hear the words of the Vindica, sacred message keeper of fire, earth, water, and air. I…"

Instinctively, Cain threw her against the brick wall. The protection request spell reserved for Vindica members couldn't be finished or the secret would be erased from her conscious memory, becoming a forgotten irretrievable thought. At least that's what was believed. He had his doubts.

"I can't let that happen. I really didn't want to hurt you, but this will be mine. I've worked for this."

Blood trickled down her right temple. He leaned closer to hear her low, coarse voice. "You're too late. Valor was blessed with the key long before you knew it existed. She'll discover the truth without my message."

"Hey! Get away from her!" A voice yelled from a distance.

Cain knew it was the girl. Her voice, her stance, her step. *Angelica.*

Cain leaned down near Rainy's ear as her eyes threatened to close. "Shhh… she doesn't know who she is yet."

Cain stood and waited for Angelica to approach, and as she got closer, he took off.

This would be a test. Did she care more about the victim or the enemy?

Thirty-Two

Angelica had avoided Landon House all day. It'd been easy really. After she'd left Lysander's this morning, she'd been bombarded by Denise and Trevor with questions she hadn't wanted to answer, so she'd volunteered to go into work tonight for a few hours just to get away from them, and according to the work schedule she'd given John Landon, she should be home now. She'd heard from no one today.

She shouldn't be walking home at this hour alone. It was reckless. But even with this logical reasoning, she couldn't call and admit fear after last night. Lysander hadn't called today either, and Angelica didn't want to be the one who called first. At least not yet.

After locking up the store at ten, she'd figured if she didn't take her normal route no one could be laying in wait for her, so she turned right on St. Peter's and headed toward Royal. It didn't stop her from being startled by every footstep and rustle from a darkened doorway.

To distract herself she listed ways in her head to send Trevor home tomorrow. For his own good, of course. Her best idea involved calling his mom, and that didn't sound real grown up. But Trevor's persistent pursuit had potential to get him in trouble.

For a moment the distraction took her attention away from the street, but she shook herself when a lump of moving black fabric against a pale gray wall caught her attention.

She puzzled over it a moment before realizing a cloaked man stooped over a slumped over figure. The dead girls flashed through her mind.

"Hey! Get away from her!"

Angelica hurried toward them, tenseness gripping her. As he stood, she broke out in a run, her heart rising in her throat. She had to get to her in time. He faced her, waiting for her to get close. She could see the shadow around his face from his hood, but then he turned with a grim smile and ran from her.

She ran after him, but he out distanced her quickly with his long strides. At the corner of Royal Street, he disappeared onto the empty street. Looking around, she couldn't see an accessible hiding place.

Damn it. Why had he run? Why not stay and fight?

Angelica jogged back to the slumped over woman, pulling her cellphone out of her jacket pocket. She approached cautiously. Please not dead. Unconscious maybe. Knocked out, would be okay. But one dead body was enough to deal with this week. Angelica leaned in closer, trying to feel for a pulse under the layer of hair, when the woman's eyes fluttered open.

Angelica instinctively took a step back, fumbling with her phone a moment before her trembling fingers stumbled across the numbers 911. In the middle of explaining to the operator that she didn't know whom the woman was, the redhead woman moaned.

Angelica studied the woman's face, forgetting about the operator in her ear.

There was something familiar about her face. Maybe without the crinkles on the forehead and extra weight.

"He doesn't deserve it." She coughed, her eyes closing again. "He doesn't"

"Who doesn't?"

"Your brother," her voice faded to barely a whisper. "Your mother said he'd want it, but it was to be you."

Angelica shook her head. "I think you have the wrong person. I don't have a brother."

"Of course you do." Her jaw tightened. "You have your father's eyes, Custos eyes. I hate those eyes."

She drifted off, and Angelica's brain caught fire. This was Rainy with shorter hair, crinkles at the eyes, and plumper cheeks. The Rainy from her dream last night. Rainy, who'd been Lily's best friend. Who would've known her father and if she had a brother. What did all this mean?

Angelica felt as though she'd be sick any moment.

Thirty-Three

Kline knew it wasn't fair, but it was necessary. He lay in wait, monitoring the scene as that detective interviewed Angelica. Kline had seen this detective before, at the other scenes where the girls' corpses had been placed. From the detective's movements, Kline knew he worked for one side or another. From the broad, confident shoulders, grim expression, and hurried swagger, Kline deduced that the detective was in with the Vindica and displeased with the nature of the progressing investigation.

The ambulance left quickly after arrival, but crime scene and the detective swarmed the scene and held Angelica up for two hours. Kline watched all of this from his vantage point on a nearby roof. He'd arrived late and had missed how Angelica had ended up here, but he couldn't afford to lose this opportunity.

As Angelica walked alone, away from the crime scene, Kline moved fluently into place, dropping down thirty feet in front of her.

She stopped short and immediately did a cursory sweep of the street, returning to him quickly.

They were alone.

She tilted her chin upwards. "You come back to make sure the job was finished?"

Kline released a low growl. "Wasn't me. I don't perform sloppy work."

Her left eyebrow rose in doubt, but Kline felt the tenseness of her muscles straining in their alertness. She was gearing up for a fight. Good.

He lunged at her, studying her quarter second delay and her jerky step to the left to avoid contact with his extended arm.

They now faced each other. For the first time, Kline could feel her breath, see the starburst pattern in her eyes. He hesitated with his next move.

Telekinetically, she flung him backward, but only five feet or so. She'd need more force behind that to tackle a Custos.

"You really need to let go of fear for your abilities to kick in. You have to release all those doubts."

She put her hands on her hips. "I'm not afraid."

But he could see the fear twitching at her eyes. He hadn't moved as she'd expected. Fear for her own safety had crept in.

"Try it again," he said, facing her relaxed.

She hesitated only a moment before he felt himself going backwards again, but not as far as the first.

"Fear will do that every time."

She narrowed her eyes at him, and her thoughts turned angry. "Who are you?"

"Consider me a friend, Angelica."

"My friends don't attack me on the street."

"Not attack," Kline said, closing in the gap. "Teach."

"Who are you?" she asked again. He felt her anger replacing her fear.

"That's it. Use that anger. Channel it into overcoming the fear."

"I told you I'm not afraid!"

He flew backward, and this time he had to use his own telekinesis to avoid landing on his backside.

"That's what I mean. No fear that time. Fear causes hesitation and doubt and weakens the follow though. Now onto lesson two. How are you at mind control?"

"Don't like it much?"

He frowned. "Your enemies will be masters. You need to be better."

"Enemies?" He could see the fear twitching at the corner of her eyes again.

"All those dead girls." He grimaced. "We don't want you to be one of them."

"Why do you care?"

"Who doesn't want to stop innocent people from dying?"

She stared at him without response.

"Start small," he said. "Try changing the color of your eyes and then change it back."

"That's crazy. I can't change my eye color."

Kline moved in close. She tensed, but she didn't strike back.

"Can't you hear my heartbeat?"

Her head tilted. "Yes."

She wanted to say more, he could tell, but she didn't trust him.

"It's your quantity of Custos blood. Makes you stronger than others."

"Like you?"

He nodded.

"Work on it," he said. "I'll be in touch for your next lesson."

He turned, tucked his hands in his pockets, and began to walk toward a side alley.

"What's your name?" She called after him.

"Let's keep our lessons between us for now," Kline said not turning around.

"It isn't fair for you to know my name if I don't know yours."

He hesitated. It was risky, but he wanted her to look at him. To look at him as so much more than a trainer. He longed for it, although he shouldn't.

"Kline."

"Well, until next time Kline."

His name on her lips felt warm on his insides. He was in trouble.

But he needed to keep her alive long enough for it to be a problem.

Thirty-Four

Rex stared at Rainy through a large glass. After a few hours of doctor's work and a discreet phone call, the nurse had led him to this woman barely recognizable beneath the erupting tubes and wires.

She didn't resemble the woman he'd seen twenty-four years ago, when she'd sought him out.

Rainy's husband had been a give-peace-a-chance protestor who'd made a nuisance of himself when Rex's wife had left him the first time. Rex hadn't planned River's death, and had truly only sent someone to shake him up and make him reveal Lily's location. Accidents had happened often back then though when a fever of renewal had swept through the Dark Soldiers, and the men would partake in the hunt with exuberance.

That night, Rainy had been distraught, ranting about how she'd given him the benefit of the doubt, interrupting her speech with a cackling laugh when the tears choked her. He'd believed she was intoxicated, but after his own experience with grief and rage, he understood the fuel burning through her.

Lily had been there. She'd come into the room as if summoned by Rainy's pain. She'd held her friend in her arms in the middle of the tapestry rug, but Lily's eyes had fell on Rex. Disappointment and hate had filled them as Rex had watched powerless to stop it, for to quiet Rainy would have been to nail a final spike in the coffin of Lily's love.

Lily and Rainy had been like sisters, meeting as roommates at Landon House. Rainy alone had accepted Rex and Lily as a couple from the beginning days of secret love on the staircase. Rainy had deserved more from him.

He'd stayed away from Rainy since. The woman had earned that much from him. Besides, she was all he had left of Lily's memory, and he rather thought they shared the grief of all those mistakes.

Rex's frown deepened.

This had to be his son's doing. No one else would be so daring. Cain must have developed his own ideas. Dangerous ideas, more than likely. Rex had not come this far to have this son jeopardize everything he'd worked toward.

The prophecy said the Vindica controlled the future of the world, and Rex would possess the Vindica. He would not be beaten to it by his own son.

If Cain wanted to play in the big leagues, Rex would make sure he knew what the price was.

Thirty-Five

Angelica set the box down. More touristy tee shirts she supposed. She'd come in this morning to stock new merchandise, but she couldn't stop thinking about Rainy last night and Kline, of course. She'd been too shaken to call Landon House when she'd locked the door behind her at 2:30 A.M., and she'd slipped into bed and pretended to sleep so when Trevor and Denise returned from going out on Bourbon Street, they couldn't ask any questions.

Her mind was ravaged with questions and the no one to talk to about her arbitrary wanderings was driving her crazy.

Madame Regina sashayed from the back curtain. "My thoughts are not clear today, Cherie. The city is cloaked for me."

Angelica smiled. Madame Regina's voice was smooth liquid with a wonderful thickness of honey. "Do you have many appointments today?"

Madame Regina coughed as she gently ironed out a blue brocade dress on one of the dolls. Madame Regina's other obsession besides seeing the future was collecting antique dolls. Since these dolls were over priced, Angelica didn't believe they were sold often due to the eclectic woman's difficult time parting with them.

"Not until this afternoon," she said, squinting, the soft crinkles around her eyes folding together. "I believe I'll go rest upstairs until then if you don't mind."

"Of course not," Angelica said, opening the box, "I'm here until two o'clock and then Secily is coming in."

She smiled with unfocused eyes. "Good. You've done good work here, and I believe you could be trained to use your inner sight. I have seen hints of it, and we must work on it in the future."

Angelica smiled as she folded a tee shirt to place it on the shelf. She'd prefer her inner sight to work less often. She wondered if Madame Regina could teach her that skill. Kline may disagree though. She didn't know what to make of their encounter, but she'd felt the strength flow through her that last time. She also had to admit to trying to change her eye color this morning. At first, she'd believed they'd darkened, but then she'd changed her mind and figured it was only the light.

She hated controlling someone's mind. Implanting suggestions felt dirty enough, but to go in and take control and feel them fighting you made her feel sick. Maybe that's why she'd failed at the eye trick.

She was nearly finished the last shirts in the box, when the bell jangled another customer. Angelica put the box to the side and stood to see the customer. Gabney towered over the front shelf display looking around the store as though something would jump out and bite her.

"Are you shopping today?"

Gabney jumped, startled. Her gaze fell on Angelica, and she smiled uneasily. "Sorry, I'm a little jumpy today. Uncle John didn't want me to come alone, but I insisted. So now I'm super nervous."

Angelica wondered if Gabney was born gabbing her mouth and that's where her name came from. She'd never heard of babies talking, but Gabney's name was certainly fitting.

"I'm surprised no one was there to escort me to work this morning."

"Uncle John's working on it." Gabney grinned. "His time's been absorbed by that detective and the council members lately though."

"How has everything been since the party?"

Gabney approached and shrugged. "Crazy. The Council members want to interrogate everyone to see who controlled Peter, but after several statements they do believe that it was a case of mind control. Serena has locked herself in her room except for one time yesterday when she screamed at anyone who'd listen that you'd controlled his mind, and that Uncle John was controlled by you, too. It's been interesting so to speak."

Angelica smiled. "So I haven't missed much?"

Gabney laughed and relaxed a bit. "Uncle John would like to see you today. He said if you'd come at about five o'clock, the house would be cleared of our extra guests."

Angelica placed the last shirt on the shelf. "Did he say what about?"

Gabney shrugged. "I just assumed it was to settle everything. He doesn't blame you for anything if that's what you're worried about."

She supposed she should feel lucky about that. And a little guilty. She'd thought it over last night while watching the officers and detectives work to process the scene. Landon had placed an awful amount of trust in her considering her lies were some of the simplest she'd told, and she knew a man as clever as him could see through them.

It didn't feel right. He deserved the truth since she truly knew that she could trust him.

"So no one will be there?"

"Everyone who lives there, but the council members are meeting tomorrow so they flew back to France."

"There was another attack last night."

Gabney nodded as she played with a bin of tiger's eye. "Uncle John was going to the hospital when I left. She lived at Landon House a long time ago."

"Had she been back recently?"

Gabney seemed fascinated by the smoothness of the stones as she brushed her fingers over each one.

"No." Gabney shook her head. "She'd been hiding from Reximortum for years. What do these do?"

Angelica picked one that caught her eye from the bin and held it up. "They're supposed to ward against evil."

Angelica reached in her shirt and pulled out her corded stone. "My mother gave this one to me when I was young. It's a tourmaline stone."

"Maybe I should have one of those."

Angelica moved behind the glass counter and pulled out a case of jewelry supplies. "My mother showed me how to do this when I was young, so pick a stone."

Gabney chose a smooth, lapis lazuli stone with dull gold specks. Spiritual enlightment.

Angelica took the silver jewelry wire, wrapped the stone just as her mom had shown her, and created a loop at the top to hang the stone. She then pulled a piece of leather threaded it through the loop and tied the ends together.

"Now you have one like me."

Gabney's grin was huge. "You should go into jewelry design."

Angelica busied herself putting the case back under the counter. "It's what my mother did. I used to watch her."

"Cool." Gabney placed the chain around her neck. "Wait, didn't you say you never knew your mom?"

Angelica grimaced. Mentally deciding not to lie anymore was easier than admitting you'd lied. "How about I explain to you and John at five o'clock today."

Gabney studied her, a puzzled expression on her face. "Sure."

It really felt like time to stop running. After last night, she wanted answers more than ever. And the answers lay in the truth about herself, no matter what that might be.

Thirty-Six

Rex's pen scratched the thick linen paper as his hands advanced with great speed. The ticking clock above the chair tapped at his thoughts. His hand paused with the distraction, another thought lost.

This was unlike him. His concentration, his focus was a source of pride. Worry was nagging at the corners.

Lucilius had handled target number two, but target one and three were still alive. Others had died, but to make an impression, young women who fit the prophecy must be sacrificed. Otherwise, the Vindica council would discount the deaths as random Dark Soldier killings. He needed the Vindica to declare someone as Valor, so they needed to believe that they were to blame for the death toll. This was an important element of his plan. Once Valor was declared, she became the leader in charge and capable of making changes. Controlling one person would be easier than five council members, although he had one of those on his side as well.

He didn't like to admit that the Rainy situation still bothered him. He'd nursed the idea all these years that if he still had her, he hadn't lost Lily completely. The last update had mentioned head trauma. Doctors hoped a medically induced coma would help give her body time to heal. His retaliation on his son would take careful planning.

Tom shuffled in. "Mr. Ronald White is here, Sir."

Rex nodded. "Have we heard from my son yet?"

Tom frowned. "He has not returned our calls yet, but I hear that the council members are leaving today, so he may call after."

Rex nodded, although he frowned. He didn't understand why Cain must be so difficult. When the boy was younger, he'd hoped he'd have more of Lily in him.

"Tell me as soon as he calls. You may send Mr. White in."

Ronald White entered moments later with his thin, greasy hair and rat-like face. Rex found the man disgusting.

Ronald's head barely leaned forward in a bow. "Have you read through my proposition?"

Rex frowned. He hated modern day protocol and would have preferred how things were done at the height of the Vindica in the seventeenth century. To have that time back again. Maybe one day when the Vindica came under his control.

"I've made inquiries about gene therapy, and I've been told that it's to treat diseased cells."

His proposition was to use gene therapy to implant their abilities into another. It would mean Dark Soldiers could possess all abilities and be unstoppable. Appealing offer, if it were true.

"My doctor has found a way for it to work." White was sweating, dripping down his forehead. He swiped at it with a dingy white handkerchief. "He's performed the experiment already, and it has worked. I sent you his report."

Rex nodded and sighed. He wished he'd found this doctor first, eliminating the middle man would be so tempting if he had to deal with this man daily.

"I've reviewed the details of your proposition, and I have made several inquiries. I do have my concerns, but it involves little risk to me. If you're successful, of course, I receive all results."

Ronald's thin lips curved into a smile, disfiguring his face. "As you wish. I'll be honored to work with you."

Rex cringed. The man should have stayed in the FBI. "This will be kept between us for now. My men will be offered for their DNA samples, but they're not to be aware of the reason yet."

His smile faded. "Of course."

Rex glared at White and he squirmed under the scrutiny. "I want results before this information is released."

"We will have results."

"That remains to be seen."

Ronald jerked his head in what couldn't be classified as a bow and then backed out of the room.

Rex stood and walked to the French doors leading to the balcony; He was careful not to allow the sunlight to touch his face, wishing to remain cold.

Control was slipping away. His men no longer trembled as he approached. The young ones spoke with ease, and his own son dared to carry on behind his back. Rex needed to make a statement that caused terror to sweep through them all. He'd start with Lucilius.

Rex returned to his desk and picked up the phone.

Thirty-Seven

Beside her thundering heart, Angelica could hear the ticking of an antique grandfather clock from the belly of the house. Books weighed the shelves reaching toward the ceiling. Rich browns, greens, reds, and blues peppered the walls. Now that she was here, her doubts ate at her resolution. Lily's lessons weren't going away without a fight.

"I've convinced the Vindica that you weren't at fault," Landon said. "Truthfully, it didn't take much. What you did with Serena was actually enough."

Gabney chimed in, "Apparently, that ability is rare, like only once every fifty or so years has someone been able to do that."

"Someone taught me when I was young," Angelica said, glancing away from the books. John's fingers rubbed vigorously at his cane and her insides twinged.

John frowned. "I'm afraid everyone is talking. The phone hasn't stopped ringing, and people have been inviting themselves over to hear first hand the goings on. I simply despise gossip."

"Maybe we should put out one email," Angelica said. "Take care of everyone at one time."

She couldn't help the bitterness from sinking into her tone, but she regretted it. John Landon had been good to her.

Landon was quiet. Angelica could feel his sadness drenching the air of the room. In the short time she'd known him, she'd come to understand that it never went away.

He sighed deeply. "Gabney says you wanted to talk to us about something."

"I do," Angelica said, swallowing against her nerves. She turned toward the bookcase. "But first, when I was younger, I dreamed about a book. It's been bugging me since the first day I came in here."

Angelica stood and trailed her fingers along the edges of leather. The smell of dust, leather, and old mingled together.

"What dream?" Gabney spoke up against the silence.

"It was this library. It struck me the first time as familiar, but I couldn't have been here before, you know, but this woman told me that I had Custos blood in me and I just needed to remember."

Landon cleared his throat. "You're not making any sense."

A weird sensation seeped into her forehead, and she paused. The navy blue leather bound book was not the cinnamon brown, untitled, size of a children's diary from her dream. She slid it out anyway and its embossed letters read New Orleans Custos. Angelica peered behind in the dark shadows and shoved flat against the wall was the small volume from her dream.

"This is the book."

Landon peered closely at the cover, his eyes registering the location and the color. "That's Rosemary's journal. I believe you would have just been born when she sent that to me."

Angelica flipped through page after page of the journal in neat lazy scrawl: the same handwriting from her mother's journal. A yellowing page stuck against the back cover scratched roughly against her fingertips. As soon as she touched it, she knew it was from Lily. Long ago it hadn't been a dream. None of her dreams had ever been dreams. She must face that fact and change her thinking.

"I lied before," Angelica said, feeling the words ring in her ears. It was time to face it all. "My mom didn't leave me when I was a baby. She left me when I was seven."

She could feel questions floating in Landon's thoughts, but he waited. Gabney's thoughts were empty, waiting for more as though they were sitting around a campfire. Angelica must continue.

"I've always lied. It's what she trained me to do. When I was young, she told me to play up the sweet, innocent act. Big blue eyes, with an open face, that was never afraid to pretend I didn't know. When I was older, I learned that lying wasn't as easy as playing innocent. Practice makes perfect though."

"Why did you lie about your mother?"

Ah, nothing got by Landon.

"Rule number one was that I could never call her mother. I was someone she'd escaped with or the daughter of someone else or whatever story she created for us that time. Rule two was to never tell the truth and never trust anyone."

Landon's hand trembled on his cane. "Who was your mother?"

Angelica pulled the yellowing letter out of the journal. "I watched her write this to Rosemary in a dream. When I was born, we shared this room barely bigger than a closet. Seven years later when I dreamed he was coming for us, this letter was part of the rotating sequence of my dreams. I'd see her sitting over a desk with little light, her belly swollen with me inside, writing it to Rosemary. I told her about my dreams for two weeks, and I could tell she believed me."

Landon reached his hand out, and Angelica handed him the letter. "I'm Lily's daughter. My last name would have been Vale if Lily wouldn't have been too afraid to be caught with me."

Gabney sucked in air and then coughed.

Landon clutched the paper tightly. "I'm the only one alive who knew she had a daughter."

Angelica breathed deeply, swallowing the tears. "Why didn't you try to find me?"

"I did." Landon's frowned deepened. "I found Serena during my search, but it was as though you vanished. I thought…well, I thought he'd found you and you were dead like Lily."

Angelica gripped her stone. "I'm protected. My mother made this for me when I was young."

Angelica could sense John's alarm. "Have you ever told anyone this?"

"No, I wasn't sure if it worked."

John stood and hobbled to the fireplace. Something awakened in him; something she hadn't felt before. "Good. Your mother had another child, and he may be able to wear the amulet."

Angelica had known this, she supposed. Had always known this, in fact. Just something else she'd buried. Sadness clung to Lily when she spoke of a mysterious boy, but she'd never said he was her son. At seven, Angelica hadn't asked many questions with the life they lived. "Why did she leave him behind? I don't understand why."

"He was Rex's son completely." Landon sighed. "Lily tried several times to escape with the boy, but the connection between Rex and the boy was too strong. Lily was always found and punished."

"He's not my father."

Landon studied her. "I knew Lily for a long time, and she never strayed from Rex until after she was pregnant with you."

Angelica looked away from him and studied the worn edges of the leather book. "She told me my father was a good man, and she never lied to me."

"Rex would have killed your mother if he would have even suspected she'd strayed. Just because Rex is your father, doesn't mean you have to be like him."

"Rex is your father?"

Mark stood in the doorway. He'd opened the door without any of them hearing.

Angelica's alertness kicked in and she gripped the book tighter. She'd meant for Gabney and Landon alone to have the truth. She wasn't ready to extend it further until she trusted it wouldn't blow up in her face. Baby steps.

"No," Angelica said. "Lily Vale is my mother."

"Mark, close the door," Landon said, gesturing toward the open space behind him.

Gabney's leg swung back and forth in a quick jerky movement, which caused Angelica's nerves to fray along the edges.

"Lily Vale was Rex's wife," Mark said, focusing intently on Angelica.

Angelica felt an intense urge to knock him off his feet. She was pretty sure she could do it if he didn't see it coming.

"Lily hid Angelica from birth," Landon said. "No one knows she's alive, and I'd like to keep it that way for awhile."

Mark nodded. "I'm sure she's going to let Lysander know, and I don't think it fair for me to lie to Serena. She's my girlfriend."

Angelica narrowed in on him. "I didn't plan on telling Lysander right now, so I don't think Serena needs to be brought into this either."

"You are going to hide this from him?"

Angelica raised her chin, challenging him. "He doesn't need to know right now."

Landon nodded. "Caution needs to be taken, so I think we will wait a few days. There will be repercussions and I need to make inquires first with the council."

Mark grinned. "Serena may get to be Valor after all."

"She can't be someone she's not," Gabney said, then gulped, eyes widening.

She'd surprised herself. Angelica nearly smiled. Angelica couldn't wait for she and Mark's next sparing situation. She could certainly fuel it with the anger of this moment as Kline's lesson had taught her. She'd decided to keep Kline a secret a little while longer, at least until she'd learned a little more.

Thirty-Eight

The dark soldier's chatter rumbled through the warehouse, and Cain searched the leader's faces as they discussed matters in the far corner. Though shadows fell over their faces, he could tell from their stances who was who.

Dark Knight was a heavyset man who held his shoulders back and his weight with his knees. Dark Shade held his fit body with his muscles flexed so he always stood out. Two others from distant territories had come in for the convergence and had not impressed Cain. Cain was unable to identify these two apart yet. Rex stood with his hands gripped behind his back, and his slight build stooped only a nudge forward toward them as he listened to their reports. Rex had come down hard on them tonight, and now it was the leaders turn to provide answers as to why they were no closer to finding Valor before the approaching Reckoning within days.

The meeting had come to an end and still he hadn't been able to find the opportunity to talk to his father. Typical, but not practical for tonight.

He felt a nudge on his arm from behind.

"Are you ready to return?"

"Give me a minute," Cain said without looking up at Falcon "I need a moment with Rex."

Rex glanced in their direction and nodded assent toward him.

He'd overheard. Sometimes Cain forgot how little escaped his father.

Cain approached and Rex dismissed the four surrounding him. When Rex readily agreed to see him, it usually didn't bode well for Cain, but Cain had his own agenda tonight.

Rex studied him closer. "You've been avoiding me."

"I've been busy," Cain said.

"Your actions haven't gone unnoticed." Rex's gaze burned through Cain, but Cain held still under it.

"Research," Cain said. "I've met your daughter."

Cain studied Rex, but not even the muscle in his jaw that usually gave him away twitched. Cain had suspected Rex already knew as the news had whipped through Landon House in hushed whispers. Nothing ever made it past the man.

"So she did live," Rex said, as if he spoke of a piece of gum beneath his shoe.

"You never thought it might be important to mention that I have a sister before I heard it from someone else?"

"Someone like your psychic friend."

Cain flinched. "How do you know about her?"

Rex smiled. The shadows only increased the absurdity of the gesture. "Nothing is secret from me."

Cain clinched his fist, pumping it tightly to relieve his anger. "You didn't know your daughter was still alive."

"Oversight." Rex frowned. "I assumed that when your mother gave up it was because the girl had died. Some block must have been put in place so I couldn't sense her."

Anger surged through Cain, but he steadied himself. "Would you have killed her, too?"

"Your mother chose death. I tried to get her to choose differently." Rex forced a deep breath through his lips. They'd had the same argument over and over.

"Maybe she just wanted to get away from you."

Rex glared at him and Cain returned the stare.

Cain felt the old anger driving him to recklessness. If he wished to escape this life, he needed to free himself of this tie to his father, but every time he was driven back to it.

"I expect you to follow orders like everyone else," Rex said, his voice calm now. "It's obvious our father-son relationship needs work, but being a Dark Soldier means you follow orders. Consequences will be implemented for your renegade antics, especially in concerns to Rainy, your mother's oldest friend."

"I'm sure I don't know who you're talking about since I was shortchanged the experience of having my mother around to even know her friends."

"Ignorance has never been an attribute you could claim."

"Yet, my intelligence hasn't earned me leadership because I'm your son."

Rex sighed. "Leave the girl alone, I will handle her."

"You will have a difficult time handling her being she's stronger than you."

"We shall see," Rex said, walking away, dismissing him.

That hadn't gone as Cain had planned. For once, he'd like to be the calm, collected one in a face off with his father. But at least he knew his father had known, and had also kept her a secret. Why? Something didn't feel right about this situation.

A shoulder rubbed his. "We need to return. It will be dawn soon."

Cain nodded. These were just more loose ends to tie up. His time ticked like a clock in his ear, but he could make this happen. It was the time for a new order.

Thirty-Nine

Teacups clanked against blue herring bone saucers. Angelica peered above the rim of her cup at the cotton top woman across from her, and Trevor's ebony flesh contrasted on the settee next to her. Angelica had never felt more uncomfortable in her life, and that was saying much considering several situations she'd landed herself in the recent past.

John set the teacup down on the table. "How long do you plan on gracing us this visit, Ms. Cammie?"

From his thin smile and deep creases around his mouth, Angelica didn't think he wanted a long stay. On the other hand, Ms. Cammie Dubois had arrived in her white designer suit and oversized sapphire princess cut diamond ring accompanied by her servant lugging six suitcases.

Ms. Cammie's teacup clanked against the tabletop as her drawl crawled into the corners of the room like a cat. "I simply must protect myself John. I'm sure you understand with everything happening, the very idea of being alone is unbearable."

Gabney's hand covered her mouth, but not before Angelica observed the smile. It seemed to take the woman ages to spit out a sentence. At this rate, she may recognize Angelica from the past. All she needed was Denise here, and all her worlds might have collided in one afternoon.

"This house is like a magnet." Trevor snorted. "I come to visit and I have to come here to find her. Is there some funky mojo around this place I need to know about?"

Gabney snickered before she gripped the armchair with her fingertips.

Landon cleared his throat, grimacing at Gabney in a cursory look. Gabney studied the insides of her teacup.

Ms. Cammie peered at Trevor. "Who are you again, my dear? I don't think I quite understand the connection."

Angelica glared at Trevor. "He's a college friend of mine visiting."

Thirteen years ago, Ms. Cammie Dubois had spackled her face with the same make up with her hair combed back and hair sprayed in a curl. Being only a child back then, Angelica had grown into a different look today. She hoped it was enough not to be recognized.

Serena mumbled. "Questioning her loyalty, no doubt."

"Because gossip is so reliable," Angelica responded, for a moment forgetting Trevor's existence. She glanced at him after and noticed how intently he listened. As a player in a con, he'd learned never to reveal his ignorance. A lesson she'd taught him herself.

Landon cleared his throat and tapped his cane on the wooden floor. "Enough. Ms. Cammie, I assume you'd like your old suite on the third floor."

"Oh, of course, John." Ms. Cammie studied them. Angelica could feel her doubt at the level of protection offered here. "I think everyone should stay here until the murders end."

Angelica shuddered. Another woman had been murdered last night. Angelica had awoken in cold sweats as she'd watched the girl's body break as she'd hung in the air. Again, she'd felt him coming from behind, but the woman had not. The sun had nearly broken the horizon this time, the cloaked individual becoming more brazen. She wondered if it were Kline, and again questioned herself if keeping the secret was the right choice.

"Is that why you've been here?" Trevor's eyes widened with his familiar grin. "Shoot, girl, why don't we stay here then? I'm not looking to be murdered in New Orleans."

Landon smiled, but it never reached the coldness of his eyes. "Angelica is welcome to stay here, but our guests must be invited first."

Angelica stood at the same instant Gabney stood. Gabney smiled, the laugh reaching her eyes. "I must excuse myself. I have a paper to prepare."

Angelica smiled, avoiding Ms. Cammie's eyes. "I'm going to walk Trevor out."

Trevor stretched out his legs out. "I'm not ready to leave."

"Now, Trevor."

Trevor chuckled, but followed her to the door.

Angelica waited until out of earshot before she turned on him. "Are you crazy? What are you doing?"

"I want in on the action." He grinned his huge goofy grin. "It's not fair to leave me out."

"Trevor." Angelica gathered herself and attempted to push down her frustration. "I told you I'm not doing a job. This is not a scheme."

"But look at this house." Trevor looked around. "The guy must be loaded, and he looks like he could croak any minute."

"Do you even hear yourself?" Angelica studied him in disbelief.

"You're good." Trevor laughed. "I almost believed you cared."

"I could hit you right now." Angelica strained against the intense anger shooting through her. She didn't want to throw him into the air accidently. "My mother thought of him as a father. This is personal."

"Oh." His face crumpled. "I'm sorry. I didn't know. Hey, it's not my fault. I come down here, and you've never spent any time with me, and you've been over here. I just figured I'd get in on it, and it'd be like old times."

Angelica released a deep breath. "I don't want it to be like old times. I don't want to do the con anymore. I tried to tell you that, but you wouldn't listen."

"It's who you are."

"It's who I was in the moment," Angelica said. "How about we spend tomorrow afternoon together, and we can discuss it. I made plans to help Gabney out tonight."

"Promise? You're not going to leave me hanging?"

"I'll be there. Just don't show up uninvited anymore."

"I don't know about these people, Gel." Trevor reached for the door. "Be careful. They seem weird in the horror movie way."

Angelica smiled. "I'll see you tomorrow, Trevor."

Angelica shut the door behind him and crossed toward the stairs.

In the sitting room, Ms. Cammie and Serena were discussing the birthday ritual.

Serena leaned in. "I think she's hiding something. No one knows anything about her. Seems to me she could be a spy for the other side."

The thought only flickered behind her tongue, but Serena's chair tipped back, spilling her onto the floor. She attributed it to the stress, the recent anger, everything really. Her control had slipped for the moment. She hurried up the stairs before they could realize what she'd done.

She rapped briefly on Gabney's door and then let herself in. The clatter downstairs followed her inside.

"What's going on downstairs?"

Angelica bit her lip. "I flipped Serena out of her chair."

Gabney burst into laughter, rolling forward on her bed. "You know, Ms. Cammie is like the Vindica godmother with money and connections. She'll have told everyone by sunset."

Angelica picked up Rosemary's journal on Gabney's desk and

jumped onto the bed. "I'm sure there will be other stories during her stay."

Gabney furrowed her brow and bit down on the corner of her lip. "Serena and Ms. Cammie are very close."

Angelica shrugged. For the moment, Angelica needed to avoid Ms. Cammie until John could smooth things over with the Vindica. Ms. Cammie would be tomorrow's concern. "So what are we doing tonight?"

Gabney crossed to her desk and pulled out a sapphire book from a drawer. "I want to try a protection spell for Uncle John tonight."

Angelica could feel Gabney brace herself for objections. Angelica didn't even have to open her senses to feel Gabney's thoughts anymore. Gabney needed to work on closing herself off better. "Have you ever tried a spell before?"

Gabney's fingers brushed the raised letters on the cover of the book. Embarrassment burned her cheeks. "No, but I just can't help but feel that Uncle John is in danger."

"I agree."

Gabney's head napped up. "Really?"

"I don't know anything about rituals so I don't think I'll be much help, but it can't hurt to try."

Gabney held the book toward Angelica. White felt applique letters spelled *Book of Enchantment* across the front. "It belonged to my Aunt Beth. She gave it to me as a graduation present when my dad told her I was coming here."

Angelica would love nothing more than to flip through its pages. Since Landon had mentioned magic and that other creatures existed, she'd wondered if other things were possible. Magic offered another possibility. "Is the spell in this book?"

"Aunt Beth wrote a spell to protect a loved one when she was a teenager. She's really quite good at it."

"You wouldn't want to try one on yourself?"

"I'm not all that important."

Gabney believed she wasn't important, but Angelica didn't doubt that she was in danger. Gabney was one of those twenty-one year old women in the window. It didn't take much to figure out the target of the attacks. Beyond age, Angelica was uncertain of the criteria.

"You're in on this big secret," Angelica said. "Of course you're important."

Gabney opened the book where a dried flower was wedged between the pages. "I need to gather some things, but we'll perform it tonight at midnight."

The pressed flower teased at a distant memory. Long ago, Lily had held a book open to a dried lavender stem. Lily must have had a book like this, a book of spells, one to create the protection amulet she wore around her neck. What had happened to Lily's personal effects was another one of those unanswered questions.

When she'd first arrived at Gram's house, she'd clung to the fantasy that Lily would return for her. At seven, she'd been trained for so long to share her senses with Lily that she'd tell people on the street to be careful at the red light or stay inside later in the day because a thunder storm was on the way. Grams would stick her chin out in the air and apply pressure to the back of Angelica's neck with a stiff hand.

Before the first time Angelica attended Sunday tea, Grams warned her that the women were to see nothing peculiar or she would be on the first bus to an institution. Angelica managed to control herself the first six weeks. The women were really boring anyway. One's son would make the school basketball team, and another would have a cold next Sunday. Nothing interesting.

Then Cammie Dubois came to visit Mrs. Joanne, Denise's mother. Heather Jasper, the preacher's daughter, declared Ms.

Cammie spoke so slowly that Tubby McPhee would be cute before she finished a sentence. Tubby was the pimply faced, tuba playing son of Donna McPhee, a regular at afternoon tea. Mrs. Donna hadn't laughed the loud hearty laugh Ms. Cammie burst with at the declaration.

At one of their teas, Ms. Cammie was in the middle of one of her stories when Angelica flashed to Ms. Cammie being robbed of the rings twinkling on her fingers. Angelica squirmed in her seat, then put her hands under her bottom, all in attempts to keep this piece of information from bursting from her lips. Grams had glared down on her after she'd bounced up and down. Somehow Grams always knew.

When it was time to fetch the coats, Angelica rushed into the coatroom scooping up Ms. Cammie's coat. When Ms. Cammie leaned forward to thank her for retrieving her coat, Angelica whispered, "Don't turn down Peach Tree tonight on your walk, a bad man wants your rings."

Grams, who'd stepped over at that moment, stiffened with a frown twitching at the corner of her lips.

Ms. Cammie had laughed, patting Gram's arm. "Children have wonderful imaginations."

Grams had eased some, but Ms. Cammie had winked at Angelica.

It was so brief, Angelica thought she'd imagined it, but Ms. Cammie hadn't gone down Peach Tree that night. Some other woman on a job had been robbed of her engagement ring. The article had appeared in the newspaper, and Grams had left it open on the table near her breakfast.

Angelica had been eight by then. Thirteen years must have disguised her by now. Angelica had never been allowed to another tea party when Ms. Cammie was a guest, so one incident should not allow Ms. Cammie to remember that long ago child. But Angelica couldn't deny that her past and her present spent much time crossing these days.

Angelica busied herself reading Rosemary's journal for the rest of the evening. She read and reread passages attempting to understand who this woman was. The journal appeared to be a message, the last words from a woman who knew death approached. The writing was cryptic at best, but Angelica could distinguish hints of regrets.

She couldn't focus on the words as they blurred before her several times as her thoughts drifted to everything going on here. She'd hoped to see Lysander here today, but he hadn't dropped in. She didn't want anything to be weird between them as she figured she'd be sticking around awhile. Kline always circled in her thoughts as well. Her curiosity over him threatened like a fever, and she wondered about their next encounter.

Finally, midnight arrived. Gabney and Angelica lay outside on a quilt spread near the stone altar on the patio. Angelica's nose tingled at the smell of the mothballs and coconut. Was this the same night sky she'd lain under at her grandmother's wishing on a star, hoping it would be heard this time?

"This is all I brought with me from Gram's house."

Gabney was perfectly still. "Were the two of you close?"

Angelica studied the white fog encasing the stars. "Not particularly, but she was the only family I had."

Gabney propped herself up with her arm. "The worst memory I have is discovering the Vindica on my seventeenth birthday. I'd already committed to college here, and I was completely intimidated after learning what I was coming into at Uncle John's."

"How is John your uncle?"

Gabney laughed. "When I was really young, my dad told me he'd lived with Uncle John while he attended medical school. My mom was only child, and my dad's sister, Beth is eccentric. She flies into town every now and then with some new fascination. Being lonely, I wanted family so I began calling him Uncle John."

"I guess we all want what we can't have."

Angelica could feel Gabney's concern eating at the stillness in her head. "Did Lily ever tell you why she was leaving you at your Gram's house instead of somewhere else?"

Images, memories clouded her head. Each new town sitting across from her in a booth and a new lesson over a chocolate covered doughnut and a small glass of milk. What is your name and how old are you? *I'm Daisy and I'm four. I'm Holly, I just turned six. I'm Angel and I'm seven. If they ask you about your past, what do you say? My mom died in a car accident. My mom and dad are missing.*

Angelica shook her head and knocked the haze away. The memories had become clearer the more she embraced the idea of having Custos blood. She didn't want them yet though. They stole her breath. "Isn't it magic time?"

Gabney glanced at her watch, which Angelica knew read three minutes before midnight. Gabney knelt down on her side of the altar stone, and Angelica settled opposite her. Angelica took the matches they'd placed earlier on the altar and lit the white altar candles.

As Gabney placed vervain, argue root, and yarrow in the metal bowl on the altar, Angelica removed Landon's hair from the plastic bag. Angelica then poured the brewed rosemary over the contents. Gabney completed the concoction by placing lavender stems across the top of the bowl. Angelica and Gabney's fingertips touched as they reached upward.

Their voices rose in unison with their heartbeat.

By the light of the full moon
In the doorway of night
We call on the presence
That protects the innocence of light
We ask protection form wrong
For one of your own

Watch over the innocent

And protect him from harm

Gabney lit a match and tossed it into the bowl. White fragrant wisps floated toward the veil of fog above. Angelica watched, feeling peaceful.

"It was as though someone was carrying it away."

Gabney hugged her aunt's book to her chest. "Vindica ritual believes the spirits of the original five guide the magic. It's believed that when it works, it's because they watched and intervened."

"Does everyone in the Vindica do this kind of magic?"

"Unfortunately, it's died out." Gabney frowned as she held her face up to the moon. "Most don't believe in the spiritual aspect anymore."

"Do you think they'd be stronger with the magic?"

Gabney blew the white candles out. "I'm not an expert, but I do know that the five books are filled with rituals and spells."

Everyone spoke about these books, but no one knew what the books contained. It could all be gibberish, but according to legend, the books equaled power. Angelica didn't recall anyone mentioning reading them or studying them. Rosemary's journal said the books held all truth if you held all five. What did that mean? How could books over four hundred years old know the truth about what had not existed? Some answers were definitely missing, and no one seemed to be asking the questions. But they were certain enough to kill for it.

"And the *Book of Shadow Souls* holds evil?"

Gabney's eyelids were heavy and her expression dreamy. "The books aren't good or evil. They hold potential and the interests of the original five."

Gabney dwelled on the *Book of Heart* with its power to cure. She'd mentioned it a few times off-handedly in conversation. With an ability to cure disease and heal people, Angelica wondered why no one searched for this book. Again, she wondered what Rex knew about the *Book of Shadow Souls* that the Vindica did not.

Maybe what she needed was a vision of the future, and that would take opening her mind up again to all that pain. Angelica wasn't seeing any other possibilities at the moment though as she felt the chilly cement through the old tattered quilt.

Forty

With his arms behind his back, Rex rocked back on his heels as he watched Angelica round the corner. Even though she wasn't alone, she didn't become absorbed in her company. She scanned her surroundings, and her forehead crinkled when she glanced in his direction. Interesting. The girl could sense the presence of a Custos. Even he only sensed them vaguely as a smell, and it had taken training himself in the presence of others.

Lily's child could not possess an ability she herself didn't possess, and Rex hadn't possessed the ability but merely honed it by other means, which begged the question where did the young woman acquire the skill. Perhaps this meant that Rex's bloodline grew stronger. It was a thought.

Doubts about being the girl's father had always circled in his mind, but he'd questioned and tortured many of his men after learning about the girl. None could have withstood his methods and withheld the truth. Lily hadn't had an affair; therefore, Rex must be the father.

Lucilius stepped up behind him. Rex sidestepped to avoid being seen as Angelica glanced in their direction.

Rex stepped back into the alley and waited.

"That one, who is she?" Lucilius growled.

Rex studied his reaction. No need to show his hand before it was time. "A long, lost daughter."

"Humph," Lucilius said. His shoulders appeared wider in the gray suit he sported, and he towered massively over Rex. "Then her mother must be a Custos."

"I assure you, her mother was human with a drop of Custos blood like the rest of us."

Lucilius glared down at him, his eyes revealing his disbelief. "I will have to report her."

Rex's spine straightened. Report her to whom? This would confirm his suspicion that more Custos existed. "Why?"

"We keep an eye on such matters to make sure our people stay pure. We will require an assessment of her blood."

"She is the key to obtaining the book."

He stepped forward. "Then I will take her."

Rex shook his head. "The prophet said only after she is declared Valor and carries out her first deed as Valor will she have knowledge of the book's location. It is why we are giving the Vindica no choice to declare her Valor."

Lucilius frowned, his face terrible in its intensity. Rex felt the disgust Lucilius felt toward the situation and knew Lucilius wanted him to feel it and that was why he'd broadcasted it. "I will give your way a short time longer, but then we will do things my way."

Rex allowed him to walk away without disagreement, but he had not gone through all this trouble to lose in the end. This plan's conception had come ten years ago, and it had grown with time. The players may not be cooperating, but Rex had worked out contingency plans. A certain Vindica council member would need to come through for him now.

Forty-One

The doorbell of the shop they were in jingled again, and Angelica studied the large, ebony woman entering. She looked normal in her red skirt suit. Angelica winced as she caught sight again of the wooden masks with red, white, and black faces hanging from the ceiling. She'd been trying to avoid glancing at them because it gave the store an even more chilling vibe than the other merchandise cluttering the shelves. The glass entombed zombie in the back was creeping her out to the point that her skin wanted to walk out without her, but she would never admit this to Denise or Trevor.

Denise smiled, but did not meet her eyes. "You can wait outside if it makes you uncomfortable."

Trevor held up a shrunken head. "This is a cool place."

Angelica checked that she wasn't unknowingly touching anything with her body parts or bag. "What are we doing again?"

Denise picked up a burnt red vial from the shelf. "Luke from film class is doing a voodoo documentary. He wants amateurs to perform some ritual to compare to the real deal."

Angelica scooted away from the shelf that promised to curse someone. "For the record, I'm not participating."

"No one asked. Besides it's not as if it's real."

Trevor laughed. "I'm in. Sounds fun Angelica, and besides you were always interested in the weird."

"Really?" Denise asked. "She used to declare loudly that none of it was real." Trevor studied Angelica, and she held still under his scrutiny. "Are you one of those people who had an accident and came out of it a different person?"

Angelica frowned, regretting her decision to spend time with them today. She could be researching her thousands of questions right now and making better use of her time. "Trevor, I told you people change."

Denise said, "Not that much."

Frustration welled. "Did you two want to spend the day with me to gang up on me?"

"We're just concerned," Denise said, laying her items on the counter. "You're barely around, and Trevor and I have gotten close, and we're both worried about you."

"I'm enjoying my time here," Angelica said. "I've made new friends, found people who knew my mother. Nothing to worry about."

Denise grabbed her brown bag and headed toward the door. "You're just different."

"I grew up. Isn't that what you always said I needed to do?"

"That and have sex." Denise smiled.

Angelica owed Denise for that nasty nickname ice princess she'd been graced with in high school. To Denise's credit, it had begun as a joke that had picked up steam as the guys in their school believed it to be a challenge.

Angelica needed to steer this conversation in a different direction or she'd be walking through all the horrible school memories all day.

"I had tea yesterday with someone we knew in Georgia, a Ms. Cammie Dubois."

Angelica watched Denise as they walked down the sidewalk. Angelia's curiosity about the connection had plagued her sleep last night. Denise didn't glance her way. "I haven't seen her in years. How's she doing?"

"She didn't recognize me. She seems fine, although a decade hasn't changed her make-up or her drawl."

Denise spoke nonchalantly. "She was always a bit eccentric."

Trevor chuckled. "If you put one of those southern belle dresses on her, you'd think she'd had stepped from plantation days."

They stopped to check for cars at the corner. Angelica's quick sweep took in way too many people on the street today to keep a firm assessment in place. "How did your mother know Ms. Cammie?"

Denise checked both ways as they crossed, avoiding Angelica's question. Angelica's suspicions grew. Did Denise know something about the Vindica? Gabney had said that others did know, but they were sworn to secrecy. Denise's intense attention on a tourist shop window was unlike her.

A hard tapping reverberated through Angelica's ears. She searched the faces of pedestrians as the volume increased. Kline's chest had given off a warm vibration. This was the sound of the chest of whatever had attacked Gabney: the man killing all those twenty-one year old women. Panic squeezed her chest. Each passing face was quiet, no drum. The sunlight would not provide cover, nor would Denise and Trevor understand if they were attacked. This couldn't be happening in the middle of the day.

"Angelica, are you okay?" Trevor asked, putting his hand on her elbow.

The pounding jarred her insides, and the fear caused her legs to shake.

A couple strolled by with silence playing in their chests. She trembled under the overpowering pounding in her head. He was near, close to them, within a few yards. A man with a black camera bag hurried by in silence.

She needed to get Denise and Trevor to safety or at least she needed to get safely away from them.

"I'm not feeling well," Angelica said. "I think I need to get home."

Denise and Trevor steered her toward Royal Street. Angelica was aware of glances exchanged between the two, but she concerned herself with keeping an eye out for the individual responsible. Her skin moistened and her eardrums felt as though they would shatter, but still her search came up empty.

They turned down Royal Street, and the tapping in her ears mumbled instead of roared. Her body eased under the release. She didn't understand why she heard it and the other girls in her dreams did not. Instinct told her that it didn't have anything to do with Valor. It was something else that she needed to figure out and fast. These women were in danger, and she needed to find out what was behind that drumming.

Forty-Two

Gint's bloodlust grew, and Kline struggled to keep him manageable under the confines of the city. Lucilius had ordered him to bring pig's blood, but Gint had hurtled it across the room in a fit of aggravation upon the smell. He'd tasted the blood of these young girls and nothing but that would do. Others had been like Gint, but always destroyed, never allowed to grow stronger. Lucilius was quickly creating a monster.

After a hot shower to rid himself of their struggle, Kline bounded down the stairs to his control room, ready to plan his surveillance route for tonight. He was closing in on identification of the hybrids working both sides. Lucilius could use this as a weakness, and Kline could use it to strengthen Angelica's fight. He needed something of substance for Lucilius right now for he felt the sinister anger growing under the calm surface, and an out of control Lucilius was more volatile than a calculating Lucilius.

Entering the surveillance room, Kline stopped short when he encountered Lucilius standing in front of his wall, peering intently at a group of photos. Those he'd snapped of Angelica.

Lucilius looked to him as he entered. Slowly, his hand rose and he tapped the pictures. "This young woman, what have you learned?"

Kline stepped inside, hoping he hadn't noticed the hesitation.

"She's quick on her feet. New to the area, but she's making waves."

"That's it? After all this time, that's all you have for me?"

Kline motioned to the board. "I've gathered intel on every one on this board. I have detailed notes."

"Ah, Mr. Kline," Lucilius said, glancing around the crowded work area. "This is why you will never be anything more than a guard. The sentries never see the importance of their charge."

Kline remained silent, simmering with the insult, but dismissing it all the same.

Lucilius pointed at the board again. "You should have focused on her. She's special, and I noticed it at first sight."

"What do you want, Sir?"

Lucilius glanced sideways at him, a condescending expression on his face. "First, I want a blood sample. Fresh. Within the next twenty-four hours. A small amount will do for a DNA analysis."

"What do you suspect?"

Kline kept his expression natural, although his fist had clinched tightly.

"Sentries don't need to concern themselves with my suspicions," Lucilius said, putting his hands behind him, causing his gray suit jacket to wrinkle around the collar. "But I see no harm in revealing that I'm concerned with her lineage. I performed somewhat of a simple test earlier today. She responds to the war call of the Custos."

Lucilius knew the impact that statement should make. Kline held steady his thoughts as Lucilius stood staring at the board a moment longer.

"Get me that blood sample by tomorrow, Mr. Kline," Lucilius said, stepping forward. "Otherwise, I'll have to employ a detrimental method to obtain what I need."

Kline waited until he'd exited before he allowed his thoughts to relax. The war call of the Custos was strictly used during battle and impossible to ignore. It worked as a summons. To hear it though, you must be pure Custos or that's what was believed. None of the hybrids had ever heard it before.

Angelica faced trouble. Kline saw no way to avoid the blood sample as that would draw more suspicion onto her and him, but her training needed to be stepped up and the timing of his plan needed to be hurried.

Forty-Three

The Research Center was a nondescript three-story glass building. A simple sign lit up VAR with greenery planted around it. Cars bustled along the roads, and Angelica followed Gabney inside through the front lobby. A massive lobby opened up in front of them leading to a pair of glass elevators. Modern gray upholstered seating dotted the area, but no one was in sight.

"Most people left for today," Gabney whispered as they crossed to the elevators. "Dad works late when he's here in town just to catch up on paperwork."

Angelica nodded, following her into the elevator. After spending an hour in her room, pretending to be ill to convince Denise and Trevor, when Gabney had called, Angelica had willingly ducked out with the excuse that she had a doctor's appointment. Of course, Gabney's father was the only kind of doctor that could help her with the problem she was having.

Stepping out onto the third floor, Gabney headed toward the right to a door with a small placard reading *lab*. Angelica watched as she pulled a card from her purse and slid it through.

She grimaced. "I worked here this summer. Technically, I was supposed to give my badge back, but I guess it's one of the perks of my father being in charge."

Inside, a receptionist area sat empty with only a heavy metal door to the left. Gabney reached over the desk and picked up a phone headset. After tapping in a few numbers, the door buzzed.

Angelica grabbed it and pushed down on the handle. It opened.

Gabney smiled. "They haven't changed the code. I should probably talk to my dad about that since it's supposed to be changed every sixty days."

Gabney led the way through a large corridor. Several doorways lined the long hall, but all of them were closed with no sign of life. Finally, they reached a door labeled administrator's offices.

Gabney opened the door and called out to the open hall. "Dad?"

A chair creaked from the only fully lit office and a moment later, Mr. White appeared. "My two favorite girls," he exclaimed, coming forth and embracing Gabney in a hug.

Angelica allowed him to hug her loosely, but this southern gesture made her uncomfortable.

"Dad," Gabney said, grimacing. "You need to change the security code. It hasn't been changed since I worked here three months ago."

"Sure, sure," Mr. White said, "but that's not why Angelica came here today. I'm sure you want the grand tour?"

Angelica nodded. "No one's in today?"

He motioned for them to follow. "We have three geneticists on staff full time. Each one has an individual lab."

He opened a door to a sterile lab with high tech equipment and storage units along the wall. A computer station sat in the right corner on a cluttered desk.

"Each of the labs looks the same. Since the scientists aren't allowed to publish any data from the Custos research, we allow them to work on their own projects and publish that work. This allows them to remain the top in their field."

"And they are okay with keeping the secret?"

He nodded. "Confidentiality agreement. The money and the freedom to create their own research works as a powerful incentive however."

"Is it always so… sterile?" Angelica asked, looking around at the metal and glass. It didn't look like any work went on here at all.

Mr. White chuckled. "Afraid so. I believe the archive room will probably be much more impressive to see."

He motioned once again for them to follow, and they exited the lab and headed down the room to the farthest door down the hall.

Angelica and Gabney entered first and Mr. White flicked the lights on. The back wall near the entrance held bookshelves of bound reports, but the impressive element was a massive screen to their left and a row of high tech computer equipment facing the large movie-type screen.

Gabney grinned. "I worked in this room this summer. Organizing all the data."

"I'll turn you into a scientist one day," Mr. White said, moving toward one of the computer units. "Uncle John hasn't won yet with all his history talk."

Gabney smiled, but she looked pained. Angelica gathered that she didn't believe that joke humorous.

"So in the archive room is where you keep the giant family tree?"

"Uh hmm," Mr. White said. Inputting a few strokes of the keys, the big screen lit up. A moment later a massive web of names appeared as the screen.

"As you can see, the map is color coded. Any name in black means we actually have scientific proof that the person belongs where we've placed them. The individuals in red are based on circumstantial evidence such as birth certificates, etc."

Angelica saw a few green markings in the text that were too fine to read. "What about the green?"

"Ahhh." He nodded. "Those are hypothesis. I suppose what some might call rumors, but since this is our tracking method we place them here until we can prove their existence through circumstantial or scientific means."

Angelica nodded. She noticed much of the top of the tree existed in green. She imagined it difficult to have DNA from three hundred years ago. A spot or two of red existed at the top. The middle, however, formed a smorgasbord of the colors. Many of the bottom names existed in black.

"Am I on there?"

"Well, that is an interesting, timely question in fact," Mr. White said. "Just today we discussed adding you, but very little is known, so we delayed the decision a few days. We could put you up here in red, but the question remains where to put you?"

Gabney walked up to the screen and pointed to a small speck. "I'm here. Of course, I only contain 5 percent Custos DNA so it is unlikely that any offspring of mine will make it onto this chart."

"You've had the tests done?" Angelica asked, looking toward the back bookcase of reports.

"Of course," Gabney said. "Most of us have these days. Some refuse for various reasons. Lysander's right here with 17 percent Custos DNA." Gabney pointed to a different branch.

"Do you have any of the Dark Soldiers?"

Gabney and her father exchanged a glance.

Gabney frowned. "We don't really know anymore who they are. Some families are on here." She pointed to a large branch of red.

Mr. White did some fancy finger work with the computer and a section of the map zoomed in larger. "Reximortum's here. So is his son."

Angelica noticed their names printed in black. "How?"

"John Landon wouldn't say how he obtained it, but he brought it to us right after we opened the facility. I know I should have asked, but sometimes scientists get too excited about the possibilities."

Angelica stared at those names. She could know for sure. A simple blood test could settle it all. Lily had said her father was a good man. Did she mean someone else or did she have blinders on to Rex?

"If I gave my sample, who would get this report?" Angelica asked.

"Well," Mr. White said, "the Vindica Council does receive updates twice a year. However, if you were to be named Valor, as the rumor goes, the reports would be submitted to you as you would then be in charge."

"Lysander doesn't believe the council will declare someone Valor. To be honest, the more I hear, the more I agree. It seems as though the council would completely give up control if they did."

Gabney studied the names on the screen. Angelica didn't know who these individuals were. She did notice that Lily rested on the tree beneath her father's name, but they dangled as if unconnected to anyone before that time.

"Uncle John agrees," Gabney said, tracing a line across as if she were working something out in her head. "He thinks something else is going on that we don't know about."

"And that's why I like science," Mr. White said. "The answers are so much easier to find than in politics. I've always said the actual prophecy could be solved with DNA." He tapped on Rosemary's name. "She had 70 percent Custos blood. Highest mixture of anyone on this chart. You know I believe the original five... oh, I suppose I shouldn't say anything."

Gabney smiled as if she'd heard this before.

"The original five believed what?" Angelia asked.

"You may as well tell her," Gabney said. "You know you want to."

"I just believe that they didn't mean for Valor to come only once. I believe they meant for the council to name a savior every time we needed one. If you look at each generation, someone has stood out. I don't have scientific proof for them all, but the Council has grown rich and powerful by not giving up control. They don't want to change."

"But," Gabney said, her eyebrows furrowed together. "It's the Reckoning that's a game changer."

Mr. White nodded.

"Okay," Angelica said, steadying herself. "Let's get my DNA tested. I think we may be able to prove a few of our theories correct."

"Let's go to Dr. Warrick's lab. He will have time to get right on the analysis for us."

Gabney squeezed her arm on the way out the archive room. The touch revealed John Landon's unease at her having the test done just yet.

I'm trusting you Lily.

But then Angelica realized it was her own instincts she trusted, and for some reason, that made her feel more certain in going through with it.

Forty-Four

Kline didn't have time for theatrics tonight, so he hoped Angelica didn't react badly to being dropped in on. He'd followed her all day, assessing his best opportunity to get to her. He'd begun to think he'd have to sneak into her room at night, but at dark she'd set out from Landon House to the apartment on Royal Street.

"I know you're there." Angelica spoke into the night.

Kline stepped out from the doorway he hid behind. "It's the heartbeat, isn't it?"

Angelica nodded. "Why do I hear it?"

Kline could sense that she'd known he'd look for her tonight, that she'd set out to allow it to happen.

"It depends. Did you change your eye color yet?"

Angelica shook her head. "I can't."

He sensed her disappointment, but it mingled with fear. She'd need to rid herself of that fear to stand a chance against a Custos.

In one swift movement, he came up behind her and gripped her around the neck with one arm and he used his free hand to clasp her forehead.

"He will be quick. Strong. How will you get out of this one?"

"Let me go." She struggled against him. He could smell the sweetness of her shampoo and feel the slim, delicate flesh of her throat.

"You will need to relax," he whispered into her ear. She stilled under his breathe against her flesh. "Fear has no place in a battle except to feed your enemy."

She gripped his arm tightly with her hand, but the next moment she flung him over her head as she bent forward.

He rolled forward and jumped back on his feet. "Good. Now why do you fear controlling the mind of others?"

She hesitated. She didn't trust him yet, but she wanted what he had: knowledge. "When I was young, I saw what it could do. I tried...once. I lost control and the man who kept trying to study my abilities ended up dead. I didn't mean to..."

Her eyes pleaded with him to understand. She believed this one mistake defined her.

"It's happened to everyone who hasn't had proper training. It's a powerful ability that needs to be honed correctly, which is why we start with your eyes."

He approached and clasped her face in his hands. "Close your eyes and imagine the pigment rearranging and blurring together until the color is purple."

She inhaled deeply, staring into his own eyes a moment longer before she did as he instructed.

He waited as he listened to each steady beat of her heart, each rise and fall of her chest.

She opened her eyes and they were a brilliant violet under the streetlamp. He released her face and swore silently.

"Did it work?" she asked.

He nodded.

"This would have been such a spectacular disguise in my other life." She smiled, one of the real lopsided ones. "You don't seem happy."

"Who are you?" Kline asked, his mind racing quickly over the mathematical possibilities.

"What do you mean?"

"Hybrids can't do that."

"But," Angelica said, tilting her head, confused. "You told me to do it."

"Test, really. I didn't think you'd be able to. I mean at 70 percent Custos blood you'd hear the heartbeat. But you heard the war cry and now this. I don't understand how this is possible."

Angelica took a step back from him, and he could feel her defenses kicking in.

"How do you know about that? Is that what it's called?"

He'd misspoken. It was obvious she didn't know what made her different. "I'm only trying to help you," Kline said, putting his hands in the air in a gesture of surrender.

"Who do you work for?"

Kline moved closer. "I need you to trust me for now."

"I don't know you. Did you do that thing with the heartbeat in my head, driving me crazy?"

Kline shook his head. "I didn't know he was going to do that, or I would have trained you for it."

"Who's he?" Angelica asked, putting her hand up in a motion for him not to come any nearer. "Reximortum?"

"Worse," Kline said. "I need you to train hard because he's going to come for you."

"Why?"

In a swift movement, Kline moved in behind her. He pricked her finger in one swift motion and collected the blood sample with the same hand before spinning her out.

She glared at him, gripping her finger tightly.

"Hopefully this simple blood test clears you," he said, watching the little trust he'd built with her be swallowed by the anger burning in her eyes. "But I need you to train because I don't think it will."

"Clear me from what?"

"Being a Custos."

"That's absurd," Angelica said, anger rising in her voice. "Pure blooded Custos don't exist."

"That's what the Vindica wants everyone to believe," Kline said, walking backward. "But you, Angelica, are smarter than that. It's what first drew me to you."

Kline rose to the rooftop away from the street and from her sight.

"You're crazy," Angelica yelled into the air. "I knew my mother, and she wasn't a Custos."

Kline left her and headed back to their headquarters with the sample. He didn't like this plan at all. It made Angelica vulnerable, but he needed to buy some time, and he saw no other way to do it. He needed to do some quick thinking before this lab work came back.

He may also need to do some damage control with Angelica.

Forty-Five

Cain watched Simone hurry toward him, her skirt swishing around her ankles. Her quick pace and her darting glances revealed her fear. His senses heightened. Simone didn't scare easily. Steady and brave defined her. Something had happened.

Cain stepped out of the shadows. "I'm here."

She jumped, and then ran to him.

She embraced him and he held her close. She whispered in his ear. "I don't like being out 'ere at night, but I needed to tell ya."

"I could have come to you."

"No," she said, her lips trembling. "My father is watching for you because he believes I'm in danger."

Cain inhaled the spice smell of her hair. She must have been making a concoction and the smells lingered on her neck, in her hair, in her clothing. She'd come straight from whatever ritual that had scared her.

"I will not let anything happen to you."

"Something has happened to change things. Even Madame Lulu is worried."

"Change things?"

Simone buried her head in his chest a moment before pulling away. "The possibilities are gone. Up until tonight, the future held

222

all these prospects depending on the choices made. Something has happened to remove all those outcomes. The Reckoning is here and cannot be stopped now."

"What about my fate?"

"Animus, I'm scared," Simone said, rubbing her hands down his sides. "Let's just go away together. Away from all of this."

"We can't escape the Reckoning. You know I'd do anything for you if I could."

"I know," Simone mumbled, burying her head into his chest, before looking up and flashing her familiar though strained smile. "As to your fate, Valor will be named tomorrow night, but you must move quickly before your father, as he knows this, too. According to the signs, Valor will know where the book is once she completes her first deed as Valor."

Cain's mind worked quickly. He'd have one shot to come out on top. "So, I just need to make sure she completes a first deed as Valor?"

"Exactly, but before your father or he'll get it first."

Cain pulled her closer. "I promise we will leave together after."

"My future is not as clear as your own, but I will if I'm able."

He gripped her tighter. Her words fell ominously into his gut. "I want you to stay with your father until I come to get you. My father knows about you, and I don't want to take any chances."

"Our fates will always be intertwined with those we love. When it comes time, you may need the help of your sister." Simone put her hand against his chest. "Always remember why you do what you do. Do not forget."

Cain stared into her watery eyes a moment, but couldn't bring himself to ask. She'd seen something that she would not tell. He knew her well enough to know this. Cain didn't want to hear anymore about fate. From this moment on, he made his own destiny. He didn't need this double life anymore. He knew what he had to do. He just needed to make sure he kept Simone safe until then.

"I'll walk you home," Cain said. "Until this is over, I don't want you out alone. Stick with your father for protection."

She laced her fingers through his and squeezed.

Forty-Six

Angelica pushed her hair out of her face and craned her neck sideways to get a look at the clock. Two hours had passed since they'd come upstairs looking for Rosemary's journal. Lysander's strong arm grabbed her around her middle and he pulled her back in close to him.

Angelica grinned. "I guess I'll look for that book later."

"Maybe," Lysander said, trailing his finger along her chin. "I may be still enjoying your company later."

"I haven't heard from you." Angelica said, lowering her eyelashes, but keeping her eyes on him.

"Work," Lysander said, continuing the downward motion of his hand. "My father had some items for delivery in Florida."

"What kind of business does your father do?"

"Antiques, really, but enough about him." Lysander grinned. "What kind of trouble did you get into while I was gone?"

Angelica's temperature rose. In humiliation, she'd remained silent about Kline. She couldn't believe her naiveté in trusting him. Now she didn't know what her blood sample would be used to prove. The hurt pride mingled with disappointment in herself as well. She'd felt attracted to him, and she'd believed herself beyond falling for the dangerous stranger.

She couldn't admit that to Lysander, of course.

"The usual." Angelica grinned. "Apparently, people can't stop talking about me these days."

"Just remember," Lysander said, gazing into her eyes. "These people want a martyr. You don't want to be that person."

A loud rumble came from downstairs and then quieted.

"So what abilities do you have?" Angelica asked, thinking of his 17 percent Custos blood and what did that look like compared to hers. Kline's question last night had left her feeling odd, as if there was something she didn't know.

"Nothing significant," he said, grinning. "I can't predict the future or move items telekinetically. I imagine those are pretty nice."

The voices rose from downstairs and then lowered to a hum.

Angelica frowned. "The noise downstairs is distracting."

An excited squeal bounced upstairs.

Lysander inhaled and Angelica felt the rippling beneath her chest. "Is there a party tonight?"

Angelica felt his lips against her forehead. "I wasn't invited."

Chatter vibrated the walls of the house. People gathered downstairs, and although Angelica listened to the chatter, she could not distinguish the voices. Something was certainly going on below.

Lysander shifted beneath her. "I think we need to check it out."

Angelica nodded, crisis mode kicking in. Since she'd begun attempting daily to see the future, she'd felt this ticking count down, as if something was going to happen soon. And now she waited each moment for it to come. It left her on edge.

She stood and grabbed her clothing from the floor, but not before catching Lysander looking her over.

"We're coming back upstairs after."

Angelica smiled as she slipped into her jeans and sweater and swept the room one last time for the journal. It's not as if the room contained much for the book to get lost among, but it had been missing from her usual spot. She checked herself over in the mirror and forced her attention away from her eyes. Kline's trick had worked. She'd tried it again this morning. He must be able to change his eye color as well, which made her have doubts about what he'd said about being Custos.

It was all so confusing.

She allowed Lysander to take her hand and lead her downstairs. People were clustered in small groups everywhere. Ms. Cammie Dubois stood among several well-dressed men in the corner. Serena, Mark, Seth and Bruce stood in a small group in the foyer. Griffen and Jack stood with a group of gentlemen who simply looked like teachers, slightly balding and frayed at the edges. In several clusters of people she recognized no one, but that one Vindica Council member, she remembered being called Frederick, sat expressionless in a side chair in the sitting room. Gabney and Landon were nowhere in sight.

A robust, rather red-faced gentleman that Landon had said went by the name of Larkin Luke, although his real name was Luke Meyers, burst into the foyer from the training room.

"I believe everyone is here now. Ladies and gentlemen, let's gather in the training room for our meeting."

Angelica whispered to Lysander. "Did you know about a meeting?"

Lysander shook his head.

Serena followed Jack into the living room. Excitement vibrated off of her in rays. Her thoughts escaped on those beams for the room to read. They were naming Valor tonight, and it had to be her because she was the only one they'd tested. She was certain of it.

Angelica hesitated, glancing toward the formidable oak front door. She'd come clean to John Landon and Gabney, but walking into that room presented a different challenge. She didn't know if she was ready for it to be her, but she could feel herself in way too deep to walk out.

She walked into the training room.

John Landon, Gabney, and Mr. White were sitting in three of the many chairs scattered throughout. None of these chairs were here during a normal day, but this was the largest space on the ground floor so they must have moved furniture from other rooms to accommodate the large crowd.

Landon's deep frown and Gabney's creased worry line across his forehead told Angelica all she needed to know about this meeting. The Council had descended on Landon House without warning.

Larkin Luke bounced around the room as he gathered four people in the center of the room, one of which was Frederick. All four dressed similarly in gray suiting, and they wore an aura of dignified snobbery. This must be the infamous Vindica council minus one member. The question remained why was one missing.

Serena went stand behind Landon's seat as if she were the doting daughter. Other unfamiliar faces crowded around the room. Angelica stood off to the side of the doorway with Lysander.

Larkin raised his arms, and everyone quieted. Angelica looked around the room and saw many smiles. Everyone knew what was going on tonight, so why had they kept it from Landon? Angelica sensed a political play here.

"As a family, we have suffered terrible loses. Some have lost hope, but I personally never gave up. I've always believed Valor was coming to save us. Yes, friends, family, we are here tonight to finally put a face to this legend."

Triumphantly, he paused as a rumble rose through the crowd of nearly fifty. Angelica thought it odd that all these people would gather with such short notice and keep Landon in the dark.

Serena leaned forward and appeared about to burst.

Larkin raised his hand and the room quieted. "Tonight, I've been granted the privilege to announce this legend into reality."

Ms. Cammie smiled across the room at Serena. Angelica noticed others who did the same. It would appear everyone knew something she didn't. John's frown deepened, and his eyes closed. She began to relax. She wouldn't have to make a decision.

Larkin cleared his throat, waiting for the attention to return to his large eyes and bulky hands. "The council has convened and they have arrived with the news only hours ago. Their unquestionable decision is that Valor is Angelica Accacia, guest of Landon House."

Angelica gawked as everyone turned to stare.

"This is a mistake." Serena cried out. "She didn't go through the tests."

Frederick glared down at Serena with his thin nose. "Angelica has abilities that only Valor has, and she is stronger than our enemies. She is the clear choice."

Jack stood and clasped his hands before him. "But has she proven herself to not be one of our enemies?"

Landon rose gripping his cane with an expression of resolution. "While this announcement is certainly a shock and came without warning, I assure you upon my word that she is unquestionably on our side. The Council has made a wise choice."

The crowd erupted into excited talk, and their stares gradually fell away from Angelica. She inhaled deeply and released the breath slowly, her brain buzzed with electricity. She'd be lucky if she didn't lift everyone in the room. She closed her eyes and hummed a lullaby in her head. So much for hiding in the background.

Larkin stood before her when she reopened them. "The council members would like a formal introduction."

Lysander squeezed her hand. "Remember who you really are."

Angelica squeezed in return and then stumbled after Larkin. The question these days seemed to be whom and what she was.

Larkin herded her toward the suits, who she greeted with a twitching smile.

"Angelica Acacia meet Ms. Pilar Lingraf, Mr. Benjamin Sury, Mr. Mathew Donovan, and of course, Frederick Bartlett."

Ms. Lingraf's crooked nose stood high in the air as she nodded. The handsome tower on her side smiled warmly, while the balding fellow waited for Benjamin before smiling. Frederick stared down on her as if she were his prey. He really was unsettling.

Pilar's voice scratched Angelica's ears. "Arthur sends his apologies for his unavailableness. He's a bit under the weather at the moment."

Benjamin shook her hand with an extra firm grip that numbed her fingers for a moment. With his touch, she sensed his telepathy ability. He couldn't hear her thoughts although he attempted a peek. "I look forward to working with you. You must come study in France with us and acquaint yourself with our history," he said, peering into her eyes, unblinking.

Such an inconvenience. We could have done this without the girl.

Angelica looked to Pilar, whose thoughts transmitted clearly through the circle.

He'll continue killing the girls if we don't appoint someone. She's as good as any. Besides she may actually be strong enough to survive this.

Angelica glanced toward Benjamin, who smiled despite his thoughts.

Could they not tell they were broadcasting to everyone? Something was wrong here.

Easily the most handsome of the bunch, Benjamin's chestnut eyes sparkled with a confidence in himself. His broad chest and tapering waist spoke of an exercise regiment, and his chestnut hair cascaded over his forehead in that fake natural way. He took care of himself and didn't give the impression he'd ever be lax with his abilities.

Larkin chuckled, his gaze darting around the room. He also projected his mind into the circle. He wanted everyone to see him with Angelica, so they'd think he represented her. "I believe Angelica's first priority will be to take care of our New Orleans problem."

Frederick focused on her. Sadness sagged and aged his body. "As Valor, Angelica will make the decisions about what is important."

Angelica was in control now and they were afraid. Angelica searched each of them and felt the worry bouncing around their brain waves. Desperation had forced their hand, but they didn't want change nor did they want to give up control. Benjamin's thoughts had revealed it all. They were giving her up as a sacrifice to protect themselves.

Larkin cleared his throat. "Let's enjoy tonight and deal with business first thing tomorrow. We have so little to celebrate these days, we should enjoy the moment. Angelica, if you'd do me the honor, there were several others who requested introductions."

She nodded formally toward the council members and trailed behind Larkin. They drifted from group to group, making introductions that Angelica could not remember. Several stood out. Ms. Maggie lost her son in this "hard war," but Ms. Sara Crow believed it the natural universal order. A dumpy Mark Finnigan stuttered and blushed over each word of his good luck speech, and an overzealous Captain Watt pushed for a Vindica Inquisition. He reckoned they should force all the bad seeds into a deep hole with no way out. Several glanced in their direction as his voice reached a creshindo and his hands flailed in the air.

While trying to avoid a flaying, she noted Mark and Serena arguing in the corner. Tears rolled down Serena's face, while Mark attempted to block her from the view of the room. There were too many voices and thoughts to hear theirs, so she attempted to read lips. Serena's mumbled, but Mark used phrases like need to stop, spectacle, Vindica questioned, and Valor. Angelica assumed he was worried about gossip.

With the distraction, she nearly missed Captain Watt's elbow jarring her in the face. She stepped back catching Lysander staring at her with an icy stare as he leaned against the doorway.

She excused herself at the next break in the story and felt the stares on her back as she approached Lysander.

Lysander did not blink or warm at her approach. "Why don't we step outside to discuss what's bothering you."

He nodded, and she headed down the hall toward the patio. Outside the kitchen door, the sky wrapped them in its pinpricked cloth. Angelica hugged herself against the chilled air.

The idea came over her slowly, and then picked up speed. She'd been named Valor of these people. She didn't even know what it meant exactly, but it felt heavy, as if it anchored her to the ground.

"I can't believe this," she mumbled into the air.

Lysander folded his arms across his chest, frowning. "You have to tell them they've made a mistake. Tell them Serena has trained for it, and she should be the one."

The chill spread through her. "I do?"

Lysander paced in front of her. "You can approach the council again and explain that you don't want to be Valor. They'll listen, and Mr. Luke can make another announcement. It's not too late."

Angelica looked away from him. "Why?"

Lysander stopped pacing. She could feel his eyes on her. "It doesn't matter who they name as Valor as long it's not you."

"Why can't it be me?"

"Because he'll come after you."

Her insides exhaled. She could handle worried. "He's going to come after me anyway. Besides, Serena would make an awful Valor."

"Damn it, Angelica. This is serious."

She smiled. "I know."

Lysander grabbed her arm. "Why do you want this?"

Angelica swallowed hard against the pain that rose in her throat. It came down to all the death around her. All the times when she was just a kid and couldn't prevent it. And something was coming, worse than Reximortum, according to Kline. She couldn't allow more people to die without at least trying to do something. She had to believe that Lily had protected her for this moment.

"Lysander, there's something I haven't told you yet," she said. "My mother was Lily Vale, Reximortum's wife."

"What?" he asked, his face drawing back.

"I'm Lily's daughter. She hid me away when I was born because she believed I was Valor."

"And you're just telling me this now."

"I… I don't know when else I was supposed to tell you."

He closed his eyes, and Angelica could swear he was counting.

"That doesn't mean you have to be Valor." Lysander gritted his teeth. "My family… I don't believe in this prophecy. It's just another way the Vindica refuses to protect itself. Why would you want to be sacrificed for them?"

Frustration grew and steadily rolled through her. "Innocent people died so I could be here today. I'm not going to decide that my life matters more than theirs. I can't… I can't do what Lily did. I need to try and fix this."

Her chest compressed as the words sprang to life before her. She couldn't imagine why Lily had made all the decisions that she'd made and allowed all those people to die to protect her. But Angelica felt those people weighing in her conscious now. She didn't need to be Valor to fight back, but she sensed the availability of knowledge would be there to help her chances. She needed to make things right.

Lysander stepped back from her. "I need time to... I just need some time. I can't believe you kept something this important from me. How do I know there aren't all these other big secrets?"

Lysander turned and strolled toward the door. Her eyes burned and her chest swelled. Her fingers sought the cold comfort of the amulet around her neck.

Party noises filtered out as the door swung open and snapped shut. She swiped at the tears before turning around.

Roxy stood, staring at her. "Do you plan on hiding when our people need you, too?"

Angelica straightened her spine. "Which family were you?"

Anger and pride lit through Roxy. "My mother ran a gift shop, and ya'll stayed in the attic for six months."

Angelica remembered an old wooden bed frame with a lumpy mattress, but there'd been this old doll with yarn hair she'd play with while watching Lily make jewelry. "Ahh, my mother sold her jewelry in the shop."

"Yes, and when he came for ya'll, he found my mother because ya'll disappeared in the middle of the night. Doesn't sound like the hero of the Vindica, does it?"

"I was five."

"I was only eight when I lost my mother."

"I was seven when I watched mine die."

Roxy's eyes widened a bit, but she hung onto her anger. "Will you run when he comes for you? Will you leave everyone else to die like you did my mother?"

Angelica exhaled. "Nothing I am going to say tonight will change your mind about me. I'm really sorry you lost your mother. In the end, he found my mother anyway, and I imagine it seems all for nothing to you. I can't explain why my mother made the decisions she made. What I do know is that I have to do what my mother couldn't."

Angelica stepped toward the door.

"I won't let any of my family die for you again." Roxy called after her.

Angelica met Rex's eyes. "I don't plan on anyone dying for me ever again."

Roxy nodded and Angelica continued inside.

Forty-Seven

The clock ticked. A chair scraped against a wooden floor somewhere and the silence of the house echoed.

"Nothing," Angelica uttered, clutching the pillow and throwing it against the wall.

Griffen tapped his pen on the notepad. "Maybe you're trying too hard."

"You don't believe that."

"No," Griffen said, raising the end of the pen to his mouth. "Unfortunately, I think it's something deeper than that."

Angelica had asked Griffen to help her work on her premonitions; particularly she wanted to have a vision connected to Reximortum. After three sessions, she'd had no luck, she'd foreseen an upcoming relationship between Gabney and Griffen, only days away. A particular nasty vision about an upcoming argument between Jack and Griffen as well, but nothing significant. It was as if a block surrounded the future.

"What about a connection?" Angelica asked, an idea slowly forming.

"A connection to what though?" Griffen asked, chewing on his pen.

Angelica sat up looking around the room. "The past."

Griffen tilted his head.

"No, listen. I know it sounds strange, but when I went back to a place from my past, the memories were there. The energy still exists. What I need is a place from Rex's past that I can connect with."

Griffen nodded. He removed the pen from his mouth and scribbled on the page. "I'll need to do some research, but this could work."

"Good," Angelica said, feeling the softness of the gray leather sofa she sat on. "Now I have something else, but I need you to keep this between the two of us for now."

Griffen leaned closer, curiosity overpowering any caution. It's why Angelica had chosen him.

"Look at my eyes. Keep looking." Angelica allowed him a moment to look and then she closed them, took a deep breath, and imagined the pigments rearranging. When she opened her eyelids, her eyes were bright pink.

"Shit!" Griffen said, pushing backward on his chair.

Angelica blinked twice and they returned to their sky blue color.

"How did you do that?"

Angelica shrugged. "What I need to know is if anyone else can do this? Has anyone else ever been able to do this?"

Griffen glanced at his file cabinets where Angelica knew the records on every Vindica member were stored. The Vindica Council kept a digital database, but Griffen was old school with technology.

"I honestly can't recall a single person being able to and that would certainly be something memorable. I will search the database for you though."

"The dilemma is that I didn't know I could do that until a few days ago. What if others could, but never tried?"

"It's certainly a possibility," Griffen said. "How did you know to try?"

Angelica grimaced. "Well, let's just say I met someone who claims to be a friend who wants to train me. He's dropped in twice on my way back to Royal Street. I have no idea if I can trust him, but he showed me this trick and then once I could do it, he acted weird. He said I shouldn't have been able to do it unless I was pure Custos."

"Well, that's impossible."

"That's what I said, so there has to be another explanation."

Griffen nodded. "I'll spend the day researching. We can look at those with really strong mind control and ask them to experiment...."

The doorbell chimed through the house.

Griffen sighed. "Only John Landon is here now. Everyone else is at work or school."

"I'll go answer it," Angelica said. "You can get to work. I feel something coming, and I want to be able to see what it is."

Griffen nodded, already heading toward his files.

At the door, Angelica opened it to reveal a full figured woman in a wide brimmed purple hat.

"Humph," she uttered. "I'd hoped you'd look more like your mom."

"Excuse me?" Angelica asked.

"Well, invite me in young lady, so we can get to it." She spoke with her hand on her hip, but she glanced around the street as if looking for someone watching her.

Angelica stood to the side so she could enter, feeling the woman's presence fill the foyer.

John Landon hobbled to the entrance of the tearoom. "Ah, Madame Lulu. To what do we owe this rare visit?"

"The world falling apart. People going crazy." Madame Lulu gestured wide with her hand.

"By all means then." Landon motioned for her to enter the tearoom. "Come in and let's talk."

Angelica stood in the hall conflicted, unsure of what to do. She wanted to go in and hear whatever was going on, but she respected Landon too much to barge into a private conversation.

"Well, come on young lady," Madame Lulu said. "We don't have time to dally."

Angelica followed them in, feeling as if she was back in grade school.

They hadn't completely eased into their seats before Madame Lulu began. "I don't make Vindica business my business, just so you know. I made Rosemary a promise, and I've kept it the best I could all these years."

Madame Lulu paused, but Landon remained quiet. Angelica followed his lead, although her head filled with questions.

"I planned to stay away and let things fall as they may." Her chest heaved upward. "But something has happened, and I don't like it. It's not good for anyone- Vindica or Anihi alike."

Landon looked to Angelica. "I'm sure the naming of Valor last night has shifted the future."

Madame Lulu waved her hand in dismissal. "That was decided twenty-one years ago when she was born. Naming her was ceremonial and for show. Even if the Vindica would have gotten it wrong, she would still ultimately be the one to begin this domino effect."

Angelica's mind raced over all the information, but the woman emitted a vibe of intimidation and Angelica felt it all the way through her core.

Landon cleared his throat. "So what is it then?"

"Something seemingly small and insignificant that no one would have seen coming, but let me tell you this, whatever it was, has caused the future to shift."

"Shift how?" Landon asked, leaning forward.

"All the options have disappeared. The Reckoning is upon us now."

"What does that mean exactly, the Reckoning?" Angelica asked.

Madame Lulu glared at her, sending a sharp stab of fear through Angelica with its intensity. "Child, the Reckoning is when the world as we know it ends. There will be war, and with war, the world will discover that Custos hybrids live among them. Fear will reign."

Landon rubbed his hand on his cane. "Let's back up. What options are open?"

Madame Lulu shook her head. "Everything leads to the Reckoning, but how we get there and our choices have some kind of block on them. Just two days ago, we could see all these strains of choices and some of them bypassed the Reckoning. Something is going on. Something powerful, and it isn't Reximortum because he dismisses the future. He'll never have domain over it when he doubts its reliability."

"So we are dealing with someone besides Rex." John Landon sighed. "Maybe he has someone working with him?"

"What I'd suggest," Madame Lulu said, standing, "is finding out what has changed. What small thing happened that caused this mess and change it before it really is too late."

At this, she narrowed her eyes at Angelica. It was as if she knew something. Angelica squirmed under the intenseness.

Landon pulled himself up. "Will we hear from you again?"

Madame Lulu looked down at them through squinted eyes. "I told you I don't do Vindica business, and I promised Rosemary that I'd watch that girl until she was twenty-one. If our interests cross, we shall see."

Landon nodded, his eyes sagging under the sadness.

Angelica waited until she closed the door behind Madame Lulu before she spoke again.

"Who is she?" Angelica asked, returning to the tearoom. "And why is she so scary?"

Landon smiled. "She's known as the most powerful seer and belongs to the Anihi Custos. Not to be messed with. The fact that she was here is a really bad sign as they despise the Vindica."

Angelica could ask several questions, but she felt time was of the essence. She needed to get to the most important... and fast.

"So I suppose what I need to do is figure out what happened."

Landon nodded. "Something we wouldn't think important that's happened within the last few days though? I mean, we've always known Valor was the first domino to fall for the Reckoning. Some prophecies say that Valor starts the falling. Madame Lulu is a powerful seer but the future does constantly change with our choices. To have the options disappear means that it is something outside of your control because you haven't even taken action as Valor and that's what really begins it."

And suddenly Angelica could think of something that had happened in the last few days. Kline.

Kline had taken her blood. The question was for what reason.

Forty-Eight

Kline watched as the one called Falcon disappeared inside the building. He waited and he didn't come out.

He retrieved his phone from his pocket and pressed 1.

"The team is all inside."

Lucilius allowed the words to linger over the line a moment. "Good. Gint has one more task tonight, but this will ensure we have the upper hand."

"Go ahead as planned?"

"Yes," Lucilius said. "I'll deal with Gint. You get me my inside man."

Kline hung up and scoped out the area. He'd already picked out the one called Echo as his man. He'd simply need to get him away from the group tonight and spend some one on one time with him.

After searching the ground for weak points, he became aware of her nearing heartbeat. He stilled his own and listened.

She'd come for him. Her anger allowing all her senses to be fully developed.

He turned just as Angelica appeared on the roof from the elevator.

"I've come to take back what you took from me," she said, her eyes flashing under the building's spotlights.

"What do you mean?" Kline asked, fear momentarily crossing

him. She planned to fight him, and he didn't want to hurt her.

"Your little blood sample has caused the entire future to change. I need it back to prevent the Reckoning."

Kline gazed at her and thought how beautiful she looked angry.

"The sample was already destroyed. It was just enough to perform the test."

At that moment, Kline flew backward. He fought to regain control midair and rolled himself forward.

"What test? What are you doing with it?" She forced out angrily, assuming a fight stance.

Kline stood and dusted himself off. "You are 93 percent Custos blood. Something we believed impossible."

"Who are you?" she asked. "Are you a Dark Soldier?"

Kline could see her searching for a weak spot. He needed to take her off the offense, or he'd have to hurt her and they were too close to the end for her to be injured.

"I'm a Custos. A pure-blooded Custos."

"Liar," Angelica said, raising him off the ground. "They don't exist."

Kline lowered himself to the rooftop. "Why not? Because the Vindica says we don't? The Vindica has plenty to hide, as I'm sure you will find out now that you are their leader."

"So let's say in a crazy moment I was to believe you," Angelica asked, looking him over. Her thoughts were open to him as she was too angry and volatile to close them off completely. She noticed his height, his eyes, his physique. She searched for something that made him less human, but he'd been chosen to mingle with humans because he resembled them, except for his aging process being all Custos.

"Why do you keep yourselves hidden?"

"The Vindica betrayed us long ago," Kline said, putting his hands up in a gesture of truce. "We normally live quietly in our tribe.

Reximortum has brought my boss here."

"So... so..." Angelica's mind was working. "Why were you helping me?"

"Helping you helps my people. Our leader is worse than your Reximortum."

"Your boss?" Angelica asked, putting her hands down, even though he could still feel the tenseness.

Kline nodded. He'd revealed more than enough for now. He must think of his father. He'd heard nothing from his people to assume his safety. But he also knew it imperative she trust him.

Angelica exhaled deeply. "So exactly what happened to my blood sample?"

"Lucilius, my boss, had a geneticist come in and do a simple test to check how much Custos DNA creates your genetic make up. The sample was destroyed after. The Custos don't want our blood being made available."

"What would happen if people were able to get it?"

Kline shrugged. "I haven't been trained in the field of science. I'm a combat sentry."

"Okay." Angelica's eyes were distant as her thoughts ran with her. "What does it mean to be 93 percent Custos?"

Kline grimaced. "Lucilius wants to test again. He believes the small amount makes it inaccurate. I overheard him say that it would take generations of breeding with Custos to achieve that level. Custos are forbidden to breed with humans, so these situations are monitored."

"And if it is accurate?"

Kline exhaled slowly. "It means the Custos will not allow you to live freely. Potentially, you are just as much Custos as I am, but you are female. Females are a rarity in our tribe."

Angelica stared him. "So you're saying I'd be like Custos property?"

Kline glanced to the streets of New Orleans. The old world colliding with the modernity of technology: all new sights for him when he'd reached New Orleans. "We are not so modern as you. Our tribe follows ancient laws and nothing much changes as things do here."

"Well, that sure in the hell isn't going to happen."

Kline grinned. "My mother didn't appreciate it much either. She tried to change our customs for women, but Lucilius killed her."

Angelica's anger released for the first time. "I need to go before I'm missed, but I think I understand what you want from me now. I will try."

"Let me show you something before you leave," Kline said, moving toward her, questioning her with her eyes.

She nodded.

He moved behind her. "Let me teach you to fly."

"What?" she quivered beneath his touch as he wrapped his arm around her middle.

They rose from the roof and he hovered them, moving them toward the edge.

"The trick with telekinesis is to bend gravity to you."

They tipped over the side.

"What are you doing?" she asked, clutching him tightly with her arms behind her.

"To go down, use the gravity as a force, imagining it as an invisible floor beneath you."

Her heart beat fiercely against his arms as he lowered them to the sidewalk below. Her smell intoxicated him and he longed to kiss her neck left bare with her hair blowing wildly about.

And then their feet touched the cement, and she pulled away but stayed within his space to feel his heat. He felt her longing to kiss him and the confusion the emotion brought.

"I must go," she said finally.

"Good luck," he whispered, knowing she heard.

Forty-Nine

Voices hummed in Angelica's ears from all the people gathered behind the yellow crime scene ribbon. She concentrated on not covering her ears with her hands to shut them out. After a forty-five minute standing wait, John's breathing was labored. His anxiety was contagious though. He'd believed Rex would stop killing the young girls after Angelica had been named Valor, but here they were being summoned to a crime scene.

John tapped his cane on the cement. "He's coming our way."

Angelica glanced at the unshaven face strolling their way. His black hair stuck up at odd angles, and his white shirt flapped over wrinkled black pants. He looked a mess but his hardened physique gave the mess a different context.

His gray eyes scanned the gawking people behind the yellow tape. "Thanks for coming John. I needed an answer ASAP before I get off track with the investigation."

"Not a problem, Gavin. I've brought Angelica Acacia to help."

Gavin glanced over his shoulder toward the hovering officers. "I've heard of you." He nodded his head at her. "We don't have much time. The victim has the same MO as the others, but she's not on the list."

Angelica rubbed her hands together against the chill. "The list?"

John nodded. "Detective Gavin is our insider. He has a memorized list of all Vindica members."

Gavin shifted from one foot to the other, on edge.

"She's not a member?"

Gavin shrugged. "Possibly, since more of you keep popping up. I need a positive ID though."

John shifted his weight on the cane. "You said same MO?"

Gavin flipped open a notepad he'd clutched in his left hand. "Young woman, twenty-one, walking alone at night, no physical signs of a struggle, as far as we can tell no fingerprints and the murder weapon is a wooden stake."

Angelica's fingertips trembled. "A stake?"

He met her eyes for a moment, but then he returned to studying the movements of the crime scene. "Two others like her, and three other supernatural incidents. Previous five were on the list."

Angelica's stomach churned and she was glad he was standing between her and the body. She'd been spared a vision of this staking, probably because she'd been distracted by her search for Kline.

John sighed. "Angelica will need to touch something of the girl's to tell."

Panic clinched her insides. For once she hadn't seen the murder and now she would have to recall it by touching a dead girl's item.

Gavin studied her. Angelica couldn't glimpse his thoughts through his thick shield. "Crime scene is all over the area. I can't have her fingerprints on anything."

John clutched Angelica's elbow for a moment for balance. She needed to get him back to Landon House. "If we have to research it the old fashion way, it could take hours or days."

Gavin shook his head. "I don't have days. I need to steer the investigation before it goes in a direction we don't want. Serial Killer status is already on the table, which will bring in outsiders."

Angelica looked around the scene. Some still glanced in their direction. "Drop your notepad."

He glared down at her, his eyebrows furrowed. "Excuse me?"

She studied his reflective eyes. She could see the green flecks surrounding his pupil. "Drop your notepad."

He studied her a moment longer before dropping the notepad which thumped to the sidewalk. Angelica stooped down, her fingers only brushing the notepad. Her fingers connected to the concrete and a spark charged through her body.

He stooped down beside her as the cement rippled under her fingertips. Faint shadows of images layered together, overlapping. Her head throbbed attempting to sort them out.

"When did it happen?" She struggled to get the words past her lips as she felt herself sinking into the muddle of the past, weighed by the centuries of history in the area.

"About 12:30 A.M."

His smooth hands covered her hands, and she felt an anchor to the present.

She stroked the cement and sunlight eroded. Darkness encased the now empty street. She could feel Gavin's absorption of the scene, so he was gifted. His thoughts revealed he couldn't experience visions on his own, but he was able to absorb the visions of others through contact.

Two streetlights cast a dim glow around them. A car horn echoed from a distant street, and a low cloud hovered just above their heads.

The drumming crept into the stillness. Though faint, Angelica scanned the street to spy its entrance. A lone figure approached from the right of St. Peters Street. Her long dark hair flapped in the breeze as she crossed her arms tighter against her chest. She glanced over her shoulder at the empty street, her pace increasing. She felt as though she was being followed. The drumming advanced. Angelica's eyes burned straining to see the lurking stranger.

The woman stepped under a street lamp and Angelica sucked in her breath at the resemblance. Long black hair, pale complexion, and crystal blue eyes a shade darker than Angelica's. Below the layer of fear, Angelica felt the young woman's humanness. She wasn't Custos or hybrid.

A towering figure clothed in a dirt brown muslin robe loomed against gray brick. Angelica bit her lip as the drumming echoed in her chest. She blinked against the anxiety gripping her, straining to keep her fingertips anchored to the concrete.

The girl stumbled, grabbing her head as she keeled over. She crawled forward glancing over her shoulder. She didn't understand. Spotting the approaching figure, she stumbled upright, fighting against the pain tearing through her body.

His hand emerged from the folds of the robe and she rose, hovering a foot from the sidewalk.

She cried out as he spun her around. His left hand emerged from the cloak holding a two-inch stake. It levitated moments in the air before he flung it through the air. The woman gasped as she watched it approach and closed her eyes as it pierced through her middle.

Angelica studied the brown cloak as he released her to the ground. His face was not visible in the night's shadows, but his oversized hand was ornamented with a single silver band. Angelica glanced back at the girl and the pooling blood jolted her hand away from the pavement.

Angelica sank down on her backside. Black spots appeared in the streaming sunlight as bile rose in her throat. She hated it. She never adjusted to the sight of death, of the life draining from a body. She'd seen enough to know it would never be experienced in comfort.

Detective Gavin stood. He was shaky, but Angelica could feel an angriness pulsing. "She didn't fight back."

Angelica sighed. He could only see what she rewound, not what she thought. "She didn't have any gifts. He thought she was…I think he thought she was me."

Gavin paced the yellow tape. "So she wasn't on the list, but she has the same killer. I have to say I'm getting tired of not catching this killer. If you can't handle it, maybe we should try."

John leaned forward. "That would be a disaster for both parties and you know this."

"How? That girl lying over there didn't stand a chance."

Angelica stood, her legs quivering beneath her. "Here's where I'm confused. I've had visions of these attacks. Louis was murdered by three individuals in black cloaks. Rainy was attacked by one black cloak and so was Laura, the girl out on the Bayou. When Gabney and I were attacked, it was the brown cloak individual, same as these three women. I recognize the heartbeat."

Gavin stared at the crime scene. "Maybe we're talking two different perpetrators."

She lingered over the store sign advertising tourist items and palm readings as she waited for the nauseousness to settle. "And maybe there are two different purposes. We have to know more about the victims."

Gavin glanced her way. She could sense the queasiness in his gut. He didn't want to run into her for a while. "I'll work on that, but I need to get back now. Let me know if you come up with anything."

She watched him swagger back to the other officers. He had his own ideas about catching the killer though. She'd need to do something before he got himself killed.

John's grip on her elbow tightened. "Angelica, I've only known one other person able to do what you just did and he's been dead for fifteen years."

She cringed. "I know."

"What are you not telling me?"

Angelica's lip trembled. He'd been her favorite. "I was six, and he took a liking to me. He wouldn't teach anyone anything because he said everyone was unworthy, but he watched me when Lily did shifts at the diner, and he taught me a few things."

"I can't believe he never mentioned you." John's grip let up. "Stanley Harrison was a good friend of mine. I spoke to him every week."

"He died days after we left. He was the only one I tried to warn, but he said he had more talent in his thumb than any dark soldier."

He'd squeezed her chin, and gave her that big goofy smile he'd give her when she was sad. She'd laughed, believing for once that he was strong enough to survive when they came for him. Remembering may be a Custos trait, but the pain that accompanied the memories felt all too human.

John laughed. "Sounds like Stan. Listen, one day, when you're ready of course, I would really like to hear everything you remember. I have a feeling we can make sense of things for each other."

Angelica steered Landon down the street, calmness returning as they left the scene behind. "One day sounds good."

Fifty

Loose ends. So many of them to ensure he achieved success. It all came down to timing though. Preventing the Reckoning involved controlling Valor's decisions, as the letter from Madame Lulu had confirmed his suspicions and left more than a few problems to solve. Lucilius would have to be dealt with as well, and he'd worked out a solution for that, but first his son must be handled.

Rex waited until the lone patron had cleared the Voodoo shop before he motioned his Dark Soldiers inside.

He heard the shuffling and a crash as something hit the floor from the back storeroom and sent his men to retrieve the culprits.

While waiting, he looked around at all the items cluttering the shelves and thought of how useless these stood against real abilities. If the world knew this, they'd understand real fear. It would do him no good right now for the world to know though, so he must get ahead of the Reckoning.

His men returned with Arneaux and a struggling Simone. Rex had to respect her feistiness. It reminded him of his Lily when they were young during that one squabble at Landon House over some items that had been stolen. Falling in love with her when they were young had been like running up against a brick wall and sticking to it.

"What do you want?" Arneaux asked, fighting his anger.

Rex moved toward them. "I've come for the girl, as an insurance policy."

"My daughter?" Arneaux fought against the soldiers holding him. "You can't have her."

"Ah," Rex said, smiling. "I didn't say you had a choice, but since I've never had a problem with you, I may return her when I'm done. That is if you keep your mouth shut until it is all over."

Simone glared at him. "You will make an enemy of Madame Lulu and our people."

Rex motioned to the men holding Arneaux, and they forced him back in the storeroom. The echo of fist hitting ribs reached their ears.

"Soon we will all know a common enemy and alliances will be formed for survival. Madame Lulu has always understood the value of a truce."

Simone struggled as the soldiers moved her forward. "What about your son? How will he be as your enemy?"

Rex smiled. "He made himself my adversary. All is fair in war. He knows this."

She glared at him without response.

"Now sleep," Rex said, entering her mind and within moments knocking her unconscious.

Painless.

He grew soft in old age, but she possessed potential as a bargaining chip. Completely abandoning his son wasn't his intentions yet. He needed his son to lose right now, and in the loss, to become complacent. This was a win-win for Rex.

And then he had to consider the potential of Simone herself. A powerful seer in his possession could change the upcoming outcome in the direction he wanted. With a little encouragement and time, Simone might prove useful. He simply needed to take the time to turn the future in his favor.

After he retrieved the book, he'd have the time to consider the Reckoning.

But for now, the time for getting *The Book of Shadow Souls* back approached.

Fifty-One

Angelica squinted against the sunlight to get her first glimpse of Reximortum's southern home. Peering out the dusty window the sun tricked her imagination, and the house of butter flickered to its once majestic white, an upstairs window gleamed whole under the glare, and broken wood siding seemed seamless. She could squint her eyes a certain way and imagine it the way Lily must have loved it once.

Griffen had collaborated with Landon and came up with the home Rex had bought for Lily when they'd run off to get married. Rex had abandoned it thirteen years ago. Most had believed it was because he'd disappeared in Europe to study the ancient Custos legends, but Angelica would bet it had to do with him being unable to live within the walls of Lily's home. Angelica knew this was the exact place she needed to have a connection and break through this block of the future.

Roxy's car came to a grinding stop on the crunching shells, and Angelica stepped out. Angelica suspected that Roxy only agreed to bring her out to spy on her, but it made no difference to Angelica. She didn't have her driver's license, and her last teacher had told her to invest in bus tokens, so she didn't expect to have it any time soon.

She scanned the grounds, lingering on overgrown shrubs and a forest marching to seize the house's remains as its own. The only sound echoing in the stillness was the crunch of Roxy's, Griffen's, and Gabney's footsteps on the shells.

Roxy snorted. "It's abandoned. I don't know what you expect to find."

Griffen kicked at the shells, propelling them in all directions. Angelica could feel his frustration. He thought he'd test the waters with Gabney a bit in the car ride over, but he'd failed to bring up anything of significance.

Angelica smiled. Those two needed to get on with it already.

Angelica heard his footsteps before she could distinguish him from the dying brush. His gray overalls blended into the trees, and his face and hair attempted the color. She noticed his eyes were the color of a cypress leaf.

"Can I help you folks?"

Angelica greeted him with a smile.

"We were interested in taking a look at this beautiful, old home. Are you its owner, sir?"

The man's smile revealed graying gums. "Why no sha, I never afford a home like dis. I look after de grounds. I's don't 'ave a key though."

She stared into his eyes, feeling his protective guard ease.

"The grounds are beautiful. You do a magnificent job." Angelica gave her best contrite smile. "Would you mind terribly if we walked around a bit? We've driven such a long distance."

His cheeks darkened. "Well, I reckon that'd be ahright. Don't have much visitors here. Can't even git the real 'state woman to come anymore."

Angelica gave him one more of her dazzling smiles before turning and strolling toward the house. The others followed her in silence. Angelica could feel their thoughts, which ranged from *that was easy* (Gabney) to *what a con artist* (Roxy). At least she wasn't stealing from him. She'd only made a tiny suggestion that he could trust them. She could have used her abilities for far worse.

Angelica did a quick survey of the grounds, and her first assessment was no one had lived here for at least a decade. Necessary repairs had slipped and the humidity was rotting the house. Holly leaves were yellow and grass was splattered with brown patches.

She turned left onto the dirt path beckoning to the backyard. There was a layer of dust on the windows, but empty rooms could still be seen through them.

Gabney stepped closer. "Do you feel that? What is it?"

Angelica frowned. She'd tuned it out, but Gabney was vulnerable with her lack of defense. "It's lingering pain, horror. Spirits live here now."

Roxy grumbled. "What exactly are we looking for outside? There's nothing here."

Angelica felt her quick onset of fear. She was afraid the ghosts were real. Strange. Roxy didn't seem the type to be afraid.

"I need to find a connection to Reximortum." Angelica smiled. "You could always wait by your car."

Roxy laughed, echoing in the silence. "I've watched too many horror movies for that."

The house ended with a great expanse of lawn. Two hundred feet away there were three crumbling buildings. A wave of despair emanated from those buildings, and Angelica shivered as it swirled around her bones. Evil things had happened in there. She hoped to avoid connections involving torture.

Roxy's frustration seeped into her head. Gabney stood behind her, trembling with fear, and Griffen's curiosity drank in their surroundings.

Three different emotions drowning her concentration.

She closed her eyes and forced them out, then she opened her mental picture of her surroundings. Wisps of people floated around the grounds, their agony lingering in every crevice. She tried to push past the horror of the place's past, searching for something tangible. A past collection of the life lived here. Maybe a connection with Lily and Rex both. A happy one. Those must have existed.

To her left, a solid fixture began to grow within the dense shrubbery and trees. Her breath caught as people stronger than a wisp formed in the shadows. As if they were there now.

She darted toward the fixture, unsure of her purpose. Logically, she told herself no one could be there, but she'd felt their presence.

The shrubbery assaulted her at first scratch. Her arms stung as it clawed at her, but she pushed through. She stumbled upon a moss wrapped stepping stone, caught herself on a low branch, and continued toward the fixture from her mental map.

She stopped suddenly as she reached a clearing of deadness. The vines were brown, dirt covered the surface, and weathered columns reached up to the trees. The gazebo structure was empty. She'd felt spirits from the past.

Gabney burst out the bushes behind her, panting. "What's wrong?"

Frustration throbbed. Failure was worse when you had to admit to it. "I thought… I thought I saw people… well, it doesn't matter, I was wrong."

Roxy tore through the bushes, gasping for breath with Griffen on her heels. "What the hell?"

Angelica rubbed the back of her neck and winced at the burning in her arms. Driving herself should have been an option. She needed to rethink giving up on that skill.

"It must have been the past, but it felt like it was happening now."

Angelica studied the ornate structure and then glanced back toward a distinct entrance. This was hidden away, kept secret. More than likely, Lily hadn't known about this place.

She stepped forward, ignoring the buzzing of physic energy. The others were rooted to the ground, unable to look away from the structure.

Griffen removed his camera lens cover. "What is this place?"

Angelica stepped closer, but it was as though a heavy wind pushed her back.

"Reximortum's altar."

Gabney whistled as her breath drew in. "Should we be here?"

Angelica took a deep breath as if plunging into the deep end of a pool, and she stepped inside the structure. She glanced down and saw her foot had landed on a red symbol. The floor was circled with symbols. One she recognized as a rune symbolizing power. She knelt down to study it closer. She ran her fingers over the grit, but she couldn't tell if it were written in paint or blood.

Griffen's camera snapping interrupted the ominous silence.

She continued to feel the surface. What horrors had Rex done here? Her fingers brushed against something smooth. She inched closer and tugged it gently from the crack it was lodged in.

Under the sunlight filtering in from the top, she made out a dainty tarnished bracelet.

Its residual energy pulsed through her fingertips, and her head swirled as the images reached her.

They swirled faster and Angelica collapsed as they jumped in her head, as though age had forgotten its order. Three faces faded in and out. She couldn't get a grasp of them, until Lily's face, though thinner than she remembered, stared back at her. Angelica wanted to reach out and touch her cheek, but she couldn't move.

A dark haired, sky blue-eyed man glared down at the faces kneeling before him. She knew it was Reximortum by the set of his jaw and the calm craziness in his eyes. She'd seen his face in the visions of her childhood. She recognized the anger bouncing around him as well.

Next to Lily the man kneeling resembled Rex in facial features, except for his helpless blue eyes gazing on Lily with despair. The man had the same pointy nose and cheek structure as Rex, although his flesh tugged more on the face.

With Reximortum's mind control, he squeezed the look-alike's insides, and he howled in agony, folding over, kissing the altar floor. Angelica grasped for a breath, struggling to move toward them. She couldn't just stand and watch.

Rex stepped back, and the man lifted himself back to his knees with effort. Angelica could feel his quiet strength draining and something, intuition maybe, told her that at one time he'd been Rex's match. But he didn't fight back now.

The faces before her swirled. She tried to close her eyes against the dizziness, but the images would not respond to her efforts. Finally, the swooshing in her ears stopped and the faces appeared again.

It was another moment in time. Reximortum towered over them again. Tears streamed down Lily's cheeks, but she did not fight Rex as he cut off her oxygen. Rex's look-alike reached out with his fingertips to touch her, but his strength was drained. He could not reach her.

Angelica watched Lily's fingers reach towards the look-alike. With a jolt, complete blackness enveloped Angelica.

Blinded against the sunlight streaming down on her, she felt a sharp pain jarring into her back. She sat up and three whitened faces stared down at her. Gabney, Griffen, and Roxy waited for a response.

Gabney's voice trembled. "Are you okay?"

Angelica winced. "I saw…" She didn't like the quiver in her voice. "I saw him torturing Lily and another man."

Roxy, levelheaded, but still shaken. "I think we should go now."

On trembling legs, Angelica stood and followed the others through the tangled brush. She noticed the stone she'd tripped on was one of many snaking a path through the brush. The cattails had claimed the path, but the stones remained beneath the overgrowth as a reminder of what had been.

She hoped this one vision would be enough of a connection to force a premonition of the future. She'd hoped to have enough control to do it here, but the past weighed heavy with despair. Lily reaching out as red-hot pain seared through her had awaken Angelica at seven. Lily had cried out one last time before she'd collapsed and sank to the stones below, and Angelica had screamed out, knowing her mother had died. As a child, she hadn't seen the look-alike man and all that had come before. Now she had more to puzzle over.

Back near the front parking area, the old man limped toward them, flattening his hair down. "Did ya'll enjoy de grounds?"

Angelica smiled, some of the fuzziness evaporating with her attempt to focus on him. "It was beautiful."

"If ya'll come back now, I sure da owner love to show da place off."

Angelica smiled, feeling the gears turn in her head. "Does he come down often?"

The old man frowned. "Tell ya de truth, I only seen de man once."

"We may come back for that tour." Angelica nodded. "It was real nice of you to let us walk around the grounds."

She ducked into the car, feeling Roxy's disapproving grimace. Angelica wasn't looking to score any points right now though.

That ticking clock in her head told her that time was out. She needed to know what was around the corner, but all these unanswered questions brought her nowhere. On top of figuring out what had sparked the Reckoning, now she had to identify Reximortum's mystery twin.

Fifty-Two

Leaning against the brick wall, Cain scanned the passing faces from beneath his ball cap. Tonight's foot traffic was skinny for a Saturday night. With the murders being broadcasted all over the news channels today, many had stayed inside and out of harm's way. His father had kept everyone in the dark about his actions, but the Dark Soldiers whispered that there was something to fear.

A young woman bundled in a black overcoat exited the shop, and Cain caught the door before it closed and slipped inside. Simone's father stood behind the counter with a book in front of him.

Damn. Simone was supposed to be working tonight.

Mr. Auneaux hadn't noticed him standing at the door. His eyes stared into space and his hands trembled. Cain had never known the man to be anything less than alert and had always seemed to sense Cain's presence.

Cain cleared his throat and stepped forward. "I've come to see Simone, Sir."

"You," Mr. Auneaux stuttered, focusing on him finally. "Go away. Haven't you done enough damage?"

"Sir, I just want to talk to Simone."

Auneaux gripped the counter, his knuckles turning white. "They took her, said I'd get her back when it's all over." He swallowed, chocking on his tears. "So tell me, will I see my baby girl again?"

Hot anger seared through Cain, for a moment his vision went white. "Who took her?"

"Dark Soldiers." He waved his arm in the air. "Reximortum, your father himself. I told her you'd only bring her grief. Dangerous to mix with your kind."

Anger ripped through him and exploded in his skull. *His father.* "Did they say where she'd be held?"

The jars on the shelf near him rattled with the energy sparking from his uncontrollable anger.

"No," he said, trembling at the effect Cain's anger was having on the shop. "Just to keep my mouth shut or I'd never see her again."

A small jar exploded near Cain and Auneaux flinched.

"I will get her back." Cain spit out through gritted teeth. "Did she know?"

"What did she know?"

"Did she know they were coming?"

"Not soon enough." Auneaux shook his head. "We tried to get her out, but it was too late."

Another jar exploded.

Cain took a deep breath and forced the anger to tighten and focus.

"I will be in touch with you," Cain said as he turned for the door. He couldn't risk blowing up the shop. He'd rather use this energy to retaliate against his father. "I will get her back."

Auneaux nodded. "Thank you."

Cain exited and headed into the darkness.

His father had made a serious mistake. War was no longer upon them, as far as Cain was concerned it had begun.

Fifty-Three

A bell jingled on a nearby door and a passerby dropped a latte cup as he passed near her. Angelica soothed the wrinkles of her jacket wishing she could sooth her jumpy nerves. She crossed the street and froze as a car horn honked at the corner. On edge, she couldn't stop looking over her shoulder, waiting for someone to attack, even in daylight.

Last night's dream had left her rattled. After the exhausting connection at Rex's old home, her mind had swirled in a bombardment of images throughout her attempts at sleep. The *Gris Gris* shop sign, Gabney's watch, and mounds of purple velvet whirling in and out, and the feeling of being suffocated by darkness had plagued her all night.

She'd hoped the vision from the gazebo would enter her dreams so she could see it again, analyze it, and try to piece the puzzle piece where it belonged. It only dwelled in her awakened state, and the details were slipping into oblivion. She couldn't recall their faces or what they wore anymore.

She turned and retraced her steps, having passed Landon House while lost in thought.

Unlocking the door, she glanced around the deserted street. For once she hadn't walked down a street listening for an ominous heartbeat. Was the fear of a heartbeat or the images in her head worse? She wasn't sure.

Inside, she walked toward the training room. A rather intense training session was scheduled to begin in an hour in anticipation that they all needed to be at their optimal performance. She'd come early to attempt to center her thoughts, so she didn't make a fool of herself.

From the doorway, she recognized Lysander's backside in loose jeans and a gray t-shirt. He was shoving his training gear into a large duffel bag.

Angelica stopped in the doorway. "Don't you need those for training today?"

He turned, gripping a faded green shirt she'd liked on him. "I'm clearing my things."

"Spring cleaning or tired of all the old things?"

Lysander hadn't returned to Landon House since she'd been named Valor. She'd given him his space as he'd asked, but so much had happened she hadn't spent her time pining for him either.

He turned away from her and put the last of his gear in the bag before zipping it shut. "Neither, I'm taking a break and training at home for awhile."

"So you've made a decision?"

He turned toward her, but his eyes stared at her forehead. "Don't do this. I need more than two days to get my head around this. You are Reximortum's daughter. Do you have any idea what this would do to my life?"

"I'm Lily's daughter," Angelica muttered. "And it shouldn't matter."

"Do you know the death he's responsible for? People will associate the two of you no matter how much you insist he's not your father." Lysander paused and took a deep breath. "I've tried to stay out of

Vindica politics my entire life. I just want to make the right decision here."

Angelica stared at him. What she wanted to say was that if she were worth it, the decision wouldn't be so difficult. But she wouldn't appear desperate.

He walked toward the doorway and she stepped aside.

Angelica's breath caught as he passed near her. She could smell sandalwood and spice from his t-shirt. She felt him hesitate at the door. He wanted to say something.

"Don't hate me."

She closed her eyes. She could feel his conflict below the surface, but now she knew he wanted her to see it and she wasn't sure how much it meant that way.

The door creaked and closed behind him.

She shook herself. No stranger to a broken heart, she'd recover, but she needed to survive first. All the signs pointed to something happening soon and being distracted was a sure way to invite failure.

She crossed to the beanbag bin in the training room. Time to try her hand at focusing.

The training room walls held several hand to hand combat weapons such as poles and swords. A bookcase of bins held other instruments of training, including the bags Angelica used for her focus exercises. During training, Mike stressed her inability to block out external stimuli. Perhaps she should have asked Kline for a training tip since Mike hadn't offered anything she'd been successful implementing. But then she'd kept Kline's existence hidden from everyone at Vindica house, so she'd have to explain where she learned control. She needed to face that secret soon. A pure blooded Custos attack scared her, and she was certain the others would not want to believe her because of their own fear.

She stood in the center of the room, closing her eyes to visual

VALOR

distractions. Of course, Mike chided her for closing her eyes to an enemy, but she hadn't figured out how to shut everyone's thoughts completely out yet. Training with Mike had been a lesson in humiliation more than skill.

With a deep breath, she focused on the bags and visualized them rising. They rotated above her hands, then she lifted them eye level. She spun them like a whirlpool; and then commanded them to stop. They halted mid-air. Her neck muscles relaxed, and she again rotated them and then lifted them above her head.

Her mind settled, leaving her troubles on the side for a moment.

A shriek pierced through the house. Angelica's command wavered; she attempted to hold her pace, but the shrieking grew in intensity.

Serena burst into the room. "This is your fault. You're trying to destroy me!"

Footsteps thundered from all corners of the house. John was in the doorway before Serena's words could sink in, and Trevor stood right behind Serena, concern etched across his forehead.

What the hell was he doing here? He had some serious stalking issues.

John cleared his throat. "What's going on in here?"

"Look at my hands!" Serena's voice screeched through the silence. "She's cursed me. She's no Valor. She's some evil monster you let take Valor away from me!"

Serena sobbed and wailed. Trevor's eyes bugged at the twisted, horrible position of her fingers. It was difficult to look at, but no one looked away.

Roxy pushed herself into the room, and Jack followed. Roxy looked from Angelica to Serena, and her brain spun faster. Angelica could tell she was moments away from making a decision. One that would protect her family.

267

"Angelica, what the hell is this?" Trevor asked, unmoving.

Jack grabbed Serena's hands and glared at Angelica. "Does she pose a threat to you that you need to get rid of her?"

Angelica looked to John and sadness weighed the creases of his eyes and his lip trembled. Gabney was right. He was too old for all of this.

"I need to know what happened."

Serena wailed. "She's trying to cripple me."

Angelica's flesh flushed as she felt everyone's eyes upon her waiting. "I did nothing to her."

John raised his hand, sensing the objections coming. "We are all on the same side here, and we must stop this pettiness."

Jack stood, glaring at John. "Are you sure? Angelica's loyalty may rest with her family."

Everyone looked from Jack to Angelica. John's face drained of all color.

Serena perked up, looking to John. "What is he talking about?"

John squirmed.

Jack's face reddened. "I possess the intelligence to infer her parentage. She resembles him, and that does not place her on our side."

Something triggered inside Angelica; it shot straight through, burning her all the way down. She didn't need to hide from the truth. It didn't matter. As Madame Lulu had said, she was born Valor, and it didn't matter who her father was.

She strode toward Serena and grabbed her hands. Serena cringed under her touch, but the answer clung close to the surface, difficult to hide with her pain.

Angelica faced everyone. "She tried to curse me, and it rebounded on her."

Angelica lowered her voice and glared into Serena's twitching, crestfallen face. She made sure her voice was heard in the silence of the room. "I'm protected from curses because my mother, Lily Vale, left this to protect me." Angelica rubbed her finger over the stone around her neck.

Angelica looked around the room. "My mother sacrificed herself to protect me from my father, Reximortum Vale."Angelica focused on Serena. "I have reasons to want to kill my father, what are your reasons to continue hurting your father?"

Serena's eyes widened and she trembled violently. She yanked her arm away and sprinted from the room. Jack glared at John a moment longer and then followed Serena.

"Soon everyone will know." John wobbled to a chair. "This could be a disaster."

Roxy stared at him stunned. "You knew?"

"Of course, I knew Roxy." John closed his eyes. "I figured you did too with all the hints you were trying to pass along."

"But…" Roxy looked toward Angelica. "Is it wise to trust her?"

John said, "Some will probably take issue with it. The same ones who will remember my mistake with trusting Reximortum."

Angelica looked at Roxy. Only time would gain trust there. "I don't need to be Valor to go after Reximortum."

Trevor's hoarse voice said, "Could someone explain what's going on?"

Angelica sighed. "Trevor, I need you to go home today."

He grimaced, looking around at everyone in the room. "I told you, I'm here until Saturday."

Angelica faced him, squaring her shoulders, although she barely reached his chest. "Listen to me, everyone will know who I am by sunset. If someone wants to get to me, they can use you to do it. You don't stand a chance against these people. I want you on a plane in a few hours. No arguments."

Roxy nodded. "I'll take him."

He seemed to be about to argue, but Roxy glared at him, grabbing him by the elbow. "Say your good-byes or they become permanent farewells."

Trevor said, "I'll call you, Angelica. I'm coming back for Christmas, too."

Angelica grinned as Roxy herded him out the door. She had to admire his persistence.

John looked to her. "I still wish the others could have remained ignorant."

Angelica bit down on her bottom lip. Knowledge was what they could use right now.

"I think maybe ignorance has been the theme for too long," Angelica said, sitting in a seat near him. "Recently, someone has been dropping in on me on my walks home, offering training tips."

Landon squinted down at her.

Angelica put her hand up. "I know. I never felt like I was in danger, and he asked me to keep it between the two of us, so I gave him a few days in hopes that I'd figure out more about him and what he wanted."

"And did you?" Landon asked, struggling not to lecture her.

"He claims to be pure Custos."

"Impossible," John uttered.

"I thought so at first," Angelica said. "But, he knows things, John. He knows how to do things that even Griffen can't find records of anyone doing. He's stronger and faster than anyone here."

"Is he a threat to the Vindica?"

"He says that his boss, another Custos, is worse than Reximortum, and he will come for me."

John gripped his cane. "We need to let the Vindica know."

"Not without proof," Angelica said, shaking her head. "Do you know how crazy that will sound? They will believe I made it up to detract from Rex."

"So what do we do?"

"We need proof, but we also need knowledge," Angelica said. "I need you and Gabney to get me actual specifics on the originals. I need to know what I'm dealing with."

Landon nodded. "I have someone who may be able to help us."

"I don't want you to worry about Rex being my father anymore. Everyone will come around to me in time."

Landon sighed. "I know. Just so you know, you may resemble him in appearance, but you have nothing of your father's personality."

Angelica laughed. "Lily always said I was my father's child. I'm beginning to think Lily knew a different man than everyone else."

"Maybe," Landon said, quietly.

Fifty-Four

The pen scratched the thick linen paper as Rex's hand advanced with great speed. The ticking clock above his chair tapped at his brain, and he paused, losing his thought. This was unlike him. His concentration was a source of pride, a strength. He could feel his hold slipping with each new obstacle he approached. So much to orchestrate with details falling just so.

A sharp knock rattled the door. He leaned back into the leather chair and cleared his thoughts for the visitor.

Lucilius entered and cast a shadow over the dim-lit room. Rex nodded in greeting and Lucilius frowned.

"I grow tired, Rex."

"I know," Rex said, careful to maintain eye contact. "I've been taking care of loose ends so that everything goes as we planned."

"Your people have grown weak," he said. "I don't know why we thought you were a threat."

Rex raised an eyebrow. The Custos afraid of Dark Soldiers created an interesting scenario. Rex could only imagine it would be caused by numbers because in abilities, they would be no match.

Lucilius waved Rex off. "Even your thoughts can't be guarded from me. How did your people allow this?"

Rex bristled. "We are exploring methods with DNA trials to

strengthen our abilities."

Lucilius nodded. "I'd be curious what you'd learn about that long lost daughter."

Rex didn't like the easy grin he'd had when he said it.

Lucilius said, "Three young women dead and now I want my book."

Rex didn't blink. "You will have it when it is all over tonight."

Lucilius stared down at him a long time before exiting.

Rex stood and walked to the French doors leading to the balcony, careful not to allow the sunlight to touch his face. Rex stood on the precipice of the future he'd envisioned over twenty-five years ago. A future that brought the Vindica and the Dark Soldiers back together under one umbrella and created the most powerful organization in existence. With this merger, the world would be theirs to envision however they chose. But, he felt the vision blurring and becoming a remote possibility as his men weakened, his son betrayed him, and now Lucilius expected him to turn over the book he'd searched for over twenty years.

He saw the years passing, leaving him empty-handed. A potential outcome, and one he needed to plot an exact course of action to avoid.

A short rap rattled the door and a cloak swooshed against the wood floor. Rex sensed Dark Knight before he spoke.

"Did you summon me, my Lord?"

"I need you to take four of our men and visit Larkin Luke at his hotel. He'll bring you to the young woman, and you are to bring her to me."

"What about the young lady that is our guest?"

"I believe she may be able to shed some light on what my son has been up to, so I'm going to spend some time with her now."

Dark Knight bowed low. "As you wish my Lord."

Rex sighed, stepping near the shadows of the sun. This moment was turning out to be bittersweet. Lily should have been by his side as he finally, after centuries, united the Vindica people. She'd loved him and in a moment of weakness, he'd ruined it all. The delicate balance between love and power had come as a lesson too late in life.

What he did now was for her though. She'd wished for a united Vindica. One where everyone united to become stronger.

This was her legacy.

Fifty-Five

Cain felt the chilly air coming off the river, lapping against the large chunks of concrete. A tugboat traveling into the gulf signaled its approach. He felt like that boat, easing gently into treacherous territory, only certain of his destination. His fate and Simone's fate rested on a sister that he felt no curiosity or desire to get to know. The sister stood in his way, and that's all he needed to know about her. After spending all these years hanging onto the anger over his mother being taken from him, he'd believed that he'd feel something about discovering a connection to family, but after a few days to get used to the idea, he knew he'd forgone the idea of family long ago.

A shuffling footstep behind him drew his thoughts back to the men waiting for his orders. Hiding their faces from passerbys, they stared at the sidewalk. The mark of a Dark Soldier was to hide oneself from sight even during daylight when they didn't wear cloaks. Cain hoped to have a different breed of soldier one day.

Cain spoke to the wind. "I admire your courage for choosing to follow my leadership. I respect the faith in me that it requires."

Lars's voice trembled. "Won't we be punished for our betrayal?"

Cain assessed his choice. He'd been used for muscle up until now, but his fear caused sweat to bead on his forehead. "When we finish tonight, they will fear what we possess."

Falcon cleared his throat and spoke evenly. "What is our next step?"

Cain paused and studied the two he'd chosen. He'd been selective due to trust, but he needed more strength in numbers. Many would come once he had the book. He was sure of it.

"Getting the book requires Angelica Acacia to take action as Valor, and then we will give her reason to give it to us."

Lars asked, "What do I have to do?"

"You will keep our guests comfortable until tonight. Make sure no one realizes they are missing."

Lars nodded and hurried off.

Cain turned toward the river. "Do I have your loyalty?"

Falcon stepped even with him. Confidence and loyalty swelled within his chest. "I'm loyal to our cause."

Cain nodded.

Falcon's thoughts turned toward tonight's confrontation and his inner turmoil at betraying Landon House. In the end, the betrayal was irrelevant because fear drove them all. Falcon feared a future that prophecies condemned him to die. A New Order could save him. Tonight Angelica would learn the fear of losing someone, just like he feared he'd lost Simone. Everyone feared something. Even Rex feared a prophecy that predicted failure.

Cain remembered before fear ruled his father. At four or five, he remembered running into the drawing room and seeing Rosemary dead. He'd never seen a dead body before, and he couldn't take his eyes from her crumpled form on the chair.

Facing the fireplace, Rex had turned to him, frowning. "Are you supposed to be running in the house?"

Cain had stared at his dirty sneaker. "No sir, I'm sorry. I promise I won't do it again."

Rex's lips had curved slightly. "I do believe you said the same thing yesterday afternoon when you ran in from killing your pet toad."

Cain had peeked at Rosemary again. "Rosemary dead?"

Rex cleared his throat. "What did you run through the house to show me at this late hour?"

Cain pulled his gaze away from Rosemary again, and he'd raised his palm to show the two marbles resting in his dirt-smeared hand. He'd focused, and they'd risen and floated inches above his palm. "I've practiced all day."

His father had smiled, and Cain had tingled with pride. "You possess the same gift as your mother. She'd want you to use it well."

Cain had perked up. "Is Mommy home yet?"

Rex had sat and motioned for Cain to climb in his lap. A rare invitation, Cain bolted into place, still clutching his marbles. "I know you miss her, but I'm sure she'll return soon. If you have any dreams about where she is just tell me right away, and that way you can help me find her and show her all you've learned."

"Can I really help you?"

"One day, you can be my partner. How'd you like that?"

"Really? You promise?"

But Rex never fulfilled that promise. After Rosemary's death and the disappearance of the book, fear crawled through the Dark Soldiers. Rex changed as he delved further into finding the book to beat a ridiculous prophecy. No one would be Rex's equal as long as he feared losing more of a foothold in the Custos world.

Cain had stopped wanting it though. He'd grown disgusted with the antiquated traditions and proceedings of a dying organization.

This was his opportunity, and Angelica, sister or not, stood in his way.

Fifty-Six

Angelica chewed on her lip as she folded another shirt. An overflowing suitcase rested on the bed before her, and she didn't believe all her belongings were going to fit. She'd managed to squeeze it all in a few weeks ago, but it would seem she'd collected a few more items in New Orleans.

Denise flung herself across the bed causing the suitcase to bounce. "You can come back if it doesn't all fit. You're only moving a few blocks away."

Angelica smiled, busying herself with pushing down on the clothes to stuff them all inside. "I just want to get it over without tears."

Denise pursed her lips, clutching an art magazine against her chest. "I don't want you to think I wanted you to go even if we haven't... well, you know."

Angelica paused in folding. Denise would never say it aloud, but Angelica sensed her sadness. Denise had believed they'd recapture the closeness of high school, but neither was that same person. "I'm only moving a few streets away, besides don't they say separation makes the heart grow fonder?"

Denise shrugged. "The apartment will be empty, that's all. Trevor gone and now you."

Angelica laughed. "I promise I'll visit, and Trevor threatened me with Christmas."

"You'll be careful, right? I mean, I'm still not sure about these people."

Rodney appeared at the doorway, frowning. "Angelica, there are suits here to see you."

Angelica tossed the last items in the suitcase. "Suits?"

Rodney's voice dropped to a whisper. "Five of them. I don't like the looks of them."

Angelica's muscles tensed. Since her genealogy revelation, she'd been anxious, waiting for something to happen. At this point, it could be anything from the Vindica calling to say they changed their mind about her being Valor to a Custos showing up to drag her into some tribe she'd disappear into like some television after school special. John had insisted she move into the house today for protection so he would not have sent anyone to retrieve her.

"Denise, stay here," Angelica said, assessing the audience she'd have.

Rodney's mouth opened, and his eyebrows furrowed in his defiant way.

She nodded. "Stay out of the way." No use arguing with him and wasting time.

Angelica breathed in deep and focused on what waited. She crossed toward the living room, lingering over the vivid painting, her heart thundering.

Waiting in the living area, Larkin Luke stood in the middle of the floor flanked by four men in black with hands behind their backs. They'd sucked the oxygen out of the room with their stiff postures and sunglasses. If these were Vindica henchmen, the organization had more secrets to share.

Larkin's voice trembled, as he wiped his moist head with a white handkerchief. "After recent events, a decision has been reached. You have to understand that self-preservation…" He trailed off. Her parentage must have reached the Vindica's ears. A message would have sufficed telling her that her services weren't needed anymore; the henchmen were overkill. Unless they weren't just delivering a pink slip.

"What decision?"

He stumbled forward. "He promised no one else would get hurt. No more girls…"

One of the muscle men shoved Larkin from behind and Larkin whimpered. "What he's trying to say is that you're being sacrificed for the good of your kind. In exchange for you and the amulet, we won't kill all the residents of Landon House."

Anger surged through her. Larkin had sacrificed her to save his own neck. Bringing them here made her vulnerable with no one else to help her.

"Larkin doesn't own me, so if I'm going to surrender, it's going to be on my own terms. And I'm not really one to give up."

Larkin stumbled back, droplets dripping down his temple. He glanced toward the door, and Angelica knew he was planning to run.

Two of the men moved toward her. The earlier speaker, the one with the crescent shaped scar beneath his left eye, said, "They said you were smart."

Angelica telekinetically flung one of Denise's iron candle stands at the man to her left. It thwacked him in the center of his forehead and he dropped to the ground, clutching his temple.

She focused on the three left standing.

As the man to her right lunged at her, she flung him backwards, and he bowled Larkin over as he slid toward the door.

Scar face speaker advanced, and she entered his body and squeezed his throat. He pushed forward against the pain and moved toward her in slow motion, clutching at his throat. With a well-aimed kick at his shins, he keeled over, struggling to breath.

A hard thwack hit the side of her head causing silence in her ear. She struggled against the sharp pain and blinked into focus the soldier who'd thrown an iron candleholder at her.

She lifted him in the air, feeling her focus dissipating.

"Rodney, get the door!"

Rodney lunged over the leader and swung the door open as Larkin gaped at the room. Angelica flung the floater out the door where he disappeared below, falling the two stories as she couldn't hold him anymore.

Scar face struggled to his feet and backed away. Angelica allowed his lungs to fill with air, but with his first breath, he threw his right hook.

It stung and anger surged. She pooled her strength and flung him forward. He catapulted backwards, slamming into the railing.

The man lying next to Larkin's feet picked himself up and stumbled to the door. He was sprinting by the time he reached the iron staircase.

Larkin trembled, straightening the collar of his suit jacket. "I'm so sorry… I didn't have a choice… I'm glad it all worked out."

Angelica glared at him, stepping forward.

He bolted for the door, not looking back.

Angelica assessed the room. Candlestick man had passed out on the floor, and the one in the courtyard wasn't going anywhere. Scar face had hobbled off after the sprinter.

She'd need help cleaning up this mess. Detective Gavin would not be happy to hear from her so soon.

"I knew it!"

Angelica's ears throbbed at the piercing sounds. Denise stared at her from the doorway, with sheer madness gripping her face. Rodney huffed, pumping his fists, unsure what to do next.

Maybe if she knocked Denise out, Detective Gavin could clean up this mess, too.

Fifty-Seven

The new recruits created weakness among the Dark Soldiers. At least that's what Rex surmised after observing the intense regiment of an initiate. Many barely passed muster, yet they laughed and carried on as if they had earned entry-level status already.

This would not do; order must be restored. Before the split, these soldiers served as the Vindica's great army, the protectors of all knowledge. Before ideals had split them into two alliances in opposition to each other, these men carried out all manners of tasks for the Custos hybrid to maintain secrecy. If Rex's plan succeeded, he'd unite the two once again, and wished only the best to serve in the position.

Rex looked up from the sparing sessions as two soldiers entered the warehouse. One limped but kept pace with the other. He recognized them as two of the four soldiers sent to return with Angelica Acacia.

They approached him, wearing grim expressions.

Bowing their heads, they waited for permission to speak.

"Where is she?" Rex asked, looking to the door for the others.

The limper cleared his throat. "Our mission has failed. We lost two men in the struggle. She is more powerful than we were prepared to encounter."

Rex rose from his seat. "Are you not trained and capable Dark Soldiers? Why is it that my men cannot defeat a young girl?"

The one with dried blood near his ear put his head up. "But sir, she's not normal. We can't be expected…"

"Silence." Rex shouted forcefully, cutting off his words, his breathe.

Dark Knight excused himself from the training recruits and hurried over. Rex swept across the product of the laxness of this institution that had been allowed to grow while he delved into his search for their future. It would not do.

"You are expected to follow orders even if that requires death. It is the oath you swore as a Dark Soldier."

The soldier's face reddened; he clutched at his throat. He fell to his knees as he became lightheaded.

The initiates stopped mid spar to gawk at the scene.

"Lord," Dark Knight squeaked. "His father…"

"I don't care who his father is," Rex said, feeling his muscles grow taunt with the surge of control. "It is time we weed out the weak. I demand quality of my men, of the people I choose to back me up. You, Dark Knight, have allowed weakness to fester. If we are to rise and survive the Reckoning, we need to be merciless with our code."

The initiate fell to the ground, still.

No one spoke; the warehouse quiet under the strain of fear.

"Now gather your best men, Dark Knight," Rex said, stepping around the corpse. "I want to see what qualifies as your best."

"Where… where are you going?" Dark Knight squeaked again.

"To see the girl," Rex said. "I was gentle before, but now is not the time for manners. I will have that book."

Rex walked to the back storage container where Simone rested. He'd been easy earlier today, believing that he'd have Angelica and his book by nightfall and then he could return the feisty young Anihi to his son. Maybe even forge a bond between the two and achieve that much more.

But that time had passed. He would not allow Cain to swipe that book from him or even this unknown daughter to defeat him.

Sometimes sacrifice was necessary. He'd learned that lesson many times before.

Fifty-Eight

The sky burned orange against the backdrop of the Quarters as streetlights flickered. Angelica jangled her key against the brass doorknob, and it creaked as it clicked open. The darkened entrance of Landon House was silent except for the slow ticking of the grandfather clock.

Home. She breathed in the eccentric smells of old books, antique wood, and spice. For better or worse, she now lived here, among the other hybrids. John believed it safer for everyone involved if she stayed in the house, but the other residents may have felt differently.

After hours of cleaning up at Denise's, Detective Gavin had finally released her, and with Denise's silent, crazy eyes following her around the room, Angelica had to agree that it was probably best she stay away from the outside population for awhile. Detective Gavin, however, had warmed to her as he'd assessed the scene and realized he now had two Dark Soldiers in custody. He'd ordered police guards on each man as they were bused to the hospital.

Angelica dumped her suitcase by the staircase and strolled toward Landon's library door. Pushing the door open, she blinked against the dim lighting where Mark studied her from John's favorite chair.

"Where are John and Gabney?"

Mark unfolded his hands. "John's resting, and I haven't seen Gabney today."

Angelica hesitantly walked into the room. "I guess you heard about today?"

Mark nodded. "I hear you performed your first act as Valor. At least that's how everyone is labeling it in the gossip."

Angelica shrugged. "I did what I had to do."

"You'll of course get to decide Larkin's punishment."

"I think the council would be better suited for that."

Mark smiled, but his eyes remained cold. "Pick your daisies carefully."

A shiver ran through her. The line teased at a memory. "What?"

He laughed. "It's the moral of a story I was told when I was young. A little girl climbs over a fence to pick daisies in someone's field, but she can't get back over the fence without ruining the daises."

"What does that have to do with Larkin?"

"Now that you've opened the golden doors of Valor, you can't walk out when you get squeamish. The traditions are firmly in place."

"The traditions could always use updating."

Mark stood up and slipped a book back onto the shelf. "At the beginning of the prophecy, Valor was a quality to be exhibited with actions. It required a willingness to fight and die for our people. Don't you think it should mean the same today?"

The iron clad invisible wall he maintained around his thoughts was firmly in place. "I'm really tired. If you have a lesson somewhere in this, can we not do it fortune cookie style."

He shrugged, looking over the room. "Just my thoughts on the whole Valor debate. Everyone has an opinion these days."

"Valor's a legend, and I'm going to do the best I can to help people, but we all need to show a certain willingness to protect ourselves."

"And we should look out for ourselves at times like these." Mark nodded as he crossed to the door. "I'll see you, Angelica. Bruce is waiting for me."

Angelica reminded herself that Mark's loyalty belonged to his girlfriend, and Serena hadn't made this easy. Angelica would imagine that Mark had received the brunt of Serena's anger. Serena could just wait it out, as it appeared from the circulating gossip that Angelica's days as Valor were numbered.

She shrugged away the conflicting feelings of rejection and failure and faced the fireplace, gripping the metal key in the palm of her hand. She could feel the prongs edging into her flesh. After the dark soldier incident, this calmness had descended over her. It was this unexplainable feeling that she was where she was supposed to be.

A younger Lily than she remembered stared back at her from the mantle, smiling. Clear, hopeful eyes instead of the creases and sadness that had always edged around the corners of the Lily Angelica knew.

Angelica had forgotten about this key. At first, she'd thought it opened Landon House, but it didn't match the key John had handed her this morning. When she'd found Lily's journal among Gram's things, the key had been taped inside the back cover. Weeks ago when she'd removed it, she'd figured it was something lost along the way, but today when she'd gone to toss it into the bottom of her suitcase, it had occurred to her that Lily wouldn't have included it in this journal if it didn't have a purpose.

Angelica looked into her mother's photographed eyes, seeing them again the night she'd said good-bye. "Help me out Lily. Where does this fit?"

A thump vibrated the floor behind her. She whirled around to John limping into the room. "Where does what fit and was that Gabney leaving?"

Angelica dropped into the red velvet chair. "Just Mark. Another one who thinks I need to prove myself. It seems to be an epidemic."

John sank into his chair, closing his eyes. "Ms. Cammie's at the young lady's apartment. She volunteered since she knew the family."

Angelica shuddered. "I wish her luck as Denise was psychotic when I left."

John's fingers rubbed the carvings on his cane as they did when he worried. "Rex daring to go after you means he's afraid or wants something. Either is dangerous."

Angelica clutched the key tighter in her hand. "Did Rex lose the book at the same time Lily ran away?"

John frowned, his forehead wrinkles becoming more pronounced. "The rumors began after Rosemary's death which was a year later."

"Did Rosemary stay in touch with Lily? I didn't see it, but maybe it was kept secret."

John shook his head. "It would have been too dangerous for the two of you. What are you thinking?"

Angelica frowned. She needed a connection, but she needed something to actually connect.

"Lily left me with three things on Gram's front porch."

John cleared his throat. "I know about the amulet and the journal, but what else?"

She held out the brass key, her palm tingling where it had impressed its outline. "I have this feeling it has to do with that book."

John's legs swayed as he stood. "Does it have an inscription?"

She studied the ridges of the key. Carved crudely in the top were three letters. "AVA, why?"

John swayed forward abandoning his cane, but he did not pause until he reached the bookcases. Her mouth fell in a silent gasp as he yanked books away from the bottom shelf. When the shelf lay empty, he pulled a hidden door open. Angelica went and knelt down beside him and helped ease a wooden trunk from the darkness of the hole.

They carried the trunk to his empty desk. The trunk had a small brass lock affixed to the front.

John's hands rubbed the lid. "Before Rosemary disappeared, this trunk arrived with a brief note. It said that it was to only be opened by the person bearing an inscribed key with AVA. It was unsigned, but I am the Vindica secret keeper, so I don't question, I keep things hidden for our people according to their instructions because it is the oath I swore. I've wondered all these years, but I had to fulfill my duty."

Angelica's trembling fingers slipped the key into the lock, and with a deep breath, she turned the key right and it clicked. She lifted the lid. Her heart beat in her ears. She reached inside with trembling hands, and grasped a worn green leather book with *Field of Shadows* burned black onto its cover. The cover squeaked as she flipped it open.

She ran her hand over the first sheet. It was not a page in the book, but was stuck to the first page in an off-centered way as though added in a hurry. "It's the prophecy Lily had in her journal. It's the same handwriting."

She glanced down the page, noticing a scribbled message. "Wait, there's more. It says Dear Angelica Acacia Vale. We will have never had the opportunity to meet, but our paths did cross. In each generation, our people could have named Valor. Events set in motion before your birth, allowed for you to have this right. Be thankful to those who've given you the opportunity, but do not grieve. Repay them with fulfilling the prophecy. Use your abilities well. Love Rosemary."

She traced her finger over the loopy letters. "This was Rosemary's book. She recorded her life inside."

Angelica peered into the chest, spying mounds of purple velvet. Resting the book on the table, she reached into the chest and brushed against crushed velvet soft as fur. Pulling the velvet up, she felt it catch, held back by something inside. She brushed the velvet away and gasped at the gold lettering on the worn book binding that read *Book of Shadow Souls*.

John's fingers trembled as he reached out and touched the cover. "It's been here all this time."

Angelica smiled. It was an eighteen-inch square book that didn't look in the least scary, but she couldn't bring herself to open it. "Wait until Gabney sees this."

John studied the book. "Where's Gabney? She called and said she was staying with you."

Angelica pulled herself away from the book to look at him. "What? I haven't seen Gabney since yesterday afternoon."

"Gabney has never lied to me. Where could she be?"

A roar sounded in Angelica's ears. Her dream. She'd been dreaming about Gabney and the purple velvet. Fear encroached on her peace of only moments ago. Gabney was in trouble. Angelica knew it, just as she'd known this key was important.

Her dream. She needed to recall the details. She closed her eyes and strained for the images to surface. The watch. Twelve thirty-five. Angelica had been staring up into the sky at the Gris Gris sign. But there was always something else. Something she couldn't remember when she awoke.

Images became a whirlwind and she felt as though she was caught in a tornado. Her mother's eyes, a dead cat, a cot, a silver ring.

Gris Gris.

Hang on to that one. Gabney floating in the air. Gabney pointed at her watch, and three cloaked figures approached. As they closed in they lowered their hoods, and Lily's face stared at her from each.

Angelica's eyes popped open and she stared at John and Griffen. Roxy stood further behind.

John waited, worry creasing his face.

"They have Gabney."

Fifty-Nine

"You're right," Kline said, bowing. "Something will happen tonight."

Lucilius threw his goblet across the room. "I knew it. Yet, Rex hasn't contacted me. He believes he can double cross me."

"Our inside contact Echo confirmed that all parties are moving forward."

Lucilius glared off into the empty fireplace for a moment.

"I'm ready to leave this city."

"Sir?" Kline asked, unsure of the statement.

"Tonight we will wrap up our own business here, and I believe it's time we return home."

Kline hesitated. "How do you want me to proceed?"

"Gint will take care of the task." Lucilius looked to him, his cold eyes burning through Kline. "Bring me that young woman. She will return with us."

"To the tribe?" Kline's tone revealed his surprise, and he hoped Lucilius's assumptions had nothing to do with the truth.

Lucilius nodded. "She needs to be studied. She has too much of our blood to allow her to remain free. Bring her to me tonight, and I will handle the rest."

Kline hurried from the room; fear that his thoughts would broadcast propelling him deep into the compound.

He couldn't sacrifice Angelica. The idea made his gut boil with acid. His feelings had gone where they shouldn't, and it was too late to reel them in. But to protect her from Lucilius would mean sacrificing himself and his father.

His only chance would be if Angelica succeeded tonight.

Sixty

Angelica clasped the purple velvet cloak tighter around her chest as she felt the stares of the elderly couple as they hurried pass them. John had given it to Lily for her twenty-first birthday. Lavender and vanilla clung to the fabric, Lily's scent, and Angelica knew she had to wrap herself inside and bring her along as she faced the people behind those three faces of Lily in her dream.

Her face prickled from the chilled air, and Angelica felt the darkness stealing her breathe. Tonight she'd have to prove herself.

"Someone's following us," Roxy whispered.

Nodding, Angelica closed her eyes. "Griffin."

He was twitching with nerves and his heart raced, but he would not let anything happen to Gabney, not before he told her how he felt.

Angelica would consider it sweet, if it wasn't so dangerous.

Serena grunted. "He's going to get himself killed."

Angelica shivered. Fear sat in her middle. Too many people to protect tonight, and she could only hope everyone made it through.

The book weighed against her back in the backpack she wore under the cloak. She thought she'd feel a thrill or at least a curiosity about the book, but she had this sick, ugly feeling when her fingers touched the pages. She didn't want it, but she didn't want them to have it either.

Roxy scanned the empty street, looking up to the sky when she was done. "Do we have a game plan?"

"Don't get killed," Angelica said.

Serena grunted. "Nice plan. Do you have a way to prevent that? It'd be nice to hear since we don't even know who we're going up against."

They stopped near the backstairs of *Gris Gris*, and Angelica searched for prying eyes. Roxy quickly unlocked the gate.

Serena had been that voice of negativity since Angelica had announced her intentions to go to the rooftop of Gris Gris. Having their doubts, others had brought up many questions, including not knowing who waited for her. Angelica knew it was Lily's son. She'd known as soon as she'd touched that book. Pieces had fallen into place.

"The plan is to get Gabney. Fight like your life depended on it, and get out safe."

Roxy nodded. Angelica watched her mentally calm herself with a forced breathe through her mouth. The two of them could probably get along under different circumstances. Hopefully, they had the chance later.

Serena grunted again. Angelica would have preferred leaving her behind, but once Serena heard Angelica's plan, she'd insisted she come as back up.

Angelica climbed the stairs with the other two following close on her heels. On the first step of the roof, cold night air and the midnight sky swallowed her and chilled her all the way through. She scanned the top, taking in three cloaks standing together, waiting for them.

Gabney sat huddled in the north corner, hands and feet tied, eyes wide. Someone else was slumped at her feet, but the body was half-covered with a thick brown cloth.

She returned to the three standing before her. Familiarity bounced from their brain rhythms. These were people she knew.

Her mind ran through the possibilities. Rodney had known about the Vindica earlier. Mark had behaved strangely. Larkin Luke had betrayed her. Detective Gavin had looked at her fascinated. Lysander…she couldn't finish that thought.

Her heart ached.

Roxy and Serena flanked her, and Angelica said, "I believe it only fair you show yourselves. The time for disguises has passed."

A terse laugh came from the middle hood as a silver ringed hand pulled the hood back to reveal Mark. "What's really fair these days, Sister?"

The bitterness chocked his words out, and Lily's eyes glared back at her.

She should have noticed this about him long before, but it was the hardness around his eyes that wiped out the kindness Lily had always looked at her with.

"How could you betray everyone? Betray John?"

He grinned. "Mother named me Cain. I guess she always knew I would betray everyone."

To Mike's right, Bruce Meek lowered his hood. After Mark's reveal, Angelica had thought of Bruce since he didn't do anything without being by Mark's side. Cain. She needed to call him Cain, his real name. A brother.

To Cain's left, trembling fingers reached up, pushing the hood off. Angelica's mind froze as she stared into Lysander's eyes. He'd asked her not to hate him, and he'd meant at this moment.

Cain clapped his hands together once. "How does it feel to lose everything?"

Angelica narrowed her vision, looking away from Lysander, focusing on Cain. "I haven't."

Bruce had moved toward Gabney, and now with a flick of Cain's finger, Bruce lifted the brown cloth, revealing an unconscious Trevor.

Anger lit through Angelica. "Roxy, I told you to put him on a plane."

"I did," Roxy said, anger pinching her voice. "I watched him walk through the gate."

"Then how did Mark... Cain end up with him?"

Serena stepped forward and smiled. "I told Trevor you were in trouble and needed his help."

Angelica now stood face to face with Serena. "Why?"

Serena turned and walked towards Cain. "I'd rather be on any side than yours."

Roxy stepped forward. "Serena, are you crazy? Your family is at Landon House."

Serena laughed. "John abandoned me when he supported her as Valor. Cain is my family now."

Cain nodded as he touched her on the back. "You have something that belongs to me."

Serena smiled. "She has it in her back pack."

If Angelica had a quick thirty seconds with her, Serena wouldn't be smiling right now. Angelica's instincts had been right about Serena all along.

"It belongs to me. Lily chose me."

Angelica forced her ability to flow through her, severing the ropes cutting into Gabney's hands. Gabney squirmed, meeting Angelia's gaze.

"And you haven't done anything to deserve it." Cain spit out. "You didn't want any of this. You needed that family that you lost, but this organization knows nothing about loyalty. Don't let them fool you."

Gabney's bindings fell away and Angelica returned her full focus to Cain. He'd transferred his anger from their parents to her. She could see it in the intensity of his eyes and the twitching of his fingers.

Suddenly, all at once voices rose up in her inner ear. The voices of people in pain. Clutching Roxy's arm, Angelica pulled her to the side, knowing the third face of Lily had arrived.

A tall, lanky shadow rose from the staircase. "You didn't think you'd have a family reunion without me, did you now?"

Cloaks spilled onto the roof from the stairs until four stood to her right and eight stood to her left. The odds were not stacked in her favor.

The man of her childhood nightmares stood among his men, her same blue eyes staring back at her. His face had burned into her memory with the shrieks of his victims, haunting her early years with Lily.

Angelica could feel Cain's anger surge. "Who do I thank for your invitation?"

"It's amazing what Simone will reveal with prodding. I must thank her later for the opportunity to meet my daughter."

Cain's anger nearly imploded and he sent energy waves through them. Startled, the others looked at him, feeling it move them like wind. Angelica wasn't sure who Simone was, but she'd store that tidbit away for later.

Angelica sucked in air, allowing the label to settle, for her to turn it over and feel something at the word daughter. She'd wondered about this moment, feared it. But in this moment, disgust welled inside of her

"Some father," Cain snorted. "When have you ever acted fatherly?"

Reximortum focused on Angelica and blocked everyone out. "I've come to offer you a partnership, as together I believe we can make the Vindica the great organization it once was. Everything you've wanted since you were seven can be yours."

"I remember that speech," Cain said. "It never became reality."

A vein on Reximortum's temple throbbed. "You're impatient, arrogant, and defiant and never earned the right."

"No, I had to take it." Cain said, forcing the words between his teeth. "Just like you."

With a wave of Rex's hand, Cain's face purpled. "I'm through with the past. I've come about the future."

With a chilled gasp of air inflating her insides, the scene before Angelica came into sharp focus.

Gabney crept unnoticed towards them, and Griffen now hung at the top rung of the landing. She and Roxy were in danger if she wasn't smart about this. Reximortum turned to her, and she knew that she needed a plan.

Angelica exhaled. "The only part of my mother you had a chance with was Cain, and you don't seem to have done a good job there, so congratulations. As for me, you lost me when you killed Lily."

Cain collapsed to his knees while some of Rex's men advanced toward Serena, Bruce, and Lysander. Reximortum stepped toward her. Gabney jumped toward them and someone swung at her with a long stick.

Buzzing grew in Angelica's head as the people around her blurred and focus became difficult to keep hold.

"Enough!"

Her abilities stretched, yelling shrilly through their minds, causing their hearts to stop.

The Dark Soldiers fell to their knees. Reximortum released the pressure on Cain's lungs, although he barely blinked against the intrusion.

Gabney moved in behind her and Roxy.

Reximortum laughed. "Quite impressive, but I knew you would be."

Angelica glared back at him. "I'm not giving you this book."

"Consider your options," Rex said, turning around to look at everyone frozen in place. "The monster's coming, and since my son betrayed me, he's coming for all of us, I imagine. Join with me and avoid the fate of the other young women. If you join me, I can make that one wish you've always wanted yours."

She'd only ever wanted more time with Lily, to ask her all the questions, to look into those eyes again.

Reximortum smiled. "Yes, I can give that to you."

"No!" Angelica and Cain's eyes met as they cried out in unison.

Angelica returned to Reximortum and searched his face. What was he saying? Could this book bring back the dead?

Rex stepped closer to her. She could see the crease across his forehead. "We can do it together. Just make the right choice."

For a moment, she only felt the stillness. The stillness of the air, of her chest, of the people gawking at them. Through the stillness, visions of the future swirled before her. A future she'd be responsible for if she allowed him to get this book.

Her heart stilled and ached. She couldn't choose the past.

All eyes turned to her. She couldn't think about loss, only what she could save.

"I made my choice a long time ago. I choose to stand between you and anyone you intend to kill."

His laugh sped up her heart. "You will beg soon, but it will be too late."

The Dark Soldiers advanced. Griffen stumbled into the fray as other soldiers ascended from below. Angelica shrugged the velvet cloak off and lifted the sword of Jeremiah. Gabney swept up the cloak and clung to it, trembling.

Rex stepped back, allowing two Dark Soldiers to advance. Roxy nodded to Angelica and countered the one to their left. As the other one swung at Angelica, she lifted the sword to block him. Impact pushed her back, and she telekinetically flung him fifteen feet back into the fray of the others.

Griffin struggled to make it to them. He ducked as a sword swung in his direction, and Angelica moved in and blocked as the soldier swung again. She followed it with a swift kick to his abdomen, and he tumbled backwards, breathless.

You're going to need my help to win this.

Startled, she glanced around and Cain met her eyes. Another Dark Soldier lashed out at him and he blocked with his arm.

I seem to be doing all right on my own.

A swoosh near Angelica's ears made her duck as a sword came down near her shoulder. She pivoted and knocked the soldier from behind, but he was prepared and swung again. She blocked the blade, but he pushed backward, attempting to knock it from her grip.

You can't save them if you're on your own.

Serena was backed up against the roof edge. Lysander's opponent had beaten him back as well, and Cain struggled against a mind walker.

You're not doing so well yourself.

Angelica entered her attacker's mind. His blood boiled, and he seized. She pushed him sideways, and then scanned the rooftop.

She'd need to get to Trevor. Only four Dark Soldiers remained standing. Hope bubbled within, and the approaching Dark Soldier flew against the building ledge with an effortless wave of her hand.

A slow drone vibrated her eardrums. She felt it rattle through her toes. He'd arrived.

Cain searched the area. He heard it, but he didn't know what it was. Angelica watched the stairs for the monster to emerge.

"Roxy, we need to get Trevor now and get out of here."

Roxy lunged toward Trevor and Griffen followed.

The three Dark Soldiers left standing, retreated to Reximortum's side. They knew he was coming.

Cain's voice broke through Angelica's alert scan of the roof scene. *We need a plan.*

Angelica glanced to Cain. The monster was on the rungs of the ladder.

We need to take it out before it has a chance and get everyone out of here in case it does.

I get the book.

No deal.

I could leave and let you save everyone. I wonder how you'd do.

Angelica studied Reximortum's crossed arms against his chest. He planned to get rid of both of them and end up with the book. He'd had a plan all along. Angelica had seen that version of the future only moments before.

You know I'll come after you for the book.

I'm counting on it.

He emerged, a giant stepping onto the side of the building and the drum increased in volume. She gaped at his opalescence and the clearness of his eyes under the moonlight. He wasn't human. She knew it from the glow of his flesh, the beat of his heart, and the unnaturalness of his size. Kline's claims of full-blooded Custos felt believable at this moment.

Limping under Trevor's weight, Roxy stopped and gawked.

Looking at Trevor's groggy limp form, the dream fell into place. The piece that had always slipped away when she'd wake flashed before her. She lunged toward Roxy and Trevor, but it was too late.

Trevor lifted into the air, away from her reach. Angelica froze. Trevor's brown eyes opened and stared into her own. She looked into his fear.

The creature grinned a hideous smile and flung Trevor over the edge of the building.

"Noooo!" Angelica felt it hurl from deep within her chest.

Cain restrained her from lunging at the Custos. "Everyone down the stairs. Do not look back, just run."

Everyone stood frozen in paralysis.

"Go!" Angelica cried out, her chest heaving from the breath that would not come. "Leave the book Gabney."

With hands trembling, Gabney set the backpack down, and Cain snatched it up, throwing it over his shoulder. The others looked from him to Angelica.

"Roxy," Angelica said, forcing air into her lungs, although it felt like scraping against glass. "Get my people home safe."

Roxy nodded, tears glistening and her mouth set. She propelled the others forward, and one by one they began to disappear down the stairs.

Suddenly, Bruce Meek flew through the air, screaming as he went over the side. The others scrambled down, disappearing quickly down the side.

A gruff, husky voice spoke. "Always fight your own battles. Never let others stand in front of you."

"But doing someone else's work is okay," Angelica snapped.

The Custos growled and focused on them.

Cain and Angelica's eyes met, and they nodded. The energy began in her abdomen, and she molded it into a thick ball. Humming a lullaby, she pushed out the drumming of his heart as he moved in toward them. The ball grew tighter in her chest, consuming her anger, her anguish, and the pain thrashing her insides. She felt as though she was on fire.

"Now!"

Cain and Angelica's hands connected and the power surged through them and tunneled toward the Custos. As the energy crashed into him, his eyes widened and he flailed through the air, gaining speed as Angelica pushed the energy from her until she felt his shock overpower his fight.

Angelica flinched as he disappeared over the side of the building, and moments later a thud pierced through her as he rammed the sidewalk below.

Anger darkened Rex's eyes. "I will have that book!"

"Not as long as I'm Valor."Angelica enunciated each word, letting them echo through her.

Angelica backed up to the edge of the building, and Cain followed.

Rex moved forward. "Are you ready to die as Valor?"

Trust me. Angelica looked to Cain, eyebrows raised.

He hesitated a moment and then nodded.

Angelica stepped up to the ledge of the building.

For one moment, she thought she should have tested Kline's lesson before, but she was willing to go on a little faith now that Dark Soldiers surrounded her.

Rex put his hands up. "You don't have to jump. If you give me that book, we can all walk away."

Cain stepped up onto the ledge, looking down below. *I hope you know what you are doing.*

Angelica grabbed his hand and jumped. A rush pushed her head back a moment. She released a breath and activated her telekinesis, keeping herself near the building. Cain's weight made it difficult at first, but he caught on after the initial shock and dulled the force of gravity pulling them down.

They glided to the sidewalk below and dust rose up around their feet.

Cain yanked his hand away. "How…"

He trailed off and then began stepping backward from her.

"I'm going to want that book back," Angelica said, standing her ground, hoping the fear that had crept into his eyes would work in her favor.

He stepped further back. "For now it's mine."

"I'm going to come for it."

He nodded and jogged toward the touristy area, her backpack bouncing against his back.

You're not Rex. You are half Lily.

She felt him sever the connection. It was just as well. Opening that line could get confusing now that he'd betrayed Landon and the others.

Wanting to go to Trevor, she hesitated at taking off before the Dark Soldiers made it down the stairs, but she couldn't bring herself to see him. His death would be her fault. She'd need to call Detective Gavin. She couldn't just leave him there.

Hearing the footsteps echoing on the stairs, Angelica hurried away. A block away, arms closed around her from behind, and she struggled as she was pulled into a narrow alley.

"Shhh…" Kline whispered in her ear.

The panic seizing her lightened some, but her senses stayed in hyper mode.

"What's going on?" Angelica whispered, when he released her. She kept an eye out on the street, expecting Rex's men to pass.

"I was sent to take you back to him." Kline studied her, his gaze unnerving.

Angelica's muscles tensed. "That monster is dead."

Kline shook his head. "Gint's not who we fear. I will go to him and tell him you got away. It will give you some time, but for my failure, I fear he will send someone else."

"Come to Landon House with me," Angelica said. "I can protect you."

Kline's face softened, and Angelica saw something in those eyes. A contradiction of innocence and seductive power and determination.

"I can't." Kline reached out and touched her hair. "I need to go in and see what his next move is."

"Will I see you again?"

"I will come back." He smiled. "You need more training."

Angelica nodded.

He moved toward the entrance to the alley and peeked out. "They've gone now. Get back quickly."

"I lost the book of Shadow Souls. Cain has it now. Maybe he'll want to go after him?"

Kline smiled. "That book only means something to the hybrids. Lucilius only wants a page from it, but I may be able to use it. Now hurry before word travels."

Angelica hesitated at the entrance to the alley, wanting to touch him for some reason. To see if he were real. To check that it was really his heartbeat she heard at a murmur. To assure herself that her instincts that he shouldn't go back to the Custos were wrong.

She passed though. Lysander had twisted her heart enough for tonight, and she wasn't ready to open it up just yet.

Their eyes met one last time before she scurried off in the direction of Landon House, alert to every noise around her.

Sixty-One

The wind kicked up debris around his legs and the plane's engines drummed out any possibility of conversation with the others loading bags. Cain gripped the backpack tighter as he advanced onto the runway. The black bounded, yellowing pages held with hand stitched leather called to him from within the zipper. He couldn't wait for the pages to spill its secrets and bring him closer to his end goal.

Serena brushed against him as she turned to look behind them again. Her nose twitched and the line wrinkled across her forehead as she searched for a familiar face.

"They aren't coming," Cain said.

Serena looked up at him and her eyes watered.

"If you want to change your mind, I'm sure Jack or John will take you back."

She shook her head and swallowed. "You are my future. I love you."

He rubbed her arm, and his gut knotted. Simone should be on this plane with him as Serena had never been part of his plan. Knowing his father, Simone would be kept alive as a bargaining tool, which worked for Cain because it bought him some time with this book and a way to figure out how to hold onto it and get Simone back.

Simone may have changed her mind about him after Rex finished with her, but Cain had to do right by her. He needed her back.

Five of the young recruits that hadn't shown much allegiance to his father boarded the plane with their duffel bags, and Cain guided Serena to the steps. A silent tear rolled down her cheek, and Cain felt her guilt at betraying her father.

John Landon had taught Cain much of what Rex wasn't capable of teaching him. In fact, Cain owed John more than his father for this desire to have something different. Only John had this passion to change the Vindica to make it fit the modern world instead of keep outdated practices. Of course, the organization had fought him on every suggestion and it had floundered because of it. Cain had understood the necessity for change from John. Hopefully one day the man would understand.

Cain would use what the man had taught him to begin anew. The help from others had already begun to come as several had joined him and he now had a benefactor supporting him. The Vindica neared its death, just as the Reckoning promised, and now others would look to him to give them a way out.

Cain stepped into the entrance of the plane and looked out at the tarmac. He planned to return to this city, but he knew it wouldn't be the same for a city doesn't stand still while you're gone.

Angelica would be waiting for him. Half Lily, half Rex, just like him. The two sides swirling inside like oil and water.

Cain closed his eyes and felt the humid Louisiana air against his face.

Goodbye little sister. I'll see you soon.

Sixty-Two

His mind registered the approach of muffled footsteps, but he did not look up to see. A voice scratched the surface of his fugue state. "Lord, the car is ready."

Rex glanced at the twitching Tom as he remembered that before his mind had drifted, he'd been filing documents into his briefcase. Pages and pages of handwritten notes outlining his takeover arrangements of the Vindica. Arrangements he'd postponed after tonight's dismal outcome.

He released a deep breath, anger pulsating through his temple. He must maintain control.

His meticulous gaze swept the library, noticing dust draping the books like a sheet. The volumes had gone untouched this stay. Darkness swallowed the balcony's French doors. Night had hidden their indiscretions in its shadows.

The anger boiled and rose up into his throat again.

"Lord?" Tom asked, his concern etched in the wrinkles of his forehead.

He exhaled his anger, holding onto only his desire for revenge.

"Has our guest been secured as well?"

Tom nodded. "The young lady had to be sedated, but she's already been transported."

Gripping his briefcase in his fist, Rex strolled pass Tom, the rooms blurring as he passed. Fear flickered in his Dark Soldier's eyes as he passed them. With each click of the clock's hand, his men waited for punishment, knowing it would be swift and destructive. They'd failed him.

Failure did not settle into his bones well. Especially when betrayed by his own blood. He'd learned this lesson before, but he'd believed his own offspring would be different. Back then he'd done what was necessary, and Cain and Angelica were no different because that truce on the roof would not last.

Rex could see the possibility within them though. He only needed to push them in the right direction, and he'd have what he wanted.

Out front, a prickle touched the back of his neck as he sensed the eerie presence even before his gaze departed the midnight Rolls Royce. He searched the empty St. Charles Street as he picked up the faint echo of a drumbeat. In the shadowed corner of a two-story white home, Rex found the intruder, a lone figure with only his colorless face glaring from the darkness.

Their eyes met and Rex nodded.

Of course, another was sent. Was it to punish for the loss or to replace the loss? He doubted the latter as Custos didn't work for hybrids; it wasn't in their nature. The loss of Gint and the surfacing of the book had rippled through their world. A convergence of energy as great as Cain and Angelica had unknowingly projected had been felt by anyone with strong abilities. Soon, any number of enemies would be brought down upon them.

"Sir, should I send the men?" Tom asked, staring at the lone figure as well.

"No, the men have their orders. We still have some time."

Rex slipped into the back seat and Tom closed the door.

Rex could use this to his advantage. He understood desperation well, and with the Reckoning upon them, soon so would they.

Rex's time would come, and it would seem sooner than he'd thought only twenty minutes ago.

Sixty-Three

Kline should have returned to Landon House with Angelica, but Magis could not assure him that his father had made it out through the network. He could not take that chance. He'd return to her after his family's safety was guaranteed.

As he entered headquarters, he noticed the dim lighting spilling into the foyer and the silence. Kline walked toward the great room in search of Lucilius, steeling his mind, tucking away any yearning for Angelica deep in the inner recesses.

Entering the ornately finished room, Lucilius sat waiting in a high back chair in front of a raging fire in the marble fireplace. But it was the two other sentries on each side of the door that gave Kline pause. Lucilius had sent for more men. Two Kline didn't recognize.

"Join us Kline." Lucilius motioned to the room. "We have been waiting for your return."

"Sir, I bring bad tidings," Kline said, bowing his head to him. "Gint is dead as are several others. Angelica has escaped."

"Has she now?" Lucilius's eyebrows rose.

"She made a deal with Cain," Kline continued, choosing his words, feeling Lucilius's contempt. "She traded *The Book of Shadow Souls* for his help. The two defeated Gint."

"So Cain has the book?" Lucilius taped his fingers on the carved arm of the chair.

Kline nodded.

"I see." Lucilius sighed.

Kline cleared his throat. "How do you wish to proceed?"

Lucilius sat in silence, studying Kline's face. Kline stood statuesque against the assessment.

Finally, Lucilius stood. "I require very little from my sentries as I know the intelligence required to obtain the position. Trust and loyalty and very little else isn't too much to ask. You have failed at both."

"Sir?" Kline asked, his jaw clenching.

"Tonight was a test of sorts as I had begun to have my suspicions about you. I have to admit that I didn't expect Gint to fail. I'd sent him to terminate everyone but Angelica. I figured that way she would come to me since that part of her that is human wouldn't be able to resist justice and all that nonsense. But what to do with you? You who have developed an obsession with using her for my downfall."

"That's way out of line," Kline uttered, fighting to keep the anger and panic in check.

"Careful Kline," Lucilius said, smiling. "You don't posses the rank anymore to speak to me in such a manner. I believe it was a human woman similar to Angelica that stripped your family of their royal status. A second offense would likely cost you your family's bloodline."

"Angelica posses enough Custos blood to dismiss any allegations and punishment."

Lucilius chuckled, filling the room with his wretched menacing sound. "You may be right but you have no evidence. I've destroyed the blood test. No, she will die like the other hybrids when it is time, and you are going to return to a Labos prison cell for your betrayal and treason against your people. I'm sure your father will serve your death sentence just as your grandfather served his."

Gathering his strength, Kline shoved forward, throwing Lucilius into the mantle, flipping the chair over as he flew through the air. Lucilius bounced off the mantle and landed before him.

Kline felt Lucilius enter his head, and Kline struggled against the intrusion. Pushing forward, Kline shoved him physically, unable to take his attention away from the fight over control of his body.

Pain shot down his back as a hard blow landed behind his neck. Kline turned and faced the broad shouldered sentry whose fist was coming down.

Kline blocked his throw and landed one in his gut, all the while fighting Lucilius's attempt at control.

The other sentry approached and drew a dagger from his leg. Kline slipped and telekinetically tossed the dagger to the side, giving Lucilius his way in.

Kline felt the intrusion right before he felt his lungs tighten.

He couldn't breathe. He fell to his knees, gasping for oxygen.

"That was the wrong move," Lucilius said, glaring down at him. "But I will keep you alive for a little while because I have plans for you."

Everything went dark. His last thought being he'd failed Angelica and his father.

Sixty-Four

The night air numbed Angelica's flushed cheeks. She sipped from her glass of red wine, feeling it warm and relax her jittery insides. She leaned forward over the balcony railing, weightlessness swallowing her. Closing her eyes to the bare street below, she could touch a freedom beyond gravity.

It lasted only seconds before sadness crushed her chest again. The numbness she kept imposing on her body eventually evaporated into crushing loss.

Trevor was gone and it was her fault.

An aching traveled over her body, and a familiar longing encapsulated her chest. She peered into the shadows of the street lamps, and Lysander gazed up at her from behind a street post.

The cold tightened its grip on her body, and her flesh warmed in remembrance of his touch.

Their eyes met and she couldn't look away.

Why had he returned? Guilt. Regret. A need to betray her again.

The doorbell echoed through Landon House, and Angelica's heart sank immediately sensing more bad news coming. Lysander nodded, and Angelica pulled away from the balcony wrought iron railing, feeling an aching in her bones.

Downstairs, Gabney stood fidgety by the door as Madame Lulu shrugged off her overcoat.

Angelica stepped on the bottom step and sipped from her wine glass.

John came from the sitting room, where he'd probably been sitting in his study writing notes for himself.

"Madame Lulu," John said surprised. "What do we owe this late night visit?"

"You should know after tonight's events." Her eyes were big and her lips set in a stiff line.

Gabney hung the overcoat and looked to Angelica. Roxy brushed up against Angelica as she reached the bottom landing, and Griffen came around the staircase at the same time.

"Why don't we all enter my study to discuss it?" Landon motioned toward the doorway.

Madame Lulu strolled in that direction, head held high, a frown creasing her face. Angelica could only think that the Reckoning had come, and she had not figured out what small event had transpired so that she could correct it.

Angelica looked to Roxy, who raised her eyebrows and tucked her short hair behind her ear. They followed her into the study with Gabney and Griffen trailing behind.

Inside Mr. White sat on a chair near the fireplace with a briefcase in his lap. He looked up as they all entered and his hands immediately folded on top of the brown case.

Madame Lulu sank into one of the overstuffed high back chairs and twiddled with a handkerchief in her hands.

"I swore I'd never be involved in Vindica business, but due to personal concerns, I have changed my mind." She stopped and swallowed.

Angelica, who watched her closely, felt something off.

"I don't wish to discuss these matters as of yet." Again, she paused.

Angelica allowed the room to open for her. Thoughts flowing around, but Madame Lulu remained a black hole.

"However, I do need you people to prevent the world coming to an end, so I've decided to offer a bit of help."

Angelica cleared her throat as the rest of the room remained silent. "Help in what form?"

Roxy nodded her head as she glanced from Angelica to Madame Lulu.

"It's your blood." Madame Lulu focused in on Angelica. "The Reckoning begins with your blood. I can see that you don't cause it, but it's what your blood is used for that does. The visions have not been definitive, but the glimpse shows this."

Roxy looked to Angelica. "So we need to make sure wherever your blood has been has been destroyed?"

Angelica nodded, her thoughts drifting to Kline. Had the sample really been destroyed? She'd need to see him and make sure of it herself.

"Mr. White, we will need to have that sample destroyed at the lab."

"Of course, of course," he said, his fingers twitching. "Preliminary results are in, so we'll just have to say whatever we have done is enough. Dr. Warrick said he was nearly finished anyway. Doesn't usually take this long, you see." He came to a sudden stop, looking at Madame Lulu.

"Preliminary results?" Angelica asked. "Anything I need to know yet? I mean it may help answer why it's my blood."

"He'd only tell me unnaturally high Custos levels." His eyes didn't meet Angelica's. Her cheeks burned. Kline had told her the truth.

"Madame Lulu, did you see why it was my blood?" Angelica asked her.

Madame Lulu shrugged. "I'm only a seer. That answer hasn't become part of the future yet. Let's hope you can stop it before it does."

Gabney squeaked. "What about the book? Did losing it change the future?"

Angelica felt the guilt squatting inside Gabney. She blamed herself for the loss of the book. If she hadn't believed Cain needed her help, she wouldn't have gone and been captured.

Madame Lulu's forehead wrinkled deeply. "The books bring trouble."

She stood. Angelica could feel her anger right below the surface.

"Those books," she spoke deeply, "contain ancient practices you no longer believe in, but they also hold secrets. Danger comes with acquiring them, but you must possess them if you hope to survive what is coming."

She looked down at Angelica through narrowed slits, studying her for a moment. Angelica did not blink.

The woman hid her own secrets.

"I'll see myself out." She nodded to John, "When the time is necessary, you may find me."

She spoke this last bit to Angelica and then strolled out the room.

"That woman is unnerving," Gabney said, rubbing her jaw as if she'd been clenching it the entire time.

Griffen nodded and took her hand in his. Angelica had noticed that they'd disappeared together earlier and that they'd chosen seats together now. Finally, something good.

"So it's not over," Roxy said, her lips set in determination.

"It is for tonight," John spoke slowly, considering his words. "Eleanor told me once that it was best that our enemies have a face. No matter the heartbreak, it is important to know who our allies are."

Roxy glanced to Angelica and smiled. "I agree. I'm angry that we didn't see it before. I mean, all their things were cleared out before tonight. They planned all of this. I feel…"

"Betrayed." Gabney finished.

"For the most part though," Griffen said, squeezing Gabney's hand and smiling at her, "we were really lucky tonight. Things could have been far worse with all those people showing up. What was that thing?" He looked to Angelica.

John said, "Detective Gavin has the body of our mystery guest. He assures me we will know something by morning."

Angelica looked to John and even without his mind open to her, she knew he wanted the answer to come from scientific proof. He was hedging to lighten the fear he knew would set in.

Some of whom they'd feared had disappeared from the city tonight; first she'd felt Cain and then Reximortum leave. She'd felt a slight sting as they'd abandoned her to what was coming. She'd lost the book, but instinct told her not to worry yet.

"So this is our team," Roxy said, looking around the room.

Mr. White coughed. "What are we going to do about the book though?"

"For now we don't need the book," Angelica said. "Rosemary left us what we need."

John leaned forward in his seat. "You found something in Rosemary's book?"

Angelica pulled a folded piece of paper out of her pocket. A paper she'd transferred words and notes onto in an attempt to cling to the hope that she hadn't lost. The truth of the books had been locked inside that trunk this entire time. If only she'd trusted her instincts instead of Lily's warnings. She wouldn't make that mistake again.

"Rosemary was a fan of Stanley Harrison's musings on the Vindica, and he said history lies in the five books. To find our origins and our future, one must find where the books lead."

Angelica paused, as the printed words burned through her anguish and aching. Rosemary's words looped through her memory.

"Rosemary believed that the books were only part of what

originally existed. I believe the books lead back to something, another book perhaps and that's the book we need."

Kline had said his boss only wanted one page from the book. This had to be why.

Griffen's forehead scrunched into the three lines of thought she'd come to like. "So the books contain clues on how to find the original?"

Angelica clutched her notes tightly. "The original that belonged to the Custos not the hybrids. Rosemary knew Reximortum hadn't figured it out because he was interested in the book's other attributes, but I believe Cain may figure it out."

Gabney frowned. "But we don't have the first clue because Cain has the book."

"Rosemary copied what we needed into her book."

She rubbed her thumb against the folded sheet.

One must lose to let another believe they've won.

Rosemary's words written above her notes. Perhaps she'd foreseen the loss of the book. It didn't matter. She'd guaranteed Angelica could succeed even when it seemed as though she'd lost everything.

She'd be ready next time.

Valor wasn't dead.

ALSO by JESSICA TASTET

The Raleigh Cheramie Series

UPCOMING
MUDDY HEARTS

THE CUSTOS SAGA

UPCOMING
Book #2 VINDICA

JESSICA TASTET is the author of three novels and a children's story. She's worked as an English teacher for eighteen years and an editor for five years. She lives in Louisiana with her family.

For updates visit:
www.jessicatastet.com

www.ingramcontent.com/pod-product-compliance
Lightning Source LLC
Chambersburg PA
CBHW021306250626
47155CB00002B/407